# AMSTERDAM NOIR

### EDITED BY
## RENÉ APPEL & JOSH PACHTER

*Translated by Josh Pachter*

Published by Akashic Books
©2019 Akashic Books

Series concept by Tim McLoughlin and Johnny Temple
Amsterdam map by Sohrab Habibion

All stories translated by Josh Pachter except where noted.

This publication has been made possible with financial support from the Dutch Foundation for Literature.

**N**ederlands
**N** letterenfonds
dutch foundation
for literature

Paperback ISBN: 978-1-61775-614-6
Hardcover ISBN: 978-1-61775-738-9
Library of Congress Control Number: 2018931226

Akashic Books
Brooklyn, New York, USA
Ballydehob, Co. Cork, Ireland
Twitter: @AkashicBooks
Facebook: AkashicBooks
E-mail: info@akashicbooks.com
Website: www.akashicbooks.com

# ALSO IN THE AKASHIC NOIR SERIES

**NEW ORLEANS NOIR**, edited by JULIE SMITH

**NEW ORLEANS NOIR: THE CLASSICS,**
edited by JULIE SMITH

**OAKLAND NOIR**, edited by JERRY THOMPSON
& EDDIE MULLER

**ORANGE COUNTY NOIR**, edited by GARY PHILLIPS

**PARIS NOIR** (FRANCE), edited by AURÉLIEN MASSON

**PHILADELPHIA NOIR**, edited by CARLIN ROMANO

**PHOENIX NOIR**, edited by PATRICK MILLIKIN

**PITTSBURGH NOIR**, edited by KATHLEEN GEORGE

**PORTLAND NOIR**, edited by KEVIN SAMPSELL

**PRAGUE NOIR** (CZECH REPUBLIC),
edited by PAVEL MANDYS

**PRISON NOIR**, edited by JOYCE CAROL OATES

**PROVIDENCE NOIR**, edited by ANN HOOD

**QUEENS NOIR**, edited by ROBERT KNIGHTLY

**RICHMOND NOIR**, edited by ANDREW BLOSSOM,
BRIAN CASTLEBERRY & TOM DE HAVEN

**RIO NOIR** (BRAZIL), edited by TONY BELLOTTO

**ROME NOIR** (ITALY), edited by CHIARA STANGALINO
& MAXIM JAKUBOWSKI

**SAN DIEGO NOIR**, edited by MARYELIZABETH HART

**SAN FRANCISCO NOIR**, edited by PETER MARAVELIS

**SAN FRANCISCO NOIR 2: THE CLASSICS**,
edited by PETER MARAVELIS

**SAN JUAN NOIR** (PUERTO RICO),
edited by MAYRA SANTOS-FEBRES

**SANTA CRUZ NOIR**, edited by SUSIE BRIGHT

**SÃO PAULO NOIR** (BRAZIL),
edited by TONY BELLOTTO

**SEATTLE NOIR**, edited by CURT COLBERT

**SINGAPORE NOIR**, edited by CHERYL LU-LIEN TAN

**STATEN ISLAND NOIR**, edited by PATRICIA SMITH

**ST. LOUIS NOIR**, edited by SCOTT PHILLIPS

**STOCKHOLM NOIR** (SWEDEN), edited by
NATHAN LARSON & CARL-MICHAEL EDENBORG

**ST. PETERSBURG NOIR** (RUSSIA), edited by
NATALIA SMIRNOVA & JULIA GOUMEN

**SYDNEY NOIR** (AUSTRALIA), edited by JOHN DALE

**TEHRAN NOIR** (IRAN), edited by SALAR ABDOH

**TEL AVIV NOIR** (ISRAEL), edited by ETGAR KERET
& ASSAF GAVRON

**TORONTO NOIR** (CANADA), edited by JANINE ARMIN
& NATHANIEL G. MOORE

**TRINIDAD NOIR** (TRINIDAD & TOBAGO), edited by
LISA ALLEN-AGOSTINI & JEANNE MASON

**TRINIDAD NOIR: THE CLASSICS**
(TRINIDAD & TOBAGO), edited by EARL LOVELACE
& ROBERT ANTONI

**TWIN CITIES NOIR**, edited by JULIE SCHAPER
& STEVEN HORWITZ

**USA NOIR**, edited by JOHNNY TEMPLE

**VANCOUVER NOIR** (CANADA), edited by SAM WIEBE

**VENICE NOIR** (ITALY), edited by MAXIM JAKUBOWSKI

**WALL STREET NOIR**, edited by PETER SPIEGELMAN

**ZAGREB NOIR** (CROATIA), edited by IVAN SRŠEN

# FORTHCOMING

**ACCRA NOIR** (GHANA),
edited by NANA-AMA DANQUAH

**ADDIS ABABA NOIR** (ETHIOPIA),
edited by MAAZA MENGISTE

**ALABAMA NOIR**, edited by DON NOBLE

**BERKELEY NOIR**, edited by JERRY THOMPSON
& OWEN HILL

**BELGRADE NOIR** (SERBIA),
edited by MILORAD IVANOVIC

**BERLIN NOIR** (GERMANY),
edited by THOMAS WÖERTCHE

**BOGOTÁ NOIR** (COLOMBIA),
edited by ANDREA MONTEJO

**COLUMBUS NOIR**,
edited by ANDREW WELSH-HUGGINS

**HOUSTON NOIR**, edited by GWENDOLYN ZEPEDA

**JERUSALEM NOIR**, edited by DROR MISHANI

**MILWAUKEE NOIR**, edited by TIM HENNESSY

**NAIROBI NOIR** (KENYA), edited by PETER KIMANI

**PARIS NOIR: THE SUBURBS** (FRANCE),
edited by HERVÉ DELOUCHE

**SANTA FE NOIR**, edited by ARIEL GORE

**TAMPA BAY NOIR**, edited by COLETTE BANCROFT

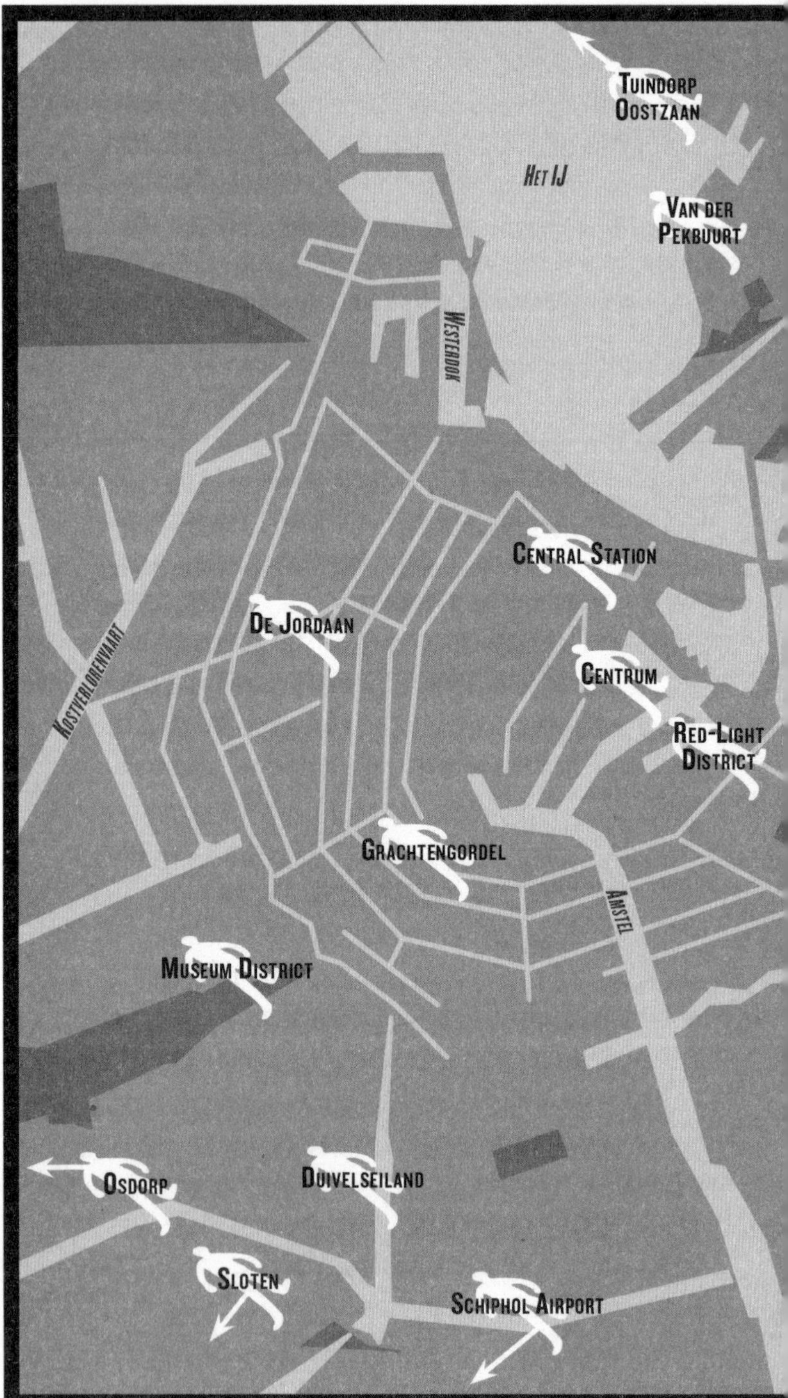

Tuindorp Oostzaan
Het IJ
Van der Pekbuurt
Westerdok
Central Station
De Jordaan
Kostverlorenvaart
Centrum
Red-Light District
Grachtengordel
Amstel
Museum District
Osdorp
Duivelseiland
Sloten
Schiphol Airport

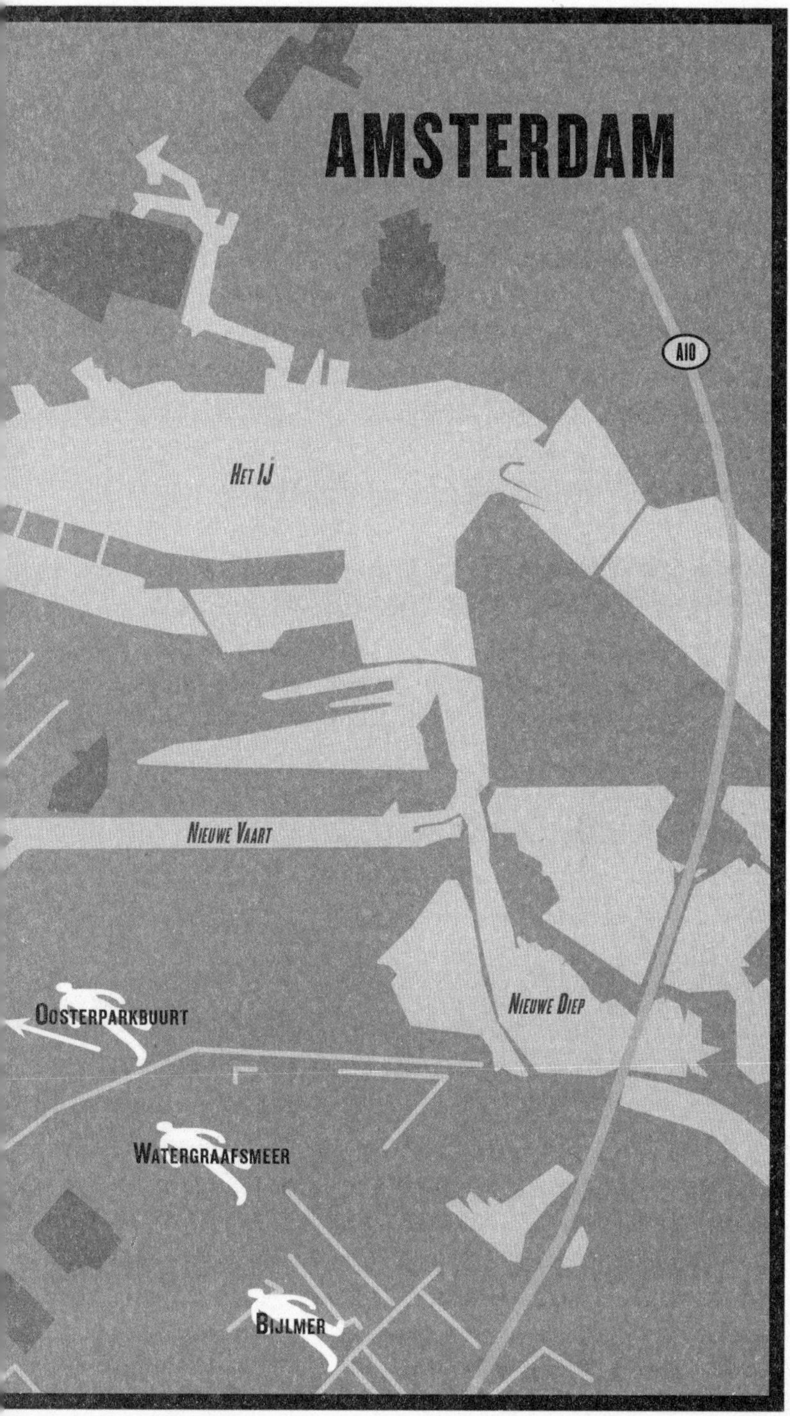

AMSTERDAM
A10
Het IJ
Nieuwe Vaart
Nieuwe Diep
Oosterparkbuurt
Watergraafsmeer
Bijlmer

# TABLE OF CONTENTS

## PART III: TOUCH OF EVIL

## PART IV: THEY LIVE BY NIGHT

# INTRODUCTION
## DARKNESS ON THE EDGE OF TOWN

*"Good evening, ladies and gentlemen, and welcome to Akashic Airlines flight 1595 to Amsterdam."*

Sometime between 1250 and 1275 AD, a small group of Dutch farmers dammed the Amstel, an unimpressive river that emptied into a nearby bay called the IJ. They built houses around the dam and the river, and so the village of Amstelredam was born. Over the years, as the village grew, its name eventually shortened to Amsterdam.

Amsterdam came into its own in the seventeenth century, the Dutch Golden Age, when it blossomed into both an important trade center and an equally important cultural center, home to many writers, such as P.C. Hooft and Joost van den Vondel, and artists like Rembrandt van Rijn and Govert Flinck.

The eighteenth century was a relatively quiet time for The Netherlands. While the country rested on its laurels, the city's population remained relatively stable. Only in the course of the nineteenth century did a new sense of vigor arise, and the 1800s are remembered as Amsterdam's second Golden Age.

In fits and starts, the city has continued to grow ever since—in 2017, its population reached around 850,000, including people from roughly 180 countries, making it one of the most international cities in the world.

In today's Amsterdam, almost anything goes. Take the availability of drugs, for example. The so-called coffee shops in which marijuana and hashish are openly sold have been in business since the 1980s. Where else in the world can you, without fear of arrest, ask a cop on the street to light your hand-rolled joint?

Amsterdam has the amenities and, to a certain extent, the feel of a major world city, but one of its most attractive features is its relatively small size. It's easy to navigate on foot, by bike, and via its excellent public transportation network, especially with the semicircular perimeter of its famous Grachtengordel, or ring of concentric canals.

Like any other metropolis, though, Amsterdam also has its dark side, its shadowy corners—in other words, there is also an Amsterdam noir. No matter how beautiful, vital, and cheery a city might be, pure human emotions such as greed, jealousy, and the thirst for revenge will rear their ugly heads . . . with all their negative consequences. Amsterdam is a multidimensional city, populated by a wide assortment of social groups, and not all of those groups agree on what constitutes normal social values and mores. This results in a lively mix . . . and, as you will see, in problems.

Amsterdam remains a trade center—and that includes illegal trade—which means there exists within its borders a criminal underclass that goes unnoticed by most citizens and visitors yet bubbles evilly beneath the surface of the city's daily life.

Gone are the halcyon days when the most common crime in Amsterdam was bicycle theft. Although the city's rates of murder, rape, violent crime, and total crime are significantly lower than the equivalent rates in the United States, there *are* murders and rapes, and there is opiate abuse and gang activity and violent crime.

It is perhaps worth noting that Willem Holleeder, the most notorious Dutch criminal in the country's history—a member of the gang that kidnapped beer heir Freddy Heineken in 1983 and held him for a ransom of some twenty million dollars—was a born-and-bred Amsterdammer.

*"Your co-captains for this flight are René Appel and Josh Pachter, and our flight crew includes fifteen of The Netherlands' finest crime and literary authors."*

In the pages that follow, you'll find fiction by winners of the Golden Noose, which is the award for the best Dutch-language crime novel of the year (Michael Berg won in 2013, and René Appel has won twice, in 1991 and 2001); by award-winning literary writers (Abdelkader Benali won the prestigious Libris Literature Prize in 2003; Hanna Bervoets has won both the Opzij Literature Prize and the BNG Literature Prize; Anneloes Timmerije won the Vrouw & Kultuur Debut Prize in 2006; and Mensje van Keulen's body of work has been honored with the Annie Romein, Charlotte Köhler, and Constantijn Huygens prizes); by established crime writers (including international best seller Herman Koch, Diamond Bullet winner Simon de Waal, Loes den Hollander, and Theo Capel), and by up-and-comers (such as Karin Amatmoekrim, Murat Isik, Walter van den Berg, Max van Olden, and Christine Otten).

*"Our in-flight entertainment system features four channels for your reading pleasure."*

In our opinion, each of the stories in this volume is a little film, and since one of the threads that ties them all together—along with their Amsterdam setting—is their noir-ness, we have chosen to organize them based on four of the greatest classic Hollywood noir films.

In *Out of the Past* (1947), directed by Jacques Tourneur and starring Robert Mitchum and Jane Greer, a private eye tries in vain to escape from his checkered personal history. Here in *Amsterdam Noir*, dark deeds from the past impact the present as a Syrian torture victim encounters his tormentor, a forty-year-old murder haunts a new homeowner, a convict on a weekend pass prowls the night, and a father wrestles with the death of his daughter.

In *Kiss Me Deadly* (1955), directed by Robert Aldrich and based on the novel by Mickey Spillane, Mike Hammer is caught up in a web of intrigue. The couples in this section of the anthology you now hold in your hands also become enmeshed in webs of intrigue, as a young mother falls in love with the wrong person, an elderly apartment dweller helps out a victimized neighbor, and a delivery boy's affair with an older woman takes a turn for the worst.

In *Touch of Evil* (1958), directed by Orson Welles and starring Welles, Charlton Heston, and Janet Leigh, corruption in a Mexican border town takes center stage. And corruption takes center stage in *Amsterdam Noir* as an innocent narrator witnesses the devil at work, a pedophile threatens innocent boys, money once again turns out to be the root of all evil, and a serial killer returns from the dead.

In *They Live by Night* (1948), directed by Nicholas Ray and starring Cathy O'Donnell and Farley Granger, an escaped con falls for his nurse. In this final section, a candlelit canal cruise turns suspenseful, an innocent Muslim girl meets her end at the edge of the city, a pair of punk teens embark on a doomed get-rich-quick scheme, and, to our dismay, we learn that not only the good die young.

*"Ladies and gentlemen, as we start our descent into Schiphol Air-*

port, please make sure your seat backs and tray tables are in their full upright position and your seat belts are securely fastened. All carry-on luggage should be stowed in the overhead bins or underneath the seat in front of you. We'll be landing in about two pages, and we wish you a spine-tingling stay in the dark side of Amsterdam."

René Appel & Josh Pachter
November 2018

# PART I

*Out of the Past*

# WELCOME TO AMSTERDAM

BY Michael Berg

*Schiphol Airport*

Aguard calls my name. I wish I could ignore him, but I know better. I get up and stagger to the cell door. "Move it!"

The other prisoners watch me go, their faces blank.

"This way!"

The guard shoves me down the passage.

I walk. Breathe. I'm not dead yet.

The corridor is long and wide. It's an open field compared to the cell I share with twenty-five other prisoners.

Saydnaya is hell. I've haven't been here long, but long enough to have been robbed of any hope. No one gets out of this place alive. Every day is an ordeal. The interrogations, the torture, the sadism of the guards. It's all just a delay tactic: at the far end of the tunnel, I'm well aware, death awaits me. It will be a release.

We descend into the cellar. As we pass the torture chambers, I hear cries of pain from behind their heavy doors. Or perhaps that's just my imagination.

"In here!"

The guard kicks me into a room I haven't yet seen. A dimly lit space that stinks of sweat and piss. A porno film is playing on a big white screen. The volume is cranked up loud. Eight prisoners are being forced to watch the movie. If any of them dares to look away, a guard smashes him in the ribs with a metal baton.

Moaning.

Screaming.

And above all else, the amplified panting of the copulating couple on the screen.

"Take your clothes off!"

The man who issues this command is big, broad, and in his midfifties. He has a bushy mustache. He approaches me, limping on one leg.

"Clothes off!"

He slaps me across the face with the back of his hand.

I take my clothes off. The guards watch, grinning. They make sarcastic comments about my body. One of them taps my butt with his baton.

"Nice ass," he says.

The man with the mustache shows me where to stand, facing the screen, my legs pressed up against a massive oak table. Two leather restraints are nailed to its surface, and he signals me to lay my hands on the leather. The straps are buckled tight, fixing me in place.

"Spread your legs!" the mustache orders. Then he turns to the prisoners behind me. "Gentlemen," he says—and, to judge by the scream, one of them takes another blow to the ribs—"be my guest!"

Dared al-Saeed walked into the departure hall of JFK's Terminal 4 and looked around. Four years ago, this was where he had arrived. Since that day, he hadn't flown again. The thought of spending hours in the enclosed cabin of a plane filled with other passengers made him break out in a cold sweat.

He had long debated whether or not to accept the invitation to present at the medical conference. The location was what finally convinced him: Amsterdam. As a young student, he and his brother Mustafa had visited the city. The Red-Light District, the pot shops, the bars, the canals, the blond girls lying on the grass in the Vondelpark with their long bare legs. Amsterdam had been a hallucinatory experience for them both.

And now Mustafa was dead.

As were four hundred thousand of their countrymen.

While he, Dared, had survived.

He felt terribly guilty.

This trip would be a testament to his brother's memory. And at the same time, it would give him the opportunity to overcome his fear of flying.

He checked in, followed the signs to passport control. The new president had complained about leaky borders and promised that—as soon as he moved into the White House—they would be dramatically tightened. But Dared didn't notice much of a difference. No gray-suited men with earpieces, no police, no armed soldiers.

The immigration officer was a rosy-cheeked white man. Dared handed over his passport and green card. As the man examined the documents, Dared saw him frown for just a moment. *Dared al-Saeed, born December 10, 1988, in Damascus, Syria. Permanent resident since 2015.*

"I hope you thanked our previous president for this," the agent remarked, returning the passport and laminated card. "Have a good trip."

"Thank you," Dared smiled in return.

Not everyone in the United States had lost their minds.

He checked the departure board and found that his flight, KL 6070, would leave from gate B32. There was a long line at the La Brea Bakery. His stomach clenched, and he suddenly felt dizzy. A panic attack. No coffee, then, and no sandwich. All these people, all this hustle and bustle. He couldn't handle it. Maybe this trip wasn't such a good idea after all.

Leaving the crowd behind, he crossed to his gate. He found a quiet place to sit, slid his laptop from his carry-on, and settled in to go over his presentation yet again. Slowly, he felt himself relax.

A voice on the PA eventually announced his flight.

It was just after four. Dared looked up. There weren't many people in line at the gate. Aboard the Boeing, he found his window seat. There was no one else in his row. As the aircraft taxied out to the runway and the flight attendants delivered their safety instructions, he set his watch ahead to Central European Time.

The engines fired up, and the plane gained speed. Dared felt himself pressed back in his seat. There was no way out of it now—seven hours in the air. He wondered if he should take one Ambien or two.

"Where is your brother?"

I sit on a wooden chair. My hands are cuffed behind my back, my ankles bound to the legs of the chair with plastic zip ties. Except for a filthy pair of boxers, I am naked. I don't care. After four months in Saydnaya, I have left all shame far behind.

"Where is your brother?"

The man with the mustache punches me in the face. I hear the cartilage in my nose break.

"Answer me!"

His eagle eyes glitter dangerously.

By now, I know his name: Karim al-Zaliq. Because of his strength and temperament, everyone in the red building calls him *Thur*—the Bull.

"If you don't tell me where we can find your brother, I'll knock your teeth out." There are brass knuckles on his clenched right fist, and, grinning, he brandishes them before me.

I've seen Thur knock more than one man's teeth out. It's one of his specialties. Eventually it will be my turn; it's just a question of time.

"Where is your brother?"

"I don't know," I lie.

"He's not at his home."

"Maybe he left Damascus."

"For where?"

"I don't know."

"Are his friends hiding him?"

"I don't know."

"Who are his friends?"

"I don't know his friends."

"You're lying."

"My brother's four years older than me. We—"

"You lie!"

When he cocks his arm, I close my eyes and wait for the blow. *Do it*, I think. *Kill me.*

"You so-called rebels are all the same!" Thur is shouting now. "Cowards, all of you! You'll never beat us!" He turns to the waiting guards. "Cut his legs free."

Before I know what's happening, they dump me into the bathtub that stands in a corner of the cell. I don't weigh anything anymore. I haven't had a real meal in weeks; I have the runs all the time. I look like the other prisoners, like a dead man.

The water in the tub is a yellowish brown and smells like piss and shit. I try to breathe through my mouth and squeeze my nostrils shut. I close my eyes.

"So." It's Thur's voice. "Now tell me where your brother is."

"I don't know."

"All right then."

One of the guards holds my ankles and another shoves my head under the vile water.

I hold my breath.

*Don't think,* I order myself. If I think, I'll go mad.

The hands that hold me under release their pressure. Gasping for breath, I emerge from the filth.

"Where is your brother?"

"I don't know. I swear—"

The hands push me down again. Longer, this time. I can't hold my breath anymore. I swallow. The sludge runs down my throat, into my lungs. Much more of this and I'll drown.

"Where is your brother? Who are his friends?"

I feel myself break, and I begin to speak.

The plane began its descent. Dared could feel the pressure on his eardrums. He opened his eyes.

"Are you all right, sir?"

The flight attendant, an attractive woman in her midtwenties, was leaning over him.

"I'm fine," he assured her, checking his watch. "How much longer until we land in Amsterdam?"

Her brow furrowed. "You didn't hear the captain's announcement?"

He looked up at her, not understanding. He hadn't heard an announcement. He had slept and dreamed—the usual terrible nightmare.

"Schiphol is closed," the flight attendant told him.

"Schiphol?"

"Sorry, sir. The Amsterdam airport." She smiled apologetically. "Heavy fog and sleet. We've been rerouted to Paris. There'll be a ticket and a voucher waiting for you at the customer service desk. The ticket's for this evening's flight to Amsterdam, and the voucher's for a hotel room in the city center. You can spend a few hours in Paris, get some sleep if you like, and still make it to your destination today. I'm sorry for the inconvenience, sir." She showed him her lovely smile again.

"I, ah . . ."

He needed time to process this new information. The medical conference didn't begin until tomorrow. A few hours in Paris. He had never been to the City of Light. Obviously he'd take the hotel room. With any luck, he'd have time to explore the place a bit, perhaps visit a museum, find something good to eat, and . . .

*Do you have plans for today?*

The question perched on the tip of his tongue.

He swallowed it.

"Thank you, miss," he said.

The rumor has been going around the red building for days. Saydnaya is overcrowded, and fifty prisoners are being moved to some other facility. One of the two affected cells is mine. Can it be true?

"Line up!"

Shortly before midnight, Thur and a platoon of guards haul us out of our cell.

"Faster," Thur orders, complacently stroking his mustache.

They herd us through the corridor, down the stairs to the cellar. The occupants of the other cell are already there. They stand in a circle, and their guards are beating them with whips, sticks, batons, anything capable of inflicting pain. It is an orgy of violence. Then the kicking begins. In the face, the stomach, the back.

And we stand there, watching.

"Second group!"

With the first kick, it feels as if my spleen has ruptured. The second is worse. *Please, kick me unconscious.* But Thur and his goons know exactly how far they can go. They take turns. Kicking, punching, spitting, pulling my hair. It goes on for an hour, maybe two. I lose all sense of time and place.

Finally, they force us to our feet and drive us outside. It's the middle of the night. The Big Dipper is bright in the sky. If I'm seeing properly, that is, for one of my eyes is swollen shut and the other is bleeding. I breathe in the cool desert air and am surprised to be alive.

We're shoved toward a large structure.

"The white building," one of my cellmates whispers.

I've never seen it before, but I know the stories. The white building is where they keep the officers and enlisted men who have refused to support the Assad regime. The tortures to which they are subjected are far worse than what we've experienced.

"Let's go, move it!"

Down in the cellar, we find ourselves in a huge space that looks like an underground parking garage. Dozens of nooses hang from the stone ceiling. Some of the prisoners begin to weep, others pray.

I feel more relief than anything else. *In the name of Allah, let it be over quickly.*

Chairs are brought out and set beneath the nooses. Fifty chairs for fifty hangings. Before they order us up, they roughly pull a burlap sack over each of our heads.

Someone helps me onto a chair.

I can barely stand.

*Yes,* I think, *it's about time.*

A noose tightens around my throat.

* * *

Dared gazed out the window. It was hard to get comfortable; he was squeezed between two big-boned women, but even that failed to dampen his good mood. The flight to Amsterdam would be a short one. He looked forward to the city, to the conference.

His interlude in Paris had been a success: a visit to the Louvre, a delicious meal, a stroll along the Seine. He'd even had time for a brief nap in the hotel room they'd given him—and, for the first time in years, he had slept soundly, undisturbed by nightmares and panic attacks. This trip, the interruption of his normal routine, was doing him good. For the last few years, he had worked like a madman, taking better care of his patients and colleagues than he took of himself. But he couldn't go on like that forever. He had to think of himself too. He had to live the life he had been given.

He glanced at his watch. KL 1244 had been scheduled to take off at 6:40 p.m., but the plane was still parked at the gate. From his vantage point, it looked like the entire cabin was occupied, with the sole exception of the window seat three rows in front of him. Low voices came from the front of the plane. It sounded as if someone was being welcomed. A delayed passenger?

Then a man walked through the curtain separating the first-class and economy cabins.

Dared felt as if a knife had been plunged into his heart.

It's the morning after the mass execution. I'm sitting in an office far from the cells and the torture chambers. The treatment to which I've been subjected has shattered me. I can barely sit or stand, but my mind is clear. Through the window, for the first time in months, I see the sun.

"Sign it," grins Thur, "and you'll be rid of us forever."

The other men in the room—the general, the lawyer, the guards—all laugh.

Before me on the table lies a statement that begins with the words: *I, Dared al-Saeed . . .*

Once I sign it, I'll be a free man.

I read through the statement. During my incarceration at Saydnaya, it says, I have been treated well, never tortured, never insulted. I have received all the necessary medical care. That's what it says.

Bullshit.

As is the reason given for my release: *General amnesty.*

What a joke.

The truth is, they are letting me go because my father, who maintains a close connection with the Assad clan, has paid them a very large sum of money. Should I be grateful? My father and I have never agreed about politics. Now I'll have to thank him for his intervention. The prospect is unwelcome. In my fourteen months at Saydnaya, I have lost everything I lived for, everything I believed in: my pride, my faith in humanity.

Worst of all, I have betrayed my brother Mustafa. I am deeply ashamed.

One stroke of the pen and I will be free.

Thur and the other men sniff impatiently.

My hand trembling, I pick up the pen. Every muscle in my body hurts.

I sign the statement.


The few seconds Dared was able to see him were sufficient. The limp, the expression, the hooked nose, the way he stroked his mustache before asking the passengers in the aisle and middle seats to let him by. Dared was absolutely certain: in the window seat three rows before him sat Karim al-Zaliq, alias Thur, the Bull.

Dared broke out in a cold sweat, and his mind raced with the images that had tormented him ever since his release: the torture, the humiliation, the dehumanization. There were no words to describe what had been done to him in Saydnaya.

As the plane lifted off the ground, he could feel an unstoppable rage course through him. *What the fuck is Thur doing here?* Had he retired and left Syria behind? How could such a bastard have escaped punishment for his crimes?

To ask the question was to answer it. All the bastards remained free men, up to and including President Assad himself. Dared remembered the interview he'd given two years before to an investigator from Amnesty International. His testimony—along with that of some eighty other victims—had been incorporated into a report with conclusions that had been impossible to deny. In Saydnaya, thousands of innocents had been systematically tortured and murdered. Students, lawyers, human-rights activists, soldiers, officers. Since the failure of the Arab Spring, somewhere between five thousand and thirteen thousand of the regime's opponents had been executed. Three hundred deaths per month, often many more than that, and the torture and murder had continued to this day.

The most loathsome fact of all was that the guilty parties would never be held to account for their crimes. Russia still supported Assad, while the rest of the world declined to choose sides and simply waited for the conflict to bleed itself out. Now that the dictator had the upper hand, he was once again the only authority the West could engage with. That thought was unbearable, and Dared struggled with it daily. Was there nothing he could do?

\* \* \*

Thur returned from the bathroom at the front of the economy cabin. He'd been there twice already. A weak bladder, Dared suspected. Or airsickness. He had considered following Thur into the narrow space and killing him. But how? Thur was bigger and, despite the difference in their ages, undoubtedly stronger. And how could Dared hope to leave the scene of such an act without being noticed?

An absurd idea.

A daydream.

Thur deserved to die, but Dared wasn't prepared to risk his hard-won freedom to achieve that end.

He watched as his enemy stood, waiting for the passengers in his row to make room for him, absently stroking his bushy mustache. For the briefest moment, Thur looked right at him, and his eagle eyes glittered. Had he recognized Dared? It was hard to believe that could be possible. Thur had personally tortured, humiliated, and murdered hundreds, if not thousands, of men. Merciless, a killing machine. And the bastard probably never lost a second of sleep over his deeds.

Dared balled his fists and saw his knuckles whiten. The women on either side of him inched away. He tried to force himself to smile, but failed.

The seat-belt sign illuminated. "*This is your captain speaking . . .*" The voice on the PA system announced that the plane would be landing at Amsterdam's airport in a quarter of an hour. The temperature on the ground was 41°F, visibility was good, and there was no wind.

Inside Dared's head, however, a storm raged. Anger, frustration—especially the latter. Sitting so close to the man who had destroyed his life and had been responsible for the death of his brother, yet he was unable to do anything about it. He craved revenge, but understood that his options were extremely limited. Perhaps he could turn Thur over to the police upon their arrival at the airport. *This man is a war criminal. Arrest him!*

They would laugh at him.

Meanwhile, Thur had visited the bathroom yet again. Visibly perspiring, he limped back to his seat. Was he ill? Dared hoped so. Typhoid fever, cancer. He would be happy if the villain dropped dead right there and then. Aisle Seat and Middle Seat stood once more to make room for him, and Thur dropped clumsily back into his place by the window.

The airplane descended through the clouds. Far below lay The Netherlands, a sea of lights. Streets, highways, homes. A network of orderly straight lines.

With a gentle bump, the Boeing touched down and taxied toward the terminal. The moment it came to a stop, the passengers jumped up and pulled their carry-ons from the overhead racks. The aircraft's door opened, and the seats and aisles gradually emptied.

Thur remained in his seat, his head resting against the window, as if he'd fallen asleep.

Dared also stayed where he was, no idea what his next move might be.

"You all right, sir?"

With a concerned expression on her face, the flight attendant bent over Thur, who mumbled something inaudible, got to his feet, took a small case from the bin, and, supporting himself by holding onto the seat backs, struggled up the aisle to the exit door.

Dared slung his messenger bag over his shoulder and followed.

"Have a nice stay in Amsterdam, sir."

As he nodded his thanks to the crew member at the door, Dared watched Thur stagger up the jet bridge like a drunkard. The man was definitely sick. Dared stayed close behind him.

They reached the far end of the jetway. The terminal was visible on the other side of a glass wall. There was still some distance to go before they would arrive at passport control. A sign on a pole apologized for the moving walkway being out of service. Thur made an annoyed gesture and stumbled slowly on, Dared keeping thirty feet behind him.

The Bull reached the restrooms, then leaned against the wall between them, as if unsure which was the right one. Then he pushed the men's room door open and went inside.

Dared hesitated. Should he follow the Bull into the bathroom? And, if so, then what?

He looked around. No travelers, no airport personnel, no crew. The corridor was deserted.

He pushed open the bathroom door and examined the interior. Three urinals and two sinks to the right, four stalls to the left. The handicapped stall's door stood open a crack.

As Dared listened for evidence of anyone else's presence, he saw Thur sitting on the floor of the handicapped stall, leaning against the side wall, his eyes closed, his face white and dripping with sweat, his jacket unbuttoned. His suitcase lay at his feet.

Dared pushed the stall door open.

"Hello?"

There was no response.

"Are you all right?"

He said the words in English, and there was no sign that the Bull was aware of him standing there. He set his messenger bag down on the floor and leaned over Thur.

"Can you hear me?"

No reaction.

"Do you need help?" he asked, this time in Arabic.

Thur opened his eyes and peered up at him in surprise.

"Are you sick?"

Thur nodded as if it was a foolish question and stammered something unintelligible.

"What's that you say?" said Dared, swinging the stall door closed behind him.

"Hypodermic," the Bull gasped.

Dared recognized the symptoms: the pale face, the perspiration, the irritation. Karim al-Zaliq was diabetic, and his blood sugar was dangerously low.

"Dextrose," the man managed to say, and he motioned to his case, which he had apparently been unable to open.

Dared undid the clasps. Inside one of the compartments, he found a vial of dextrose tablets and four insulin pens and needles.

"Dextrose," Thur said impatiently.

"I can't find your tablets," Dared replied, turning the case so Thur couldn't see the vial.

The Bull muttered angrily.

Dared took the four needles from their sterile packaging, pressed each onto a separate insulin pen, rotating them clockwise to engage their locking threads, then set each pen to the maximum dosage. When he flicked the top end of each barrel with a fingernail, he saw Thur's eyes widen in fear.

"What are you—?"

Before the man could move, Dared jabbed two of the needles into his stomach.

"What are you doing?"

"Repaying you for all the deaths you have on your conscience," Dared spat out, pressing the plungers.

Thur's mouth gaped wide. "Were you in—?"

"I was," said Dared, reaching for the two remaining pens. "I was in Saydnaya." He injected the third dose of insulin. "This one is for my brother. And this one"—he drove the fourth needle home—"this one is for me."

Thur's eyes closed, and he slumped to the floor. Dared checked his wrist for a pulse, and found only the slightest flutter. Unless the man was given sugar, he would be dead in fifteen minutes, possibly less.

Dared carefully wiped the pens clean with his handkerchief, then pressed each of their barrels against the fingertips of the Bull's right hand. He picked up his messenger bag and slung it over his shoulder, slipped out of the stall, closed the door behind him, and left the bathroom without looking back.

Following the exit signs, Dared found himself again surrounded by other travelers: men, women, children, from all directions on the compass. For the first time in years, the sight of so many people around him did not bring on a panic attack. He joined one of the passport control lines, patiently shuffling forward as he waited his turn.

The officer had short hair and wore a light-blue shirt with dark-blue epaulets. Dared handed over his passport. The officer examined it, looking back and forth between the document and the man who had presented it—checking the photo, Dared supposed.

He had just killed a man.

Anyone else would be flushed, shaking in his boots.

But Dared was completely calm. No regrets, no remorse. The only thing he felt was an incredible lightness, the burden he had borne for years at last lifted from his shoulders.

Smiling, the officer returned his passport. "Have a nice stay, sir," he said.

Dared moved on toward baggage claim. When he found the correct carousel, the conveyor belt had just begun to spit up its load of luggage. The passengers from his flight jostled for position, anxious to collect their possessions and be on their way. Dared ignored the pushing and shoving. It was as if he was wearing protective armor. As he worked his way closer to the belt, he glanced around. Somewhere among that sea of suitcases and garment bags and shrink-wrapped cardboard cartons must be a bag belonging to the Bull. How long would it be before someone found him in the bathroom? Was anyone waiting for him? Would anyone miss him? Dared couldn't imagine the man had friends or family.

He claimed his suitcase and headed for the green *Nothing to Declare* sign. A customs agent nodded him through. He walked on.

The arrivals hall was mobbed. Children with balloons, mothers and fathers, a young man with a bouquet of red roses, all searching eagerly for their loved ones.

Dared wondered if someone from the conference would come to fetch him. He'd e-mailed the organizers this morning from Paris to inform them that he'd be on the evening flight, but he'd had no response. He scanned his surroundings. There was a shop selling blue Delft plates and other souvenirs. On the walls, huge posters showed windmills and fields of red and yellow tulips and canal houses and Rembrandt's *Night Watch*.

This time, Dared decided, he would go to the Rijksmuseum and see the famous painting for himself.

He was about to give up hope of being met when he saw her. A pretty young woman with long blond hair and green eyes. She was holding a sign with his name printed on it in large capital letters.

Waving, he approached her. "Hello," he said, "I'm Dared."

"Hi, Dared." She had a lovely smile. "I'm Saskia. Welcome to Amsterdam."

# SPUI 13

BY ANNELOES TIMMERIJE

*Centrum*

*April 2016*

E lla disappeared on the day I began to live alone in the heart of the city after thirty years of marriage. The day I returned to where I came from, to the person I used to be.

I knew something was up when she didn't drop by as we'd agreed, but I drew the wrong conclusion from her absence. Ella is always on time, unless a major story breaks. Then she vanishes, and no one can reach her. That's the way it goes in her line of work.

I decided to consider her nonappearance Lesson #1 in my New Life course, so I threw on a jacket, checked myself in the mirror, and—passing through the living room where Mimi had fought for her life—left the house and walked over to the Athenaeum Bookstore on the corner, as I'd done so many times in the past.

Even before my move, I'd decided not to have anything delivered to my new digs, so that at least once a day I'd have to get out of the house. I bought a newspaper from a girl who could have been me back then: eighteen, maybe nineteen years old, working part-time for extra cash to supplement whatever academic scholarship she was getting. I grew up behind a counter, so I knew the drill. In the four years I worked at the Athenaeum, I dealt with unkempt punks and unwed mothers, sold newspapers in six languages and hash brownies. Over and above my paltry salary, I had the opportunity to meet famous writers like Harry Mulisch and John Irving, the crown princess incognito, and the king of the squatters in full regalia. Everyone who was anyone and everyone who was no one came to the Athenaeum—and there I stood in the middle of it all.

This part of the city is now clean and predictable, all the anarchy of the olden days long gone. The bookstore no longer shows customers with lousy taste the door, and *Het Lieverdje*—the beloved bronze statue of a cheerful boy of the streets—has survived the Provo riots, the happenings, even its own kidnapping. After eleven occupations by students, the University of Amsterdam's *Maagdenhuis* remains stately and forgiving, true to the line from the Gospel According to Mark carved into its lintel: *Suffer the little children to come unto me.* The square has been newly repaved with stones and is ringed by stuccoed and lacquered buildings—an open invitation to a comfortable and carefree life.

I should have been relieved that day—and happy—but what I felt when I slipped my key into the outer door was alienation. As if I no longer belonged on the "village green," as Ella used to call the Spui.

I climbed the stairs and let myself into my new home, settled onto my new couch with a bag of chips and the paper, clicked on my new television for company, and fell asleep.

A call from the police awoke me. Apparently my ex had given them my number.

A moment later, although the camera connected to my new doorbell wasn't yet working properly, I recognized over the intercom the same female voice I'd just heard on the phone. She must have called from across the street, or right in front of my door. I was surprised to see that she was alone; perhaps the police only travel in pairs on TV shows. Ella knows that sort of thing.

She was the one who'd given me the courage to leave my husband, to return to my old stomping grounds. She had kept me grounded as I ripped myself free of the suffocating relationship I had too long confused with love. She'd never pressured me, had always been understanding—though it was true there'd been times she'd impatiently stamped her foot, frustrated with my hesitations and delay.

Of the two of us, Ella is the strong one, the independent one, the determined one, the one who's always ready to lend a helping hand to a friend in need. I am the quiet one, the timid one, the mouse. It takes awhile to discover that there's more to me than meets the eye. That's the way it was even when we were childhood friends in the Haarlemmerstraat, skipping rope on the narrow sidewalk in front of our fathers' shops.

"We take this matter very seriously," the detective said.

"This matter" was a video that had been delivered to *De Telegraaf*—one of Amsterdam's largest daily newspapers—a few hours earlier.

"Was it a message *from* Ella," I asked, "or from someone else, *about* her?"

Instead of responding to my question, the detective posed one of her own: what was Ella working on?

I never know what Ella's working on, I answered honestly. Nobody knows what Ella's working on—that's why she's so good at what she does. Her secrecy, Ella says, is what allows her to do her job: her silence protects her sources, her family, her friends . . . and herself.

"We were going to watch a movie," I said, nodding at the

Blu-ray of *The Graduate* on the coffee table, "to christen my new house."

We only watch *The Graduate* on special occasions. The first time, at the Tuschinski, we were fifteen, maybe sixteen, and we dreamed of growing up to be Joan Baez. Mimi was still with us then. Before we even left the theater, the three of us agreed that we instead wanted to grow up to be Katharine Ross. Ella was already on her way, with that thick brown hair. When we were forty, we saw *The Graduate* again, now through the eyes of mature women. Ten years later, we watched it a third time, and last year we'd planned yet another showing to celebrate our making it to sixty despite all the cigarettes we'd smoked. That screening never happened, though, since Ella was on the road for the newspaper and I was busy explaining to my husband what an insufferable ass he had become.

On the day of Ella's disappearance, we'd planned a catch-up *Graduate* to mark my independence—and, more than that, without either of us having said the words aloud, as a tribute to Mimi. After that, we were going to have dinner at Café Luxembourg, Ella's favorite. That was all I had to offer the policewoman, I thought at the time.

The kidnapping made the evening news and was almost instantly a trending topic on Twitter. By the next morning, photos of the most famous crime reporter in The Netherlands were everywhere you looked. The banner headline on the front page of *De Telegraaf*, her employer, screamed, "WHO HAS OUR ELLA?" in oversized capitals.

I'd spent the night in a chair by the window, with all the lights out and the curtains open, waiting for some word from her, staring at the barred windows of the Esprit store across the road, at the soft glow of the streetlights, at the black-and-white neighborhood cat—officially the Luxembourg's house cat, who lay deep in thought across the Begijnhof's doorway— at the pedestrians, mostly solitary men who walked past my house from left to right or right to left without giving it a second glance. Some of them were visibly drunk, some hurried self-confidently by as if they were on their way to jobs that really *mattered.* Between two and five a.m., young women pedaled past on their bicycles, like Ella and I did years ago—without worry, without fear—until Mimi's fate forever changed our relationship to our little corner of the city.

Ella sometimes jokes that if twenty-four hours go by and I haven't heard from her, she's probably lying at the bottom of the Amstel River with a bullet in her head. In that case, my instructions are to get in touch with Bert.

She says it lightly, and I know she is unafraid of the dangers that are such an integral part of her world, a world with which I am completely unfamiliar. She seems to enjoy the excitement, but when no one is paying attention—not even she herself—I think it gnaws at her. Anguish stalks her at the very moments when there's nothing to be concerned about. When I stay over at her place, or when we share a room on one of our hiking trips, her nightmares keep me awake.

My ex, the son of a bitch, texted to warn me not to involve him in any way, shape, or form in *that Ella business*. Nobody seemed interested in how I was doing, another reminder of all the people who'd unfriended me. The one who walks away from a marriage is the one to blame, something like that. Only the publisher at the company for which I've been freelancing for years took the trouble the next morning to stop by. All he had to do was walk across the street, but his concern seemed genuine and I appreciated the support. We talked about Ella, and then—to convince ourselves that things couldn't be as bad as they seemed—about a manuscript I was proofreading for him. Before he left, he congratulated me on my new home and my new life. "It's so cozy here on the Spui," he said.

And that was my welcome back to the neighborhood where, once upon a time, Ella and I had majored in the Dutch language at the University of Amsterdam, where, encouraged by our parents, we had escaped the humdrum fate of Haarlemmerstraat shopgirls to which, only a few decades earlier, we would have been doomed. Here, at this exact part of the city, our freedom began. Here, for us, the *world* began.

The morning after Ella's kidnapping, it seemed as if the world converged on the Spui—I had to zigzag around knots of gawkers to reach the Heisteeg. On my way to the Lijnbaansgracht police station, I imitated the self-confident tread of the men at night: *Here I come, and nothing bad can possibly happen to me.* From the desk sergeant's reaction to my name, I could see that any hope it had all been a misunderstanding was misplaced. There's always that glimmer of hope when something awful happens, even though you ought to know better. Ella and I had experienced that with Mimi. But the desk sergeant knew exactly who I was and why I was there. There was no misunderstanding; it was all true.

The *Telegraaf*'s editor-in-chief was the only person other than the detectives who had seen the video. I watched it three times that morning, together with a man who introduced himself as Theo, a detective in the major-crimes unit, not much older than me.

It opened with a shot of my house, filmed from across the street: a narrow building, not quite perpendicular to the ground, an unimportant afterthought compared to the chic art nouveau home next door. The camera zoomed in slowly on my front door. In the next shot, I was lugging two huge suitcases, tagging behind Ella, who wore a backpack and carried a smaller bag in her left hand and a key in her right. She opened the door, took a step back, made an exaggerated bow, and ushered me in with a sweep of her arm. It was funny: we looked like teenagers moving into a dorm. That was our way of dealing with the serious nature of the occasion.

The remaining shots were almost all of Ella. She'd been filmed on the way to my house, and coming out the front door, and walking along the Spui, probably heading back to her own apartment on the Singel. I laughed when I saw her wrestling with the lamp she'd bought as a housewarming gift and had planted in my still-empty living room to surprise me. For those few seconds, I could almost imagine I was watching a rerun of *The Banana Splits*.

Theo paused the video the second time we watched it.

"She had a key to your house?" he asked.

"She still does."

He nodded and pressed play.

Ella, sitting at a wooden table, a white wall as backdrop. I was surprised to see how *normal* she appeared. It was like looking at the Ella who reports on a high-profile murder case, the Ella we all know from television: eloquent, informed, well put together. Her left eye was slightly squinted, the only clue to the nervousness she must have been feeling.

"This message is for my man," she said, straight into the camera. "I'm fine, I'm getting enough to eat and drink, I'm not being mistreated." She took a breath, cleared her throat, and continued: "I'm being held against my will. The conditions for my release will follow."

The screen went blank.

"She doesn't have a man," I said.

Ella doesn't believe in long-term relationships, they're far too complicated. Typically, her boyfriends don't last longer than a month or so; after that, she gets bored and gives up. She usually sees two or three guys simultaneously, though more recently she's begun to find that too exhausting. Instead, she's bought two additional apartments—in the wake of the financial crisis, she was able to pick them up relatively cheaply—so she now has three home addresses scattered around the city. Real estate is her current passion.

"She means me," Theo said. "My last name is Mann. Ella and I have known each other professionally for years. She's talking to me."

It was only then that I realized something Theo already knew: "They think my house belongs to Ella."

Theo raised an eyebrow.

I asked him when he'd figured it out.

"Last night, soon as I saw the video. Spui 13 is still a red flag for me, so I sent my colleague over to talk to you."

Mimi was twenty-one, the same age as Ella and me, when she was awakened by a loud noise that October night, almost forty years ago. Her boyfriend Mark was a sound sleeper, which we felt at the time explained why she had gone down to Spui 13's second floor alone to see what was causing the racket.

It came out during the trial that two men, brothers, had broken into the shop on the ground floor and climbed the stairs to our two-level apartment. One of the brothers put a knife to Mimi's throat. "Just to scare her," he told the judge. But then he raped her. And then the other brother took a turn, except he was so drunk he couldn't come. That's when—

according to the second brother's testimony—things got out of hand. He slit Mimi's throat with a single sweep of his own blade. Meanwhile, the first brother went up to the third floor and beat Mark to death with a bicycle chain.

Theo Mann was a young patrolman at the time. His supervisor recognized in him a talent for detective work and brought him along to the scene. The murders of Mimi and Mark, he told me, remained one of the grisliest crimes of his long career. What he saw that night, the butchery of two people around the same age as himself, had stayed with him for all the years that had followed.

"Mimi was my cousin," I told him that afternoon, after we watched the video.

I didn't have to think about it for long when I heard that the building was going to be auctioned off. Ella was the one who first found out about it, of course—I never hear about things like that. "Buy it," she'd said, but without putting too much pressure on me. And you don't have to know much about real estate to understand that a property like that one—a sweet little house, the smallest on the Spui—doesn't come on the market often.

"Unusual," Theo remarked tactfully. "Most people wouldn't want a house with that history."

Mimi's parents—who had died a year after the murders; of grief, my mother always said—had tried to buy it at the time, to prevent strangers from moving in. But the owner, a notorious slumlord, hadn't even responded to their repeated offers.

"It used to be our house," I said, "a long time ago. Ella and I squatted there."

If that weekend had unfolded differently, it would have

been *our* dead bodies the young Theo would have investigated. Ella and I had wanted to get away for a few days to London, but we didn't dare leave the house empty—we were afraid other squatters would take it over, or the owner would send in a goon squad to secure it. We'd almost given up on our plans when Mimi, who had moved to Groningen to attend the university there, announced that she and Mark would be happy to come down to Amsterdam to house-sit.

"Ella and I were questioned," I said, "but I don't think it was you."

Theo let that pass. "You haven't been living there for long, I understand."

"It seems longer, but I only moved in yesterday."

"From where?"

"From a marriage to an architect who treated me like I was one of his designs."

With a scarf wrapped around my head, I strolled home through the crowded Leidsestraat, lingering here and there like a tourist and barely recognizable. No one would know that I had just been to the police station. Not that it mattered, but my invisibility made me feel better.

Turning off the Kalverstraat onto the Spui, I tried to ignore the people with cameras. There were three of them right in front of me, and at least five more taking snapshots or videos with their phones—there are *always* people with cameras on the Spui, but that day there were more of them than usual. In an attempt to convince myself that I was completely relaxed, I went into the Esprit store and bought a shoulder bag I didn't want. With my old one stuffed inside the new one, I forced myself not to run across the street to my house. Scared on my own square.

Before I left the station, Theo had asked if I was okay, if there was someone who could come and stay with me. I'd lied to both questions. I couldn't think of a soul I wanted to see, except for Ella.

I shot both of the front door's dead bolts—with Ella's key in the hands of her kidnapers, the fancy three-point lock my insurance company had recommended was now worthless—went upstairs, checked all the windows on the second floor, then up another flight of steps to the bedroom I hadn't yet slept in. I turned on the radio to drown out the sounds from the street and fell into an exhausted sleep in my new bed.

In the middle of the afternoon, I called a locksmith and then the realtor on the corner of the Spuistraat.

"I have a house for sale."

"We'll be happy to help you," the person who answered the phone told me. "May I send my colleague out to have a look, perhaps sometime around the end of this week?"

As soon as I mentioned the address, he proposed moving the preliminary visit to the following day.

"I'd like someone to come today," I said. "Tonight, if necessary."

"I need you to see something else," Theo had told me, after I'd watched the video for the third time. "Can you keep this quiet?"

Keeping quiet was a skill I had mastered during the years of my marriage. I nodded.

He slid a sheet of paper across the table. "This was delivered this morning."

It was a short list of demands, addressed to *The Owner*, who was ordered to put Spui 13 up for sale. A particular realtor was indicated, complete with phone number. Even the name of the ultimate purchaser—J. de Vries—and the sales price were specified.

"So they know Ella doesn't own the house," I said.

"Or they realized it after kidnapping her," said Theo.

"No, they kidnapped her because she's famous."

"That can't be the only reason."

Theo asked from whom I'd purchased the building.

"A homesick American. I can send you his contact information if you want it."

"Please, although I don't see a link from him to Ella," said Theo.

"She was at a real-estate auction when she found out Spui 13 was coming on the market. Does that help?"

After that came a formal interrogation. We went to another room; the woman detective who had visited me the previous evening sat in. Theo wanted to hear all about Ella and me, about my family connection to Mimi, about my purchase of Spui 13. I explained how Ella had handled the bidding for me at the auction, how brilliant she was.

"Why didn't the American just use a realtor?" he asked.

"He wanted it over and done with, without a lot of hoopla. That's the advantage of an auction sale," I explained. "According to Ella."

"That's the connection," said Theo's colleague.

He nodded. "Yeah, I think Ella's kidnapper must have seen her at the auction. Was there a lot of interest? Did she get in a bidding war with someone else?"

Ella had bid so strategically that the other potential buyers dropped out quickly. Later, after too much prosecco at the Luxembourg, I asked her if she'd ever considered leaving journalism for the world of real estate. She looked at me, half smiling, took another sip, and said, "An interesting thought."

Obviously, what I really wanted to know was if she was researching a story about the Amsterdam real-estate market. But I didn't ask, because I know Ella would rather die than say a word about whatever she's working on.

I told Theo and his colleague about the impact the murders of Mimi and Mark had had on our lives. How fear had held us in its grip for years and how, as an antidote against the poison of the atrocity, we had become more ourselves than we had previously been. Already an extrovert, Ella had chosen to fight crime with pen in hand and welcome the limelight, while I—the introvert—had abandoned my dream of becoming the same type of Dutch-language teacher I had once had myself in order to avoid standing in front of groups of students. I withdrew further and further from the world and took refuge in the privacy of a home office, surrounded by manuscripts I was paid to proofread.

"I wanted to go back to Spui 13 to keep Mimi's memory alive," I said, acknowledging the guilt that had never left us. "I suppose that sounds crazy."

Theo almost shook his head.

"The American completely renovated the building," I went on. "It doesn't look anything like the way it was."

When Theo brought his questioning to a close, I asked him something that had been burning in my throat for the last hour: "Are you sure the guys you arrested really did it?"

Everyone on and around the Spui was shocked by the murders. Ella and I came back from London when we heard. Until they caught the godforsaken bastards, we returned to our parents' houses and stayed cooped up in our bedrooms behind closed curtains. Later, my coworkers told me that the

Athenaeum was mobbed during the weeks after the crime. Regular customers dropped by two or three times a day to see if anyone had new information, and the same was true of the local residents, the other shopkeepers, the bar owners, and especially the journalists who frequented Café De Zwart. Even the right-wing snobs in Café Hoppe thirsted to learn who had the murders on their conscience as much as they thirsted for another round. And the same two words were on everyone's lips: *Hells Angels.*

The day before my house—without photos or even an asking price—was listed in the real-estate website Funda's *Silent Sale* section, I found a plastic Media Markt bag hanging on my front doorknob. It wasn't quite ten o'clock, and I'd just dashed out to pick up a loaf of bread. Inside the bag was a cat, the black-and-white from the Luxembourg, its head severed from its body.

Fear—real, razor-sharp, deathly fear—apparently brings clarity along with it. I went upstairs with the idea that—for the time being, at least—I was safe. They couldn't kill me, that would complicate the sale of the house. Which gave me the courage to check every room, every drawer. Only then did I lean over the kitchen sink to vomit coffee and bile and weep until I had no tears left to shed.

With the cat wrapped in a hand towel, I crossed the square to the café. I didn't notify Theo at first, and I lied to the Luxembourg's owner about where I'd found the poor creature. "Around the corner," I said, "in the Voetboogstraat."

He disappeared into his office behind the bar, sobbing, the beheaded cat cradled in his arms. The manager made me a double espresso and asked me if I'd heard anything about Ella yet.

"What a shitty welcome back to the Spui," she said.

* * *

I called Bert. Because Ella had told me to, and because I couldn't handle the situation on my own.

"If you hadn't called today," he said, "I'd've called *you* tomorrow morning. Ella's instructions."

That was all the introduction we needed, all we needed to trust each other. Which was good, because Bert showed up at my door an hour later with a laptop, suitcase, sleeping bag, and rolled-up camping pad.

Bert has worked at the newspaper for half his life. Ella is his boss. Her silence about her work extends to the identities of her colleagues, which is why Bert and I had never previously met. I knew his name from the paper and from Ella's instructions. I could hear her voice inside my head: *He's tall, clever, and a good man—and that's exactly what you'll need.*

For the time that he stayed with me, he slept on his pad in the living room, close to the steps that led down to the front door. He watched over me, cooked for me, took on the management of my life.

I told him everything, even the things Theo had warned me not to talk about. They were, after all, *my* things. Including the cat.

"The message is loud and clear," said Bert. "They're watching you. But of course you already knew that."

He made sure the locksmith did a good job, after double-checking with his contacts in the security sector, since the lock business isn't always on the up-and-up. Then we made a shopping list for the day and walked together to the Albert Heijn supermarket on the Koningsplein. "This is how we'll do it," said Bert. "We'll show them you're still here and not alone. The paper's paying."

Amsterdammers of my generation are sure to remember

the Spui Murders, but it was different for Bert, who was about ten years my junior. After an hour's research—with his phone on speaker so he could ask questions of his sources at the same time his skilled fingers danced across the Internet—he'd brought himself up to speed on Mimi and Mark's case. He told me what he'd learned, so I could provide additional details and make corrections. Everything seemed to indicate, he said, that the police had arrested the real murderers. "But of course you already knew that."

Bert is the kind of guy who can say things like that without being annoying.

I wasn't so sure. "There has to be a reason they want me to sell the house."

"Those brothers were released after doing fifteen years, did you know that?"

"No, and I wish you hadn't told me."

"No worries, their friends got rid of them . . . um, about twelve years later. Huh, I wrote that story myself."

Bert explained that motorcycle gangs were part of his beat, even back then. "Now I understand why Ella didn't want that assignment."

"They weren't in the Hells Angels," I said.

"How do you know?"

"They always denied it, and so did the actual gang members."

"Bullshit. The police were able to identify the brand of the bicycle chain Mark was beaten with. Hells Angels all the way."

A minute later, he held up his left hand and said, "Wait a second." He studied the screen of his laptop, the fingers of his right hand working the touch pad. When he looked up, he told me he had a new idea. "Is it possible they broke in to prove something? Could it have been some kind of initiation rite that spiraled out of control?"

Three days later, the realtor called to tell me that J. de Vries had offered a hundred thousand euros above the asking price.

I was speechless, and after a moment the man added, "As compensation for your loss."

They'd kidnapped Ella to blackmail me out of my house, but now they were being *generous* about it?

"Do you believe that explanation?" I demanded.

The realtor didn't respond. Instead, dotting the i's and crossing the t's, he asked if I had any questions about the formal settlement. He knew I knew he was just an errand boy.

I told him I wanted to sign the papers as soon as possible.

"They've proposed the middle of next week."

"Make it sooner. And I want a guarantee from the bank."

"I've already got it," he said.

Something the realtor said got me thinking, and Bert agreed with me that it was strange.

"No one would talk about 'your loss' in a situation like this," Bert said. "Compensation for damages or inconvenience, *that* I would have bought."

Today, as I look back and try to figure out when and how things went wrong, it seems to me that this choice of words, which sounded almost intentional, was a clue. I still can't figure out, though, how we could have made better use of it.

The contract seemed perfectly straightforward. Bert—who like Ella had connections with the Amsterdam police—

forwarded the buyer's address and passport number to Theo.

"This Jan de Vries—that's his full name—is seventy-four and a filthy-rich old geezer," Bert told me, after an hour of research. "I can't find anything unusual about him, which is unusual all by itself. They know him on the business desk. A smooth operator, avoids publicity."

"I want you to go with me to the signing," I said that evening, as he stood in the kitchen slicing vegetables for a ratatouille. "But of course you already know that."

There was no way Bert would have *allowed* me to go by myself, so the next afternoon we strolled arm-in-arm to the realtor's office around the corner. Theo had suggested I think of it like any other business transaction, so that's what I did. There'd be plainclothes cops in the area, he assured me, quiet and invisible, ready to step in if they were needed.

The prospective purchaser of my house wore a fine Italian suit—Corneliani, Bert told me later. His face seemed vaguely familiar, like other people with money and power. The realtor asked him if he'd read the contract carefully.

The man nodded.

"Any questions or amendments?"

We both shook our heads.

After we signed, the realtor quite properly congratulated de Vries on his purchase and me on my sale.

"Now *I* have a question," I said to de Vries. "Why did you want me out? Why couldn't I go on living there?"

De Vries, the realtor, and Bert all looked at me with raised eyebrows.

De Vries got up, gave the realtor an ice-cold glare, and headed for the door.

"When will Ella be released?" I called after him.

He turned and said, "You never should have bought that building in the first place."

And he left the office.

Bert was furious at me. Theo too, though he did a better job of holding it in. They were right, of course: I should have just played the game for the sake of Ella's safety. However, a week later—as promised—a new video was delivered to *De Telegraaf*. Bert and I watched it together with Theo at the Lijnbaansgracht police station.

No Ella. Where I'd expected to see her face, light with relief, I saw instead myself, in tears, Bert's arm around me. We were crossing the Spui, approaching my house. Bert squeezed my shoulder, I wiped my cheeks. Without our noticing, some-one had managed to film us on our way back from the realtor's office. The video ended with one sentence of typed text: *She will be released the day after the closing.*

That evening, I thanked Bert for taking care of me by cook-ing dinner for once. We raised more than one glass to Ella's upcoming release, but we didn't talk about it much, as if our words might jinx her. After the third toast, I dared to ask when he planned to publish his story.

"Pretty soon. It's almost done. When they let her go, she'll call you first, then me. As soon as I hear from her, I'll post the article online. We'll save *her* piece for the print edition. That'll be the most important account, obviously."

In his journalist's mind, he was already looking beyond the actual release. That didn't surprise me: Ella is exactly the same.

Movers came to put my things in storage, and I carried a suitcase of clothes and toiletries to Ella's apartment on the Singel without looking back.

I didn't want to go to the closing, and I could have given a notary my power of attorney. But I went. The buyer ignored my stare, signed the final papers, and left without a word.

I walked back to the Spui for a sort of final goodbye, and saw him sitting on a bench outside the bookstore.

"Do you have a place to go," he asked, getting slowly to his feet, "or will you squat again?"

It was only then that I recognized him from all those years ago. Jan de Vries had begun his career as a slumlord on the Spui.

"I didn't like the two of you then," he said, "and I don't like you now."

And he turned away and crossed the square to a chauffeured limo that was waiting for him.

The brothers who murdered Mimi and Mark had told the truth. They weren't Hells Angels, and what happened wasn't an initiation gone out of control. They'd been hired to toss a pair of squatters out of a house, and *that* was what had gone out of control.

Theo cursed up a storm, immediately assigned a team of detectives to investigate de Vries, and promised me the man would never get away with it. That was a comforting thought, although I knew it was an empty promise as long as Ella was still in the man's hands.

Bert rewrote his lead and came up with a new headline: "REAL-ESTATE MAGNATE SUSPECTED OF SPUI MURDERS."

The article would go live the moment Ella was released.

After the closing, I decided to clean Ella's apartment, just to have something to do. The next morning at daybreak, I began preparing for her return.

*April 2017*

It's now a year since Bert's article nailed the ex-slumlord to the cross. After he published it, he went on to write an entire series of stories about the Amsterdam real-estate mafia, partly with the help of Ella's notes.

But Theo Mann was unable to keep his promise: Jan de Vries made a clean getaway before the police showed up to arrest him. He's now living large—and not exactly incognito—in a country that has no extradition treaty with The Netherlands.

On the first Sunday of every month, early in the morning, while the city sleeps, I've gotten into the habit of walking down the Spui and along the Rokin to the Doelensluis, where I can stand on the bridge and watch the Amstel River flow slowly by.

It's been so long since I last heard from Ella that I imagine her prediction must have come true.

*This story was inspired by an actual Amsterdam murder case.*

# ANKLE MONITOR

BY HERMAN KOCH

*Watergraafsmeer*

*Translated by Sam Garrett*

Maybe it was a mistake to go back to my old neighborhood on the very first day of a weekend leave. I could have been imagining it, but I seemed to read it off the faces of the people I came across on the street: how they glanced up at me, walked on, then took another look. I avoided the butcher shop and the bakery I used to go to. I bought a couple of buns, some sliced liver, and salted beef at the Albert Heijn on Christiaan Huygensplein—the girls at the registers were too young to remember, they were just as friendly to me as they were to everyone else.

When I walked into Elsa's Café, though, conversations literally slammed to a halt. That's what I was that first day: a conversation killer. I'm not a complete bonehead, I was more or less prepared for it, but it's still weird when it actually happens. At Elsa's they have these swinging doors, like a saloon in an old western. That's the way it felt to me: as though I was coming through the swinging doors, six-guns drawn, to settle an old account. And in a certain sense I was, but not with the people who were there, not with anyone who was at Elsa's right then.

I don't know what I would have done, though, if *he* had been standing there, prattling at the bar with a beer in his hand. Then I wouldn't have been fully accountable. In fact,

I've never been accountable for my actions—not being accountable is the thin red line in my life that's taken me everywhere, from the maximum-security facility to here again, now, in my old neighborhood.

There are about twenty of us in there, in what you'd probably call an "open block." Open to the extent that we don't have to stay in our cells between nine and six, but can just wander the corridors. In fact, it's only one corridor, a broad one, sure, more than thirty feet across. Everyone on both sides of it has his door open, some of us hang our laundry out to dry on a rack in the corridor. When you look in, the cells are like you'd expect: girlie posters on the walls, a little desk with a couple of books, an outdated desktop computer. A few of the guys don't have any photos or posters at all, so that's clear enough: posters of half-naked men or boys would send the wrong signal on our block.

At one end of the corridor is the rec room, with Ping-Pong and foosball tables and a row of shelves with games: Risk, Monopoly, that kind of thing. And about five decks of playing cards, with a couple of cards missing from each deck.

At the other end of the corridor is the point where our open block stops, clearly marked with bars and the kind of massive wired glass you couldn't bust through, not even with an ax. As though anyone here has an ax in his cell! No, but we do have other things, things I'm not going to talk about here, I'm not out to rat on anyone. What am I saying: I'm not out to rat on *myself!* Later, when I go back on Monday, maybe I'll need those things again—I hope not, but you never know. It's good to have them, the mere thought of those things and what you can do with them is what keeps you calm.

Sometimes, when they start bitching at me, I picture it

in my mind: I'm lying on my bed and a guard says something about dirty laundry on the floor, making it sound like he's my mother. Then I think about it. In my mind, I slide my hand under the mattress. He doesn't have time to get away, maybe he starts screaming, maybe he doesn't: I'm fast. Whatever the case, it's too late. I'm finished before his colleagues can get there.

But I don't do that. I won't ever do it, either. As far as that goes, we're all the same around here. *Good behavior* is the key thing we have in common. We do our little hand-washes, we borrow a book from the library, we play Ping-Pong and foosball like civilized individuals, pull some weeds in the herb garden. In any case, we never fight. We're always conscious of the cameras, twenty-four hours a day. "Wasn't that serve out?" we ask cautiously and, cool as can be of course, lay our paddles on the table. We look at each other. *Staring down* is what they call that. It's about who has the steadiest eye, the most eloquent body language. But the security cameras don't pick up a thing. "I think you're right, it was out." You make a mental note to do something later, in the showers or out in the yard, in a corner where there aren't any cameras.

The serve wasn't out, you know that—and he knows it too.

The first time he showed up at visiting hours was six months ago. A journalist, a big name in crime circles. Marc Verhoeven. He had a plan: a biography, the story of my life.

"We share the revenues," Verhoeven told me then. "Everybody wants to read about you. I expect it'll sell a quarter of a million copies."

I was up for it. I didn't have to tell him everything, nothing that would jeopardize my getting out of here three years from now.

"But I'll need you to tell me a couple of things, of course," he said. "Things people don't know. Things they want to read about." Then Verhoeven asked if I was okay with him interviewing my wife. "*Ex*-wife," he corrected himself right away. "To get a complete picture, I want to interview Chiara too. But not without your permission, of course. Not behind your back."

I sensed something at the time, I don't know exactly how to describe it: a dark cloud, people say sometimes, as in, "dark clouds gathered." But what I sensed wasn't so much dark as compact and odorless. A poisonous cloud from a chemical plant, the neighbors are warned to keep their doors and windows shut.

"She's not my ex-wife," I told him. "We're only separated."

"Okay, okay," he said. "Have it your way. I mean, if you'd rather not have me interview her, just say so."

Later on, I couldn't help but laugh about that *Not behind your back*. All you could really say was that I had been too trusting. Looking back on it, if I had known then what was going to happen, that visiting hour would have gone differently. Would have *ended* differently, I should probably say.

You have those animal habitats at the zoo that look a little like an open cellblock. In fact, there are no bars. Just a moat with a wall on one side that the visitors can lean on, and the habitat itself is on the other side. A lot of trouble has been taken to reconstruct the animals' natural surroundings: a couple of boulders have been brought in, there's some sand, one or two trees that obviously aren't native to these parts.

At the back of the habitat is where the animals lie—let's assume we're talking about *predators* here, but it could just as easily be zebras or chimpanzees—dozing in the shade. There's not much movement, a couple of sparrows are pecking around for leftovers between the rocks, but it's not enough to wake the predators from their afternoon nap. They—for the sake of argument we're still assuming that we're talking about mammals here: lions, tigers, bears—blink their eyes occasionally, as though they're dreaming: a nice dream, perhaps; they're back where they came from, Yellowstone Park, the forests of Madagascar, the rolling savannas of Kenya or Tanzania.

Then, suddenly, there is tumult. Somebody—perhaps only a child, a child who has escaped its parents' attention for a few seconds—has clambered up onto the wall and then fallen into the moat. There are screams, mostly from the parents, but then other bystanders get involved in the general panic: they shout instructions at the child, conflicting instructions, one of them shouts this, the other shouts that. *Swim! Run! Don't move!* The water is shallow, it only comes up to the child's chest. *A rope! A keeper! A ladder!*

Then one of the predators—now we can come out and say it: this is the lions' habitat—one of the *lions* opens an eye. *What's all the noise?* he wonders. *Can't a lion get a little sleep in this habitat? What's all that splashing around in the moat?*

It's the biggest lion, the male, the kind of lion we imagine when we think of a lion: from *The Lion King*, a Metro-Goldwyn-Mayer lion, a lion like the ones on a pouch of Samson rolling tobacco, with a huge mane around its head. Slowly it stretches, even more slowly it rises, one leg at a time, onto all fours; easy as can be, it wanders over to the moat to look at what all the fuss is about.

One of the last times he came to visit, about two weeks ago, that's the way I looked at Marc Verhoeven: the way a lion would. We were both in the same space; just like the child in the moat, the journalist had found his way into the animals' habitat. True, there was a guard standing at the door, but I've already told you: I'm fast, I can do it in a couple of seconds.

Right then and there, I knew. I'd known it for a long time already, of course, but now I knew for sure. I could smell it.

*Like I was sniffing his underpants.*

Yes, that's what it was like, no two ways about it. I'd fished his underpants out of the laundry basket and sniffed at them—and I knew.

And now I could smell it, even without having his underpants in my hand. Later, lots of times, I asked myself how I was able to do that. And I think I know.

First of all, because of all the years of training *on the outside*. In my professional community, the sixth sense is more important than the other five. For *survival*. You have to be able to interpret a sound without actually hearing it: the window of a car parked in front of your house is rolled down, the safety on a pistol is slid back. You hit the ground before the shot is even fired. You survive.

And on the inside too, just as much. Without turning around, you know who comes into the showers right after you. Who's moved up behind you in a flash. You slick back your hair under the hot spray from the showerhead, you keep your eyes closed and let the water splash against your eyelids—but within half a second, you turn. You yank the sharpened screwdriver out of the other person's hand, in one move you break his wrist—and, if you've got enough time, all five of his fingers.

I listened to Verhoeven. For the umpteenth time, he asked me about my connections with this guy, with some other guy, about where I was when Edward G. got plugged behind the counter of his cigar store, about whether I had used different passports during my frequent trips to Thailand, Colombia, and my place on the Costa del Sol.

Yes, I listened, I nodded, and I answered, but meanwhile I breathed through my nose as much as possible. I stuck my nose out above the grassland of the savanna, nothing but my nose, the zebra foal wandering this way would never get to see my head, the cracking of its own vertebrae would be the last sound it heard in its short life, once I sank my teeth into it.

*When did it start? How long has this been going on?*

It surprised me to realize that I wasn't really even all that surprised. That's right, I could even start to understand it a little. Ex-wife of criminal serving solid time sets out to start a new life, to forget the past. And then, one day, a journalist comes to visit. A crime journalist who is planning to write a book about her husband—her ex-husband. He is not entirely unhandsome, he's charming, patient—not hotheaded, not like *him*, she thinks, and she brushes the thought aside as quickly as it arises.

On his third visit, the journalist brings her flowers, on the fourth a box of chocolates. She notices, despite herself, that she has started to enjoy his visits more and more, that she spends more time in front of the mirror, pins her hair up and then lets it fall; when the doorbell rings, she moistens her lips with the tip of her tongue.

This time he has brought along a bottle of wine, the apartment is a little less well-lit than during his previous visit; on the coffee table which she's set with a bowl of nuts and blocks of cheese with mustard, a candle is burning.

"What did you say again, when do you have that weekend leave?" he asked me the last time we sat in the visiting area, after the guard announced we had two minutes left.

"Two weeks from now."

"And how long have you got?"

"Three days. It's a *weekend* furlough, right? Like it says. Out on Friday afternoon, back again on Monday morning."

Verhoeven took a deep breath, stood up from his chair, took his jacket off the backrest. "I'd really like to check out a few places with you," he said, watching the guard from the corner of his eye. "I think you know which places I mean."

"Sure." I wondered whether he was going to say it— whether he would dare to.

He dared; he just came out and said it: "And please, don't go anywhere near Chiara. Try not to take any unnecessary risks, you know what I mean. Leave her alone."

I looked at him, blinked once, not because I felt the need to blink, but because I thought it would put him at ease.

A lion—but a tame lion, napping in the sun. A nice lion: oh yeah, I could be real nice, charming, purring quietly and nuzzling up to my keeper, like a lion in the zoo. Or no, better yet, in a circus: the lion tamer cracks his whip in the sand and I jump through a hoop of real fire, night after night, I eat sugar cubes from his hand and let him scratch me behind the ears. I purr and I smile, a nice tame lion, but only in the knowledge that, one day, when he sticks his head in my mouth again before a breathless crowd, I'm going to snap my jaws shut. He will know, he'll feel it; maybe at first, when he can't pull his head back out, he'll think there's been some misunderstanding. But there has been no misunderstanding. The children will be the first to start screaming, then the women, the men will gag, the barf will splatter all over the bleachers, here and there some cold-blooded type will go on filming with his smartphone so we can all watch it again later on YouTube; how I spit out the lion tamer's half-chewed head somewhere in a corner of the cage— maybe the snack was a little stale, it's certainly not something I'm going to swallow, it might upset my stomach.

"She's got a restraining order," I said. "And I'll be wearing an ankle monitor."

I'd checked it out already on Google Maps: as long as I stayed on Pythagorasstraat, I was safely outside the area of the court injunction, just barely. It was only about fifty yards' difference: as soon as I turned the corner of Pythagorasstraat and entered Copernicusstraat, my ankle monitor would send out a signal and an alarm would go off somewhere.

That's how I imagined it, at least: there's this central tracking room with computers, the ankle-monitor tracking room, manned by no more than two people. One of them has just ordered a pizza and the other has gone outside for a smoke. I turn into Copernicusstraat, an alarm goes off in the tracking room, it takes a moment for the ankle-monitor tracker who stayed inside to figure out which of the maybe fifty or sixty roaming monitors has been activated. Twenty, thirty seconds, maybe? Not much longer than that, I figure, but in those twenty or thirty seconds I've already left Copernicusstraat and am heading up Archimedesweg, toward Molukkenstraat. When I pass under the steel train trestle, the tracking room loses the signal for a bit, the colleague has come back from his cigarette break in the meantime, now they've got video too.

"He disappeared . . . there," the one says; he points at the screen.

The other guy taps a few keys on the console and now, at the top of the screen, my first and last name appear. And who knows, maybe other things too—I've never been in a tracking room like that, all I can do is guess.

My age. My offense. The length of the term I'm serving. *Armed and dangerous*, yeah, maybe it says that too. I've always liked that phrase, though in my case it could be misleading:

it might make people think that, when I'm walking around without a gun, I'm *not* dangerous.

The blinking dot now reappears on the far side of the trestle.

"Where's he going?" asks the colleague who was just outside for a smoke.

Then the bell rings. "I bet that's my pizza," the other man says.

For a moment they stand there, wavering. Just how serious is this? It's not the first time someone with an ankle monitor has entered forbidden territory. Nine times out of ten, they turn around and go back after a minute or so, to the area where they're allowed to be. In the background, we hear the opening jingle for the weekend soccer recap on *Studio Sport*. The timing is perfect: at the very start of the first highlight, a slice of pizza can move from box to mouth.

I stop, turn around, walk back to the trestle.

"Look, he's realized, he's going back." The bell rings again, more impatiently this time. "Could you answer that? It's my pizza."

The blinking dot disappears beneath the bridge, disappears completely.

"What do we do? Report it? Send a car out?"

"Hold on a minute. If he comes back out on the right side, it's a false alarm. They don't like that much."

I wait under the bridge, I count to twenty, more or less as long as it would take me to come back out on the right side again. But above all I wait to hear if they've done anything yet. If I can hear a siren in the distance.

If I do, I'll call it off. Tomorrow is another day. But if things stay quiet, I'll wait those twenty seconds and race out from under the bridge, into the new neighborhood. I've already looked at it at least a hundred times on Google Street View—this neighborhood wasn't there yet when I disappeared from public life—and I could find the door to her building in a flash, even blindfolded. I figured it out. Less than two minutes. I'm an athletic person, I've been training, I stopped smoking ten years ago. Within ninety seconds, I'll be at the door. I'll ring the bell—not hers, the neighbors' on the floor above or below her.

*Hello?*

*It's your neighbor from the ground floor, they left a package with me yesterday, it's for you.*

At a household appliance store on Linnaeusstraat, I checked out a few of the carving knives in the display case. If I wanted a better look, I'd have to ask the salesgirl to unlock the case for me.

I was going to have to rely on my own strength—I could do it with my bare hands if necessary. And maybe it wouldn't be necessary. I thought about how I would put my foot in the door, the panic in her eyes.

*Just want to talk to you for a moment,* I'd say. *If you're smart, you'll keep calm and let me in.*

At the stationery outlet a little farther along, I bought a cardboard mailer and a big fat marker. The mailer was one of those you have to put together yourself; I stopped in a doorway on Hogeweg and folded it together, wrote her name and address in block letters on the label.

Back in my day, there wasn't any fountain at the corner of Hogeweg and Linnaeusparkweg. On that corner, there used to be what the people called a *seamy* bar. Now there's a patio restaurant where mothers sit drinking café lattes while their children shriek and splash in the fountain.

*Café latte*, another one of those expressions. In my day, the year I was sentenced, they were still just calling it a coffee with hot milk.

In fact, restraining orders can be a good idea. What I'm saying, I guess, is that I'm not *opposed* to restraining orders in principle. They can keep you safe from certain things, they can protect you from yourself, like an ignition interlock in a car. If you can't get the car started, then you won't hit a tree on the first curve or cream somebody at a crosswalk.

What I hadn't counted on was that the ankle monitor would warn not only the imaginary crew of the ankle-monitor tracking room, but that it would warn me too. Halfway down Copernicusstraat, about a block and half from the crossing with Archimedesweg, it started buzzing. Not only buzzing: it actually *vibrated*. It went off, like an alarm clock.

"Fucking shit!" I said, and picked up the pace. Maybe they'd told me about this, maybe they hadn't—in any case, I couldn't remember. The deeper I went into the area covered by the restraining order, the louder the buzzing (and the vibrating). Under the trestle, it buzzed and vibrated almost nonstop.

I picked up the pace a little more; by the time I came out from under the bridge, I was sprinting. The sidewalk went up an incline there. From Google Street View, I recognized the new glass building at the corner of Archimedesweg and Carolina MacGillavrylaan. Like I said, this neighborhood hadn't been built yet when I went into the slammer. Back then, the only thing along the Ringvaart, across from Flevopark, were some garden plots and a research lab where they did tests with radioactive material. Kids I went to grade school with used to claim they'd seen frogs with three legs and two heads along the banks of the Ringvaart. On Saturday afternoons, we combed out the whole shoreline there sometimes, but we never found a deformed frog.

There weren't many people out on the street, fortunately. Not a lot of passersby who might hear the buzzing of my ankle monitor. That seemed pretty unlikely to me, anyway; maybe in a closed space, a room or a shop, but not here, not outside.

I was panting by the time I got to the doorway of the brown building with its two apartment towers. I scanned the nameplates beside the doorbells, waited till I'd caught my breath, then rang the one that belonged to her downstairs neighbor, on the ninth floor.

"Hello?" a woman's voice said through the intercom, no more than ten seconds later.

"I'm your downstairs neighbor," I said. "They left a package for you at my place this morning."

I held up the package in front of the camera and started counting to ten; at four, there was a loud click and the glass door swung open.

As I was about to get into the elevator, a guy came through the entrance: a man in a blue windbreaker, short gray hair and glasses. It would have looked strange if I had let the elevator door close in his face.

"Good afternoon."

"Good afternoon."

The man pressed the button for five, I hit ten.

We started up, without another word. But there was no silence. From somewhere underneath my pant leg, at ankle height if you listened carefully, came a clearly audible, rhythmic buzzing. The man looked at me.

"My cell phone," I said. "I'm not going to answer it now. Have to deliver this package first."

The man nodded, but kept looking at me. Then I saw it

happen in his eyes: he knew me from somewhere, though he didn't know exactly *where*.

There had been a documentary about me, and the biography Marc Verhoeven was working on wasn't the first book; there was already one about my formative years in the neighborhood, out in Watergraafsmeer, a book with way too many photos in it, from back then but also from the present.

"I live downstairs," I said. "I've seen you before."

The man got out on the fifth floor. Was I imagining it, or did he reach into his pocket as soon as he stepped out of the car? Was he maybe going for his cell phone?

Time was running out. It had been running out from the start, but now it was *really* running out. When I left the elevator on the tenth floor, I heard it right away, and this time I wasn't imagining things: a police siren. Close by. At the end of the corridor I was in now, there was a little window. The flashing blue lights could be seen from all the way up here on ten.

Maybe it was a mistake, shooting myself in the foot like that by going to my ex's place on the very first day of my leave—the best way you could think of for me to blow my chance of early parole in three years.

But the moment she opened the door—I didn't even have to hold the package up to the glass peephole so she couldn't see my face or my eyes, like I'd been planning—I knew it was no mistake.

I could tell from the way she looked at me; it was in her eyes. The same way those eyes had looked at me at that sidewalk café in Corleone in Sicily, where she'd been working as a waitress. That was twenty years ago. I was there on vacation, because of *The Godfather*. Because I wanted to visit the hometown of the Corleone family, the way someone else might go on a pilgrimage to Rome. She put a bottle of Peroni and a glass down on my table and looked at me. And I looked back.

"Rob," her lips whispered now.

"Chiara," I said.

"What's . . . ?" She pointed down at my shoes, at the buzz of my ankle monitor.

The only sound from the living room at first was that of a TV, but now there was another sound too: a man's voice.

"Who's there?" the voice asked, and the next moment the man appeared in the little hallway that connected the living room and the front door.

I had a feeling then that I can only describe in one way. *This is it*, I thought, *this is what I live for*. That's what sets me apart from people like Marc Verhoeven, who will never do anything but watch from the sidelines. Like a soccer coach in the dugout: his best striker scores with an unstoppable bullet to the top corner, and all the coach can do is throw his hands in the air—all he can do is cheer.

Maybe some things had happened between me and Chiara. Technically speaking, maybe she *was* at that moment my ex-wife.

But I hadn't given her up, not just like that, that's not the way I am. Today I had come to take her back.

At what moment had Marc Verhoeven fallen into the moat? The moat that separates the visitors at the zoo from the lion's habitat? Was it during his very first visit to the maximum-security unit? Or was it later, when he hit on the bad idea of "interviewing" my wife as well?

No, it was probably right now, I thought, as in one swift movement I tore the lid off the mailer and pulled out the brick. The brick that, in a flash of inspiration, I'd taken from the pile at the corner of Archimedesweg and Carolina Mac-

Gillavrylaan, where the road workers were putting in a new section of bike path.

*This is who I am*, I thought when I saw his face, his eyes those of a cow that's grazing in the middle of the tracks and suddenly realizes there's an express train hurtling toward it, his hands making a gesture of fending off something. More like a conciliatory gesture, really: *Wait a minute, we can discuss this, right?*

But lions don't discuss.

They don't wear ankle monitors, either.

This was my life, squeezed together tightly in a couple of seconds.

And a couple of seconds was all the time he had left to sniff around in my life.

Thirty seconds, tops—it almost never takes me longer than that.

# SALVATION
BY SIMON DE WAAL
*Red-Light District*

*Translated by Maria de Bruyn*

I t's just after midnight, a warm spring night. Waldemar, a thickset man of fifty-eight, is standing on a bridge in the heart of Amsterdam's Red-Light District. He's carelessly stuffed his dark wrinkled shirt into his stained pants after rolling up the shirtsleeves a couple of times. The pants' legs are too long and the cuffs, which drag across the cobblestones when he walks, are frayed. He leans forward against the handrail of the Bosshardt Bridge, named after the Salvation Army major who, for decades, helped the neighborhood's weak and damned souls without worrying about their pasts.

Waldemar rocks slowly back and forth, to and fro, mumbling something incomprehensible under his breath. A tourist, Hiroki Ota, wearing a wool cap with flaps that say *Amsterdam*, stops a few yards away. He's hiding a small camera in the palm of his hand and waiting for the moment when Waldemar's worn-down soles lose their grip on the asphalt and the crazy old street person plunges headfirst into the murky water. He wouldn't be the first simpleton in Amsterdam to suffer that fate and drown, but when the man hasn't fallen in after rocking perhaps fifteen times, Hiroki gives up and walks on, disappointed. He disappears into the knot of people pushing their way through the busy Molensteeg.

Red lights and garish neon ads are reflected in the canal's

still water. Swans float by, slowly, elegantly, and drift beneath the bridge. They come to a halt in front of the Casa Rosso nightclub, vain and almost haughty as they wait for the bread that is thrown to them every evening. Crowds of tourists take photos of the unexpected and paradoxical scene: stately white lines of impalpable beauty on expansive black water, lit up by the simultaneously alluring yet merciless red neon lights of the prostitutes' claustrophobic windows.

Waldemar has seen it all a hundred times. Silently he straightens his back and leaves the bridge, his gaze turned deeply inward, his bearing making him unapproachable; he thinks of his daughter, whom he's missed for so long. He looks up only when he reaches the next corner. Rowdy students, unsuspecting tourists, a boisterous group of young women celebrating a bachelorette party all pass him by. He turns a corner into a passageway that leads to the next canal. No red lights here for a change, but a large, busy snack bar where a drunk boy with close-cropped hair and a dangling lower lip fruitlessly tries to insert a coin into a slot so he can open the vending machine's window, within which an assortment of typical Dutch treats beckon. Behind the vending machine, a sweaty bearded man appears with a tray of fried snacks; with practiced movements, he quickly fills all the empty windows with freshly prepared food. Bold gulls swoop low through the street, waiting for a moment of relative quiet in the passage-way so they can snatch up any fallen morsels. The boy takes a bite of his croquette, which is still too hot. Cursing under his breath, he keels forward, gasping for relief, and the food falls out of his mouth. He staggers on angrily, waving the hot croquette in his unsteady hand.

Emerging from the passageway, Waldemar comes out onto the next canal, the Oudezijds Voorburgwal. This has quite a different, almost peaceful look, dominated by the monumental Old Church, Amsterdam's oldest building, which dates back to the year 1280, its tower illuminated in the evenings. A beacon of hope above a square kilometer of misery, which is how the local police have characterized the Red-Light District for years. Waldemar saunters past the church. The dark-skinned prostitutes preside over their domain in the small alleys surrounding the stately building, just like every other group that has its own space in the district: the S&M ladies, the Thai and Filipino transsexuals, the Chinese, the Eastern Europeans. And all of that spiced up by dozens of busy coffee shops, by a café where the Hells Angels meet, by the headquarters of the Salvation Army. Belief and sin go hand in hand here.

Waldemar knows it all. The entrance to the small passageway at the Oudezijds Voorburgwal is dark and oppressive, only illuminated halfway down by the red neon lights over the prostitutes' doors. Waldemar assumes his usual spot across from the passage, a place where he can look into it without calling attention to himself. The world passes him by; it's a day just like the hundreds of others he has spent there. And here comes Aaron, a man in his fifties, sporting an extravagant dark-gray beard and a velvet suit that could belong either to an old-time town crier or a member of Rembrandt's *Night Watch*. A dashing hat with a long feather rests atop his head. He carries a wooden staff with a pennant, so he can be easily spotted in the busy crowd. This way, the tourists he is guiding can follow him with no trouble. Waldemar steps back a bit to make way for the guide and his entourage.

"We'll begin here," announces Aaron in practiced English. "This, esteemed public, is not only the Red-Light District's narrowest street; it is the narrowest street in all of Amsterdam. Exactly three feet wide! Only three feet! The name is . . .

De Trompettersteeg. Yeah, you try to pronounce that." He falls silent, because he knows that laughter and murmuring will arise as the tourists actually try to say the passageway's name.

An overly ambitious man with a face ruddy from drink begins to cough as he tries to push the last, so undeniably Dutch, syllable out of his throat.

"That G sound," Aaron finally continues, as the exuberant group quiets down, "saved lives during the Second World War. The Germans couldn't pronounce it, so the Resistance forced traitors and infiltrators to say the word *Scheveningen*, where the *Sch* sounds just like the G. Those who couldn't do it properly were Germans and therefore risked losing their lives. So remember the name Scheveningen."

Waldemar shakes his head benevolently as the flush-faced man is thumped roundly on his back after struggling to say the new word.

"Let's go on," instructs Aaron. "After we emerge through the passageway, be careful: the ladies are here to earn money, not to be ogled. And do you remember what I said at the start of the tour?"

The sightseers respond like good children on a school trip: "Don't take photos!"

Waldemar mumbles the words along with them, checking his watch. He knows that this is the last group that will be led through the district tonight. The neighborhood is growing calmer, more shadowy, the night is asserting itself.

Aaron beckons again, and someone from the herd ventures a hesitant first step into the dark passageway, toward the red-lit and seductive temptations. "I'll follow behind and continue my narration."

"It's like entering the gates of hell, where purgatory awaits you," says the red-faced man, and his words hurt Waldemar.

One by one, the tourists disappear into the passage. Aaron brings up the rear, his feather swaying above their heads, his staff tapping on the cobblestones.

"Why don't you tell them what happened there!" yells Waldemar, but no one hears him because no sound issues from his mouth.

*No fucking photo's!!* is misspelled on the passage's wall; the big graffitied letters are meant to be artistic, but their message is clear. Of course, Aaron's herd can't help themselves. As soon as they reach the windows, they gape at the young women. The red lights hide all their flaws, and their white lingerie, which really doesn't cover anything, shines brightly. The tourists stare and stare and stare.

"They're actually quite pretty," a woman whispers in surprise to her husband as they pass the voluptuous, beckoning bodies. He nods a bit too enthusiastically, to which she responds with a frown.

The red light is out at one of the windows; the paint is peeling, and the window is dirty and covered sloppily with brown packing paper from the inside. Aaron passes it by, as he's passed it a hundred times before.

Waldemar lingers by the side of the canal for a long time.

Later, as the tourists tumble into their beds, what remains are the drunkards, the bullies, and the pimps, who appear like rats in the night to collect cash from their women.

Waldemar knows them all.

It's a few days later, and there he is again. Waldemar saunters through the district at his characteristically placid pace. He wasn't gone during those intervening days, but nothing noteworthy happened, so they can be safely ignored.

Tonight, at the end of his usual circuit, Waldemar stops

at the Trompettersteeg. Quick footsteps can be heard from the direction of *No fucking photo's!!*, and Ivan, a plump young man, not yet thirty, with bushy eyebrows and a freshly rolled joint hanging carelessly from his lips, exits the passage. A modish name-brand bag hangs from his shoulder, and he's carrying a wad of brown packing paper under his arm. Ivan the pimp walks by Waldemar and bumps into his shoulder without looking at him. No apology follows, and the young man carelessly drops his bundle of paper at the side of the canal as he walks away, leaving the penetrating scent of hashish, never really absent for long in the district, hanging around Waldemar's head.

Soon Waldemar loses sight of the young man, who becomes an unrecognizable silhouette, indistinguishable in the crowds.

Waldemar bends over and picks up the paper. He smoothes it out, then folds it as neatly as possible and puts it under his arm. Slowly, his gaze shifts to the passageway's entrance, and the voices in his head fade away in an anxious premonition of what's about to happen.

He strolls into the passageway, up to the window where the packing paper had hung. The red lamp is on again above the door, soft and flickering irregularly. A poor attempt has been made to clean the window, and there she stands. Her eyes are hazy and evasive, her pose inexperienced. Waldemar's face pales as thoughts and memories and love and hate all fight with one another in his head.

People pass him cautiously; his wide frame is making passage through the narrow alley difficult. Although she looked away from him at first, the girl's curiosity triumphs. She lifts her head, doesn't seem unfriendly. Waldemar gestures to the door handle, which she turns from the inside, cracking the door slightly.

"Fifty," she says hesitantly.

Waldemar says nothing and points inside.

Unpracticed, she makes the international sign for money, rubbing her index finger and thumb together.

Waldemar, who has been standing there with his hands in his pockets and legs spread, shows her his right hand, which holds a bundle of banknotes.

That works. She opens the door wider and lets him in, then pulls the curtains shut.

"What do you want?" A light, unrecognizable accent wafts through her words; it could be foreign but could as easily come from the eastern part of The Netherlands.

Waldemar doesn't want anything. He looks around the room.

The girl stands expectantly beside the bed and finally lays a questioning hand on his forearm.

"You know what?" says Waldemar.

"What?"

"Let's just sit down."

He bends and sweeps his hand over the bed, but remains standing when she doesn't make a move to sit.

"What's your name?" he asks.

"Katja," she answers uncertainly.

"You chose a good name, Katja. A good working name."

"It's my real name."

"Oh."

A short silence follows.

"You shouldn't let just anyone in," says Waldemar.

"Maybe you should go," she says, suspicion winning out over uncertainty.

Waldemar takes a step forward and grabs her by the arms, just below her shoulders. His dark eyes hold her in a penetrating gaze. "*You* have to go," he says, laying the paper—which she hasn't really paid attention to—on her bed.

This confuses her, and she tries to get loose. "Why should I go?"

Waldemar doesn't notice the swelling panic in her voice, simply because he hasn't expected it. "It's dangerous here," he responds. "Look, this has to go up on the windows again. No one belongs here anymore."

Now her shoulders are shaking and he can see fear in her eyes, so Waldemar takes his hands away. "Don't be afraid, sweetheart. I don't want to frighten you."

"But why? Why is it dangerous here?" She looks straight into his eyes for the first time and sees his years of madness. "Why?" she repeats.

Waldemar's chin trembles and he glances away, because he can't handle her innocence and fear. He sighs and manages to put into words the thing he has never wanted to say: "A girl was killed in this room. Someone like you. A beautiful, sweet girl. Didn't they tell you that when they brought you here?"

A shiver goes through her body. "No, he didn't say anything. Here?"

"Yes, in this room. In that corner. I'm sorry. No one can ever come here again."

Waldemar wipes the tears from his eyes, shakes his head, and suddenly grabs her by the arm. "You have to leave here. Now."

He takes her to the door and opens the curtains. A prostitute on the other side of the narrow passage sees Waldemar pull Katja from her room with a crazed expression and drums angrily on her own window.

"You have to leave here. It isn't safe, it's not safe here," he mutters urgently, unaware of the commotion unfolding

around him. Aaron, who has just walked into the passageway with a fresh group of tourists, stops, so as not to put his
clients at risk. The drumming prostitute pushes an alarm button. Lights flash, and a siren drowns out everything else in the
street. People cover their ears, but Waldemar sees, hears, feels
nothing. He drags Katja through the passageway, convinced
that the devil is at her heels. He pushes people aside; Aaron
tumbles against the wall, his hat rolls away, its feather crushed
by someone's shoe.

Waldemar plows through the tourists, and there stands
Ivan. Immovable, unwilling to lose his newest acquisition because of the district's village idiot. His hand rests loosely in
his trendy designer bag, his joint dangles from his mouth, a
disdainful smile rests on his lips.

Waldemar's desperate eyes are focused on the light at the
end of the passageway. He runs straight ahead and crashes
into Ivan, knocks him into the passage wall. Waldemar hesi-
tates, growls like a wounded animal, and looks back—not at
Ivan, from whom he now has nothing to fear, but at Katja. She
runs surprisingly quickly in her high heels; he scarcely needs
to pull her along. The light comes closer. Waldemar turns
back once more, they're almost there, and now he pulls his
daughter close. This time he's there in time to save her, and
she knows it, because she hugs him tightly and smiles. The
white light dances like a spirit at the end of the passageway.

"Go!" screams Waldemar, as they finally burst onto the
Oudezijds Voorburgwal, and the tourists and junkies and
johns scatter out of their way. "Go, my darling sweetheart!"

Their hands part. His daughter runs, runs, runs, and when
she is almost out of sight, he sees her ascend, lift up into the sky.

Waldemar can still feel her warmth in his hands, and he
watches her rise up with a smile.

In the passageway, Aaron finally spots his hat on the ground. When he reaches for it, his gaze falls on Ivan, who is sitting under the graffitied wall. Ivan stashes his switchblade back in his bag, but Aaron sees it, glimpses the red on its blade. Slowly, Aaron picks up his hat, smoothes its feather as best he can, and returns it to his head. He hoists his staff and slams the end of it against Ivan's head, and the pimp loses consciousness and collapses to the ground like a rag doll. Aaron grumbles with satisfaction as he hears the first sirens approaching. He regathers his flock, who have observed his actions with alarm, and they follow him out of the alley, silent, impressed.

On the Oudezijds Voorburgwal, Waldemar takes a few uncertain steps, and then his knees buckle and he falls. Instinctively, he places his hands on his stomach, and, when he looks down, sees blood seeping between his fingers. Thick drops fall on the cobblestones.

He topples onto his back and is soon surrounded by shocked prostitutes, a coffee shop bouncer, a dozen tourists, and three drunken English hooligans, one of whom, well-meaning, tries to drape his jacket over Waldemar's head.

Waldemar fends them off with some difficulty. He turns his eyes to the gates of hell, sees that the red light above his daughter's room is out, and dies, suffused with satisfaction.

# PART II

*Kiss Me Deadly*

# THE TOWER

BY HANNA BERVOETS

*Van der Pekbuurt*

"Is this your first visit?" the girl in the red jacket asks. The elevator ride is apparently part of the attraction. Gita hadn't realized that, hadn't expected there to be an operator in the car with her.

She nods, and the girl smiles. "This is the fastest elevator in Western Europe," she says. "It only takes fifteen seconds to get to the top. You should look up."

The girl cranes her head back, and Gita follows her example, but she's not sure what to do with her hands. Oddly enough, she misses her rolling suitcase—its handle has been the only thing she's had to hold on to this evening. She checked it when she came in from the street, though, handed it off to a girl whose hair was tied back in exactly the same ponytail worn by this child who stands beside her. Gita watched her tuck it away in a corner, with another suitcase and two carry-ons, the luggage of others just arrived from Schiphol or on their way there. She wonders if anyone can tell from her appearance. Can the bag-check girl and the elevator girl see that she's a local, not a tourist?

Tourists, Schiphol . . . at the thought of the airport, Gita feels nauseous, although that might just be the light show, as bright images flicker along the car's ceiling: the three Xs from Amsterdam's coat of arms, the Dutch flag, a tree, a cat, a skull—is that really a *skull*?—a house, a child, something blue, something red, an orange dog, a pink smiley.

"We're there," the girl says.

The silver doors whoosh open. The observation deck is larger than Gita had imagined it would be.

"We're open for another hour. If you have a ticket for the swing, though, you'll have to hurry—it closes at nine."

Gita nods, and the girl retreats into the elevator. Does she still tip her head back when she's alone?

It's peaceful up here on the roof. A couple strolls along the railing to her right, two teenage girls take selfies with the city spread out below them in the gathering dusk. A boy standing beside the huge steel swing wears the same red jacket as the girl in the elevator and looks at her questioningly. She shakes her head.

*Of course*, she thinks. *Of course there's hardly anyone here tonight: it's almost dark, it's drizzling, it's practically freezing—but, God, the view is gorgeous.*

You can see for miles in every direction, despite the fence on the other side of the railing. The fence is six feet tall, she got that tidbit from Femke. The couple, an older man and woman in white sneakers—probably Americans—examines a signboard with a line drawing of Central Station and other landmarks. But the station's not very interesting anymore, since the grand renovation it's actually quite ugly, and Gita finds the other landmarks—the Old Church, the Palace on the Dam, the Stock Exchange—equally unappealing, so she walks around to the far side of the roof for the view of Amsterdam-North.

And there is the neighborhood where she grew up. The streets, the houses, the trees, all laid out in miniature; she can hold a streetlight between her thumb and forefinger. From the ferry dock, the Buiksloterweg ambles northeast, then, just past Pussy Galore, forks off to the right. To the left, it changes its name to the Ranonkelkade and then the Van der Pekstraat, a caterpillar with fat legs extending to either side. The legs are the Anemoonstraat, the Oleanderstraat, the Jasmijnstraat, the Heimansweg.

Mireille lives in a house on one of those legs. Right now, she's probably sitting in front of the TV.

Gita's parents lived for many years on the highest floor of an old building on the next leg, until the block was torn down and renovated and the prices went sky-high. Atop the new building on the site where she was raised, there's now a penthouse that seems unoccupied, since no light ever burns in its windows.

The caterpillar's head is a square, the Mosplein, and Gita knows that, at this moment in the Café Mosplein, Sjors and Maya are lowering the metal shutters across the plateglass window that looks out on the square. She wonders if she can make out her own building from here. Yes, there, the street just south of the square, that must be it.

What would happen if she went there now? Climb the stairs, slip her key into the lock, and then immediately the scream, the uproar that only she can understand. She left the heat on but turned out all the lights—had she been *hoping* for burglars? The longer she stares at her building in the distance, the more clearly she can hear the screams.

She turns away and sees Femke's complex, those buildings there on the right. Femke pointed it out to her once, from the ferry: "That one, there, with the big windows!"

Earlier this evening, Gita checked all the mailboxes and buzzers in the lobby, but she couldn't find Femke's name. She'd actually grabbed a complete stranger by the arm and said, "Sir, you don't happen to know Femke de Waal, do you?" The man shook his head and scowled at her suitcase. "Airbnb's not allowed in this building," he said severely, pulling a ring of keys from his jacket, and Gita had turned away and left but not gone home. Instead, she'd wandered aimlessly through the warren of streets until she found herself at the foot of the A'DAM Tower, the tallest building on the waterfront.

Gita fishes her cell phone from her pocket. No new messages—nothing from Femke. Without thinking, she scrolls up, past dozens of texts, maybe hundreds, until she comes to the very first one in the chain: *Red leather gloves!*

Johnny hadn't wanted to wear his rain jacket that day. It had rained all week, fat drops pelting the windows, the bed of Johnny's plastic dump truck filling with water—Gita hadn't had the energy to bring it in from the backyard. Johnny shook his head angrily when she held the jacket up for him. He made a face like he'd swallowed something gross and growled what sounded like a no. It was only a few steps from the front door to the curb, where the school bus would stop, and, if he wanted, his teachers would let him stay indoors all day. Strictly speaking, he didn't *need* the jacket, but Gita had just bought it and wanted to convince herself that the money hadn't been wasted—it had cost more than she could really afford.

Their argument unfolded like most of their arguments. First Johnny began to scream, his eyes already tearing, his cheeks flushed, and then he started kicking. His flailing arms struck her in the face, but Gita knew he didn't mean to hurt her. Finally, he broke out in uncontrollable sobs.

She was reminded of a video that had been going around on Facebook for weeks. A man tells his three-year-old daughter that steak comes from cows and the girl bursts out in tears. "Poor cows," she whispers to the camera.

Every time Gita saw that clip, she felt a mixture of anger and jealousy. She was jealous of the parents, who had a healthy, beautiful little girl with two pigtails, a child who felt empathy for other living creatures. But she was mad at them too, for bragging so shamelessly about their blessings. Why would anyone be interested in the private happiness of strangers?

The bus stood outside her door for ten minutes that morning, two wheels up on the curb. When she couldn't calm Johnny down, she bribed him with a prepackaged pancake. It was much too early for a treat—she could see Johnny's nutritionist shake a finger—but what choice did she have? The bus was waiting, with other children aboard. Thank god Johnny stopped screaming the moment he heard the crinkle of the plastic wrapper.

"Sorry," she told the frowning driver, when Johnny finally clambered up into the bus.

Later that day, she regretted the humbleness of her apology. She did what she could, damn it, and who was a school-bus driver to judge her? She wished she'd told him so, right to his face. But at the same time she felt guilty about the way she'd treated Johnny. She shouldn't have insisted on the rain jacket. He was tired, he'd had a bad night, his day hadn't even begun, and she was already nagging him. When she brought him home from Mireille's that evening, she decided, she'd give him another pancake, just because.

Had she noticed Femke come into the café that morning?

Probably not. She can barely recall taking her order—the only reason she knows now that it had been an open-faced egg sandwich was that she remembers Femke saying, "You should leave off the dill," when she paid for it. A typical remark, she would come to learn: Femke always spoke her mind, whether or not anyone had asked for her opinion. At first, Gita saw the trait as arrogance, until she realized that in a way it came from a desire to be helpful. Femke simply *knew* better than most other people, and with each observation about the things she ate and saw and did, Gita's admiration for Femke's knowledge and insight and pure bravado grew.

After the comment about the egg sandwich, though, Gita had merely nodded. *She's not from around here*, she thought. She could tell from the woman's long, formfitting raincoat, nothing like the shapeless things worn by the café's usual customers. Before heading back out into the rain, Femke had tightened her belt, but Gita didn't notice how slim she was until later that day, when the woman returned. Her raincoat was dry then, and so elegant that Gita wondered if it really *was* a raincoat, after all.

"I think I left my gloves here," Femke said.

Now that they were standing face-to-face, Gita realized that the woman was beautiful. Maybe it was her makeup, she thought at the time. But four or five weeks later, Femke gave her an eyeliner pencil, the same kind she used herself, and it didn't make Gita's eyes any bigger or more attractive.

"I don't think we found a pair of gloves," said Gita, and she glanced at Sjors, who stood in the doorway to the kitchen, shaking his head.

Femke shrugged. "Might as well have a drink, since I'm here. Do you carry Macallan?"

She spent the rest of the afternoon at the bar, reading the newspaper, playing with her phone, asking questions whenever Gita had a free moment. About the café—"You didn't have to close when they renovated the square?"—but personal things too: "Do you live in the neighborhood?"

Gita remembers finding their on-and-off conversation odd, but not unwelcome. When customers talked to her, they were mostly older gentlemen who did little more than order another drink. Femke was young—probably ten years younger than Gita—a member of a more interested generation. So when she suggested that Gita pour one for herself, Gita did something she'd never done before. She set a shot glass on the bar beside the register and filled it to the rim with whiskey.

She hadn't had much to eat that afternoon. The guilty residue from the morning's scene with Johnny stuck to her ribs like chewing gum, but the whiskey burned some of it away and gave her the courage to speak honestly for once. "Actually," she heard herself say, "I don't like the neighborhood as much as I used to. They promised us a whole new clientele after the renovation. But most of our regulars moved away, and we're not good enough for the new residents. They like the trendy spots in the Van der Pekstraat, little bistros that serve soup, where the whole menu is soup and nothing but soup, you know what I mean? Can you believe anyone would come all the way up here to eat soup?"

Femke toasted her and sipped her whiskey.

Encouraged, Gita went on: "All those chichi places are the same: a brick wall, ferns, folding chairs, a wooden bar; it's like you're in a house that's in the middle of being remodeled. They serve your drink in a mason jar instead of a normal glass, but it's not like those jars ever actually held pears or peaches or whatever, they buy them brand new by the case. Did you ever try to *drink* out of one of those things? You're lucky if you don't spill all over yourself!"

Femke laughed and shook her head. "I'll drink to that!" She emptied her glass in one swallow and leaned across the bar, her face only inches from Gita's. Her heavy perfume reminded Gita of her father's aftershave, with just a hint of Gauloises mixed in.

"We should go to one of those hip places sometime," Femke whispered conspiratorially, "and sabotage the joint."

Gita laughed, not sure if Femke was serious, too tipsy from her drink to come up with a witty response.

Femke rose from her stool and picked up her phone. "I'll text you so you can let me know if my gloves turn up. What's your number?"

Gita told her. It seemed natural but at the same time not, as if she'd eaten a piece of candy of a type she hadn't tasted in years. When *was* the last time anyone had asked her for her phone number?

When she got to Mireille's that evening, Johnny was parked in front of the TV. She'd hurried up the six flights of stairs and stood panting in the quiet living room; the ticking of the cuckoo clock was an almost sarcastic echo of her heartbeat. Johnny was watching Elmo. It was his favorite DVD, though Gita wished he would pick something else for a change. Elmo reminded her that Johnny never made any progress, which reminded her in turn that *she* never made any progress, trapped in a stuffy room where the light was always blue and Elmo endlessly showed off his brand-new shoes.

Mireille slouched in her armchair by the window, paging through a magazine.

"Sorry I'm so late," said Gita.

"You couldn't call?" Mireille snapped, not looking up. "Johnny was worried about you." She nodded at the television: Johnny was glued to the screen, his mouth slightly open, as if this was the first time he'd ever seen Elmo's big red feet. "I do this for you, you know," Mireille muttered, struggling to her own feet. "You want Earl Grey or rose hip?"

*Whiskey*, Gita thought. *Do you carry Macallan?*

That Friday evening, Johnny had splashed merrily in the tub, teasing her. She'd found the game tiring, but she'd played along: "Come on, I bet you can't get me wet!" She was mopping the bathroom floor with a towel when her phone buzzed in her hip pocket. A text. She had to scroll up to see who had sent it, and what she found, from four days earlier, was Femke's number and *Red leather gloves!*

This new message read: *Sabotage the Soepboer on Sunday?*

Gita stuffed the phone back in her pocket, as if she'd been caught looking at something not intended for her eyes.

She got to the Soepboer a little early. She'd dropped Johnny off at Mireille's with the excuse that she'd been asked at the last minute to work an extra shift at the café, and then she hurried down the Van der Pekstraat more quickly than necessary, perhaps motivated by her lie, which had made it sound like she was in a rush. She wore her tightest jeans but worried her age would be a giveaway that the Soepboer wasn't her type of place. The moment she came through the door, someone called her name: Femke, already seated at a little table by the window.

"No mason jars," Femke whispered, after the server took their order. They had to back away from most of their other prejudgments too. Yes, there was a brick wall, but otherwise the Soepboer was more cozy than run-down, and they gave up their plan to sabotage the place. They sat there all afternoon, talking and talking, while the server kept returning to refill their wineglasses.

At Femke's insistence—"You have a son? Really?"—Gita talked about Johnny. He was fourteen, she said, a sweet boy, at least most of the time. His father? After Johnny was born, she'd never seen the guy again. "Men," said Femke. "They can be such assholes, don't you think?"

Gita didn't say a word about Johnny's condition.

Femke explained in turn that she was an independent financial consultant. She'd had an office in Utrecht for a while, but had recently relocated to Amsterdam: a month ago, she'd moved into one of the new apartment blocks by the water, and now she was eager to make some friends in the neighborhood . . . which answered a question Gita hadn't dared to ask.

Over the next few weeks, Femke was a lunchtime regular at Café Mosplein. She usually hung out at the bar, chatting about the book she was reading or a movie Gita had to see, and more and more often about new clients she'd taken on, like the woman who kept fiddling with her phone during a consultation. "She was adjusting and readjusting the temperature in her house," Femke laughed, "so her Bouvier wouldn't be too cold—can you beat that?" Those were afternoons when, for the first time, Gita found herself glad that the café attracted so few customers.

One Thursday, Gita called in sick so she and Femke could take the ferry across the IJ to go shopping. That was one of the few times they left Amsterdam-North together. From the boat deck, Femke pointed out her apartment building as, giggling like schoolgirls, they brushed the windblown hair out of each other's faces. In the city center, Femke steered Gita to stores she'd never even heard of. Femke decided on a long red evening gown that Gita thought suited her perfectly, and Gita bought a jacket Femke pulled off the rack for her. *It's on sale*, she rationalized, handing her debit card to the sales clerk, *a steal at this price*. Tapping in her PIN, she felt a deep connection to Femke, who had just done the same thing herself. Pressing those little numbered keys was like sealing their friendship.

"Where'd you get the jacket?" asked Mireille that afternoon.

"Ordered it online," said Gita, tugging Johnny away from the TV. "It was on clearance."

She had by then told Mireille about Femke, there'd been no way to avoid it. "I think I've made a new friend," she'd said. Talking *about* Femke gave her almost as much pleasure as talking *with* Femke. When she brought Johnny over to Mireille's one Saturday evening, she'd explained away the almost-unheard-of occurrence by saying that she and Femke were going out.

"You look chic," Mireille had said, admiring Gita's black velvet sweater. Gita didn't know if that was a compliment or a reproach, but she understood that she'd better not ask Mireille to take Johnny again on a weekend night.

The next week, when Femke mentioned a new restaurant she wanted to try, Gita suggested they wait till after Johnny's bedtime.

That evening, Gita rummaged through the plastic crate in the bathroom for the nylon straps and metal leg braces Johnny'd worn to bed as a child—well, as a younger child. Back then, he'd sometimes had epileptic seizures during the night, and the straps and braces protected him from hurting himself. Over the years, the frequency and intensity of the attacks had abated, until the risk of an episode was outweighed by the discomfort the restraints caused the boy, not to mention the struggle it took to tie him down.

"Come on, now," she said, "give me your arm." Johnny was exhausted. She'd fed him a big bowl of mac and cheese for dinner, and that had filled him up and tired him out, so he didn't put up a fight. He remembered the routine, the tightness of the straps on his wrists and legs, though it had been a long time since they had last used them.

"Mama," he said, the word a question. "Ma?"

The moment Gita locked the apartment door behind her, she felt herself go limp. With every step she took, a shiver ran from her shoulders up her neck to her throat, and it wasn't until she finished her second rum and Coke at the Butcher— the new hot spot by the water—that her arms and legs felt normal again.

When she returned home a few hours later, Johnny was sleeping peacefully, and she kissed him lightly on both cheeks.

Gita leans in to peer through the rooftop telescope, swivels it on its axis from left to right. Do the people down there realize it's possible to peep right into their homes? The curtains on most of the windows of the apartment complex on the water are drawn, but she can see right into some of the illuminated living rooms, make out a shape here and there that could be nothing more than a houseplant but could just as well be someone's husband or father or lover. Gita releases the telescope and reaches again for her phone, presses again on Femke's name. Does a screen light up behind one of those windows?

She puts the phone away and returns to the telescope, aims it straight down twenty-two stories to the street: the black asphalt jumps into focus before her eyes. There, 367 feet below, is where their plan began. It wasn't much later then than it is now, though at that time of year it was still quite light out. It was cold, their summer jackets too thin for the crisp September evening.

"Oh no!" cried Femke.

"What?"

"It's closed. We can't go up."

They'd talked about the Tower often, laughed at the crazy idea of the giant swing on the roof, visible from every café, every house and apartment in the area. It was big enough for two people, they could see that from the ground. But could you sit close enough to hold hands, and was it really safe? They weren't going to find out, not that night—now that they'd finally talked themselves into the adventure, the Tower was closed.

A little old woman hurried past the shuttered doors, struggling to keep up with a dachshund on a leash. The dog trembled, as surprised by the cold as they had been. "An accident," the woman told them. Femke shook her head sadly, but Gita didn't understand at first. "A jumper," the woman said quickly, as if she'd already told the story a dozen times today, and perhaps she had.

Gita and Femke stood there in silence, necks craned, looking up to the top of the Tower, the observation deck, ringed by a tall fence meant to prevent the sort of tragedy that had apparently occurred despite its presence.

"That fence is six feet high," said Femke softly, and Gita visualized a man—it had to have been a man—reaching above his head, grabbing hold of the top metal bar, pressing the toe of his sneaker into one of the diamond-shaped openings in the chain link, and hoisting himself upward.

She can't remember which she noticed first, the music—a piano being played beautifully somewhere behind them—or the shadow that suddenly fell across Femke's face. Gita turned and saw the colossus: a ship, the *AIDA*, the biggest cruise ship in Europe, though she didn't know that at the time. At that moment, the ship made her think of Mireille's balcony, the only difference being that the people on the ship's balconies seemed happy, little Playmobil figures who leaned over their railings and waved at them. And where was that heavenly music coming from?

"Three concert halls," said Femke, reading her mind. "Two casinos, four pools, nine restaurants."

As they watched the enormous craft glide by, Gita was reminded of an animated film she'd recently seen, *Pinocchio*. The movie was long and too difficult for Johnny. He'd begun to whimper impatiently, and she'd put him to bed and watched the rest of it alone in her dim living room. One moment in particular had stayed with her—the scene with the whale, a sea monster so huge that it sucked whole schools of fish, sea urchins, anemones, even poor wooden Pinocchio down its gigantic gullet, the whale's jaws gaping wide and everything in its path disappearing between them. She imagined the prow of the cruise ship breaking open and inhaling her and Femke from the dock into its maw.

She felt dizzy. She might even have staggered a bit, and suddenly Femke's arm was around her waist, supporting her. It was the first time Femke had touched her in such an intimate manner. She was a little taller than Gita; her slender arm slid easily around her back, her left hand came to rest on Gita's hip and held her close.

"We should do that," said Femke. "You and me, we should go on a cruise."

"Yes," said Gita, "absolutely." And she laid her hand on Femke's, and the two of them stood there for a moment, until the ship and its music had passed out of their sight and hearing.

A *cruise*, they'd told each other several times that evening, *we really have to do that*, each time bursting out in peals of laughter—and when Femke laid a thick travel brochure on the bar the next afternoon, Gita assumed she was making a joke.

But Femke leafed furiously through the colored pages until she found what she was looking for. "This one!" she said, tapping her forefinger on a photograph of a sleek white ship with bright blue trim. "Leaves from Naples and goes all the way around the world!"

"That would be wonderful," Gita sighed, and she tried to slide the brochure aside to make room for the glass of Macallan that Femke had ordered, but Femke held it in place with her finger.

"Look," she said, "thirty thousand euros a person, all included. Around the *world!*" She drank down half her whisky and took an envelope from her purse.

Gita had seen similar mailings before. Every so often, one of them showed up with her bills and advertising circulars: *Need extra cash for Christmas?* or words to that effect.

"Fill this out and sign it," said Femke. "We'll be on our way in three weeks."

Gita looked up from the envelope and couldn't tell from Femke's expression if she was serious or trying to be funny. "That's a loan application," she said. "How am I supposed to pay it back?"

"We'll split the payments," Femke replied cheerfully. "Sixty euros a month each, that's doable, isn't it?"

Gita shrugged, and then Femke did something she'd never done before. She slid off her stool and came around the bar. From behind, she put her arms around Gita and hugged her. Femke was so close that Gita could feel her heart beating against her back, could smell the familiar musk of Gauloises. All at once, she felt truly happy.

Femke put her chin on Gita's shoulder and nodded at the brochure. "Look," she said, "that woman in the straw hat is me, and the one holding the cocktail is you."

* * *

It all went as smoothly as Femke had predicted. A week after Gita signed the application, the money was deposited into her account.

She worried that people could *smell* it on her. When she hunched down in the supermarket to pluck the cheapest brand of tomato soup from the bottom shelf, she felt like she'd been caught red-handed: was this the behavior of a woman in possession of so much wealth? Femke proposed that they open a special vacation account—putting it in Femke's name would get her a significant break on her taxes, she explained, and she was a financial consultant, so she ought to know what she was talking about—and Gita was relieved to see the enormous sum disappear from her own account, as if she'd taken off a heavy fur coat that had never really fit her in the first place.

Johnny seemed especially irritable those days, and Gita went through twice as many prepackaged pancakes as usual. He often wept when he awoke in the mornings, and at night he was anything but cooperative. When she finally got him settled beneath his Grover blanket, he stared up at her fearfully. She knew what was bothering him. The leg braces. The straps. But she never used them more than once a week, only when she went out to eat with Femke and then never longer than a couple of hours. That frightened look of his annoyed her. She was his mother, she had always taken care of him, had never hurt him. Didn't that count for anything?

Meanwhile, she had to figure out what to do with him when they went off on their cruise, an entire month. For just a moment, she considered taking him along, but she couldn't do that to Femke, she decided, or to Johnny either. He'd be terrified of the waves. What was meant to be a vacation would only make his mood swings worse.

And besides, Gita thought, she hadn't had any real time off in fourteen years. For fourteen years she'd taken care of Johnny, spent every weekday and many Saturdays on her feet in the café. In fourteen years, she'd withered from a promising young lady determined to make the best of things to a middle-aged woman who'd accepted that she wasn't entitled to the best of anything, that the future she had once dreamed of had turned out not to be a pretty pink house and a dog, but a swamp. Didn't she have the right, just this once, to enjoy herself?

She asked Mireille to take Johnny in, offered to pay her for the trouble. Mireille had been offended by the idea of payment, but she hadn't said no to looking after the boy.

Until two days before their departure, when Mireille had called her. "I've talked it over with Bor," she said, "and he won't have Johnny here for a month."

There was a long silence on the line.

"To be honest," Mireille said at last, "I don't think I could handle it, anyway. I haven't got the energy. You understand, don't you?"

So she'd had to make other arrangements.

On the afternoon of their flight, she and Femke had agreed to meet across from the airport Burger King at five. Femke had to see a client in Utrecht at noon, but their flight didn't leave until 6:30, so she'd have plenty of time to get there. Femke would bring the tickets.

At 5:05, Gita lifted her suitcase onto a baggage cart and hurried through the arrivals hall to the Burger King. The smell of frying meat made her hungry, but she couldn't stop to eat and risk missing Femke.

She waited for five minutes and watched a somber young

couple take their place in the line approaching the counter. She waited ten minutes and watched the couple settle at a table with a tray piled high with burgers and fries. She waited fifteen minutes and watched the couple revive over their meal: the girl's face became animated, the boy laughed at something she said.

After twenty minutes, Gita sat on the edge of her baggage cart. She watched the couple rise, watched the girl playfully order the boy to clear their table, watched him stick out his tongue at her.

While she waited, she sent Femke a text, then another. She asked a security guard if there was a second Burger King elsewhere at the airport. She called Femke's cell phone three times, maybe four, but no one answered.

At 6:20, Gita wheeled her cart into the departures hall. She approached the customer service counter for the airline on which they were ticketed, and asked the agent if it was possible to get a refund.

"I'm sorry," the girl said, "we don't process refunds here. I can cancel your reservation, though. Would you like me to do that for you?"

Gita hesitated, then nodded.

"What's the name on the booking?" the girl asked.

"Femke," said Gita, "Femke de Waal."

The girl typed the name into her computer, then asked Gita to spell it. "I am sorry," she said at last, "but I don't show a reservation under that name."

Gita's fingers tighten on the cool chain-link fence. It would be so easy to hoist herself upward, to climb, to perch on the crossbar at the top. From that vantage point, the view of the city would be even better: the passenger terminal across the IJ to the left, the Prinseneiland to the right . . . and below? She closes her eyes and imagines falling forward. As she falls, her velocity will increase—one of the few things she remembers from her science classes in school.

"Ma'am?" says a voice behind her.

She opens her eyes and turns around. The boy in the red jacket is pointing at the swing. "Last chance. Do you want to ride?"

The roof is deserted. The drizzle has strengthened into rain. With her hands in her jacket pockets, Gita approaches the swing. Her fingertips glide across her phone, a cool black brick that remains stubbornly silent.

Now that she is beside the swing, she realizes for the first time just how tall it is: the steel pyramid stretches far above her head.

"Have a seat," says the boy, and Gita settles onto a flat red wooden board that reminds her of the ski lifts she's seen in the movies.

"Now fasten your safety belt, please."

She pulls the black bar up between her legs, fumbles with the locking mechanism, and then she sees them. Two terrified eyes, pupils darting back and forth as if they're following a bumblebee in flight. She clicks the tongue into the buckle and sees the windmilling arms, the kicking legs, the thin wrists she wrestles with difficulty to the mattress. She pulls the belt tighter, feels the nylon press into her thigh. She can hear him screaming now, whimpering like a cornered dog. Johnny's pajama bottoms are suddenly wet, she can smell the urine, but he's finally secured, so she pulls his blanket over him, over his pajamas. She sets the iPad on the night table next to his bed and points at Elmo, who is laughing gaily.

The ski lift jolts upward. Gita's legs dangle in the darkness.

"Here we go," says the boy beneath her, and the swing begins to move, first back, then forward, and Gita looks down at the city spread out beneath her. There are houses to the left and cars to the right and boats in the water, all pinpoints of light, glowworms that wriggle across the earth and mean nothing at all to her.

*Look*, she hears Femke say, *that woman in the straw hat is me, and the one holding the cocktail is you.*

# SILENT DAYS

BY KARIN AMATMOEKRIM

*Oosterpark*

I t was early autumn when they began to cut down the trees. The wind was aggressive, the rain thin but steady. I sat at my window and looked out at their balding crowns, and then I watched them fall. It happened in silence, as if the trees were fainting, dropping to the ground without the least resistance.

The park seems wounded now. But I've lived here long enough to know that even this will pass. The gaps left behind by the fallen trees will close, the park will heal itself, and people will say they can't imagine it ever being any different.

I've lived in this neighborhood for eighty-two years. I've seen it change: the city itself, its inhabitants, their faces, even the language they speak. But at heart the neighborhood remains the same. Amsterdam-East was never flawless. It's the side of town where the Jews lived before the Germans came and took them away. Their empty homes were immediately repopulated. We all worked hard but remained poor. No one had time for sentimentality. In the summers, the heat fanned our discontent, and we invented turbulent celebrations, throwing old furniture out of upper-floor windows to the streets below. We built bonfires of the shattered remnants, the flames so high they tickled the underbellies of the clouds.

I was born over there, in the Dapperstraat. Over the years, I moved around the area and eventually landed here, on the fourth floor of a stately building on the east side of the park. I spend most of my time in an armchair just inside my living room window, looking out onto the park. Most of the city's sounds fail to reach this high, and I content myself with observing the silent stories of the world outside my window. Some things are better without sound. Even violence seems peaceful when wreathed in silence. I have witnessed robberies and drunken brawls that suggest contemporary ballet, the dancers wheeling around each other with exaggerated, expressive movements. From my vantage point, these events are almost beautiful.

I don't have many friends. Just one, really. His name is Ruud. He's absurdly fat and always in a bad mood. He doesn't walk—probably because of his weight—but putters around in a motorized wheelchair. I have no idea why we're friends. Perhaps we're both lonely, who can say? We see each other almost every day in the library in the Linnaeusstraat. I read the newspaper, and Ruud asks me what's in it, and then he curses the world while we drink free coffee from plastic cups.

A few months ago, Ruud asked me how long I plan to stay on in the house on the park. "You're old," he said, meaning maybe it was time for me to start looking for a place in a rest home. But I'm not planning on moving, and I told him so. "You'll die there, then?" he growled, and I said yes, that is indeed my plan, not necessarily right away but eventually. At which point Ruud felt compelled to tell me yet again about his neighbor, a hoarder who tripped over a pile of junk, fell down the stairs, and broke his neck. When the police searched his apartment, they found his dog half-dead, with—so the story went—its decomposing body melting into the carpet. "They had to carry the poor thing out of the house, rug and all. Finally had to put him to sleep."

"I'm not a hoarder," I said.

"That's not the point," Ruud hissed between his teeth. "You're too old to go on living there. One of these days you'll break your hip or something, and you'll be too weak to call for help, and then you'll die up there, and your body will rot away and start to stink. Everyone else in the building will suffer, just because you're too stubborn to go to an old folks' home where you belong."

"It won't take them long to find me," I shushed him. "You'll miss me, won't you?"

"You wish," he muttered, then ordered me to go on reading from the paper.

To be honest, it doesn't matter to me if I die alone in my apartment. I'm used to being alone. It would be strange to be surrounded by people when my time comes, to see Ruud's fat face before me as I take my final breath. I don't even want to think about it. No, I'm accustomed to my own company, and the prospect of dying alone doesn't bother me in the slightest. I only hope my death is painless. Violence frightens me—even the thought of it makes me nauseous.

I clearly remember that conversation with Ruud, because it happened the same day the walls of my house began to speak. I'd been reading in bed, and at the moment I closed my book and reached to turn out the light, I heard it. The voice was soft but audible, right beside my face. A vague whisper. I listened, holding my breath. It was a woman's voice, and though I couldn't understand what she was saying, I could tell that she was unhappy. The experience made me quite nervous, but after a few minutes the voice faded away and I drifted off to sleep.

A curious thing about this type of old structure is that you can't really predict how sound will travel. I didn't recognize the voice that came from within my walls. It might have been someone living two doors away, or on the ground floor, three flights below me. Or it might have come from the third floor, where the building's new owner lived with his wife. He was a lawyer who'd bought the house a few months earlier in the hopes of increasing his income. I watched him go out the front door every morning in a gray or dark-blue suit. A man of routine, who returned home each evening promptly at a quarter past six. His wife didn't work. She was a quiet woman with a pale face, not unfriendly.

The owner was almost as insistent as Ruud in his attempts to convince me to move out. He even offered me a sum of money to leave. He wanted to renovate my apartment, I knew, so he could offer it at a much higher rent to expats or some other wealthy sort. But I'm not leaving, and I politely told him so, even though that means I'll go on having to mount a discouraging number of steps to reach my nest. I don't want to leave this house, because I know it inside and out. The stairs are very steep, yet I know which ones will creak when I step on them. I know where the handrail is loose and how the front door sticks in the winter, how you have to give it a bit of a push before it will open. And although I don't know all of the residents, I do know the building's idiosyncracies . . . and that's a sort of love, isn't it? Yes, I love this house, and in a way I believe the house cares for me too.

Looking out the window one day, I saw the owner approaching. I glanced at the clock on the church tower farther up the street: it was only three in the afternoon.

Without undue haste, he chained his bicycle to the fence on the other side of the road. There was a noticeable calmness in his movements. Something in the way he checked to make sure it was safe to cross—*too* in control. A hint of pent-up anger. I stepped away from the window and stood in the middle of the living room, listening for any sound from below. I heard him open the front door and quietly lock it behind him. As his footsteps ascended the stairs, I had a growing sense of discomfort. It was the middle of the week, a workday. At this time, the building was deserted, except for the owner and his wife. And me, above them. He'd probably forgotten all about me.

Involuntarily, I held my breath. The ticking of the clock on the windowsill sliced the air. Then, without warning, a storm of violence burst out beneath my feet. The owner roared as I'd never heard before. Furniture crashed, some glass object shattered against a wall. The wife's sobbing pleas seemed to come from every direction. They leaked through the cracks in the windowpanes, crept through the mouse holes, climbed the walls, and oozed into my apartment and filled it, bouncing off me as I stood in the middle of my living room, my hands over my face, more frightened than I'd ever been in my life. When the crying stopped, the hitting continued, and I slowly dropped my hands to my sides. *Bang bang bang,* I heard, and I wondered what the woman's silence meant.

Perhaps the scene below was less violent than it sounded? Or perhaps he had knocked her unconscious? And then, in a sudden insight I couldn't wish away, I realized that she might no longer be crying because she was dead. Perhaps I—hiding behind my hands like a coward on the building's top floor—had overheard the murder of the quiet woman with the pale face.

* * *

The next day, I told Ruud that the owner of my building had beaten his wife, that I'd been afraid I'd been a witness to her death—but that later, thank God, I'd heard her scurrying around below. I was concerned, I said, that at any moment the situation could take a turn for the worse.

He shrugged. "She's the one who's chosen to stay with him," he said.

I don't really *like* Ruud, although I call him my friend. But his words contained a grain of truth: if the woman wanted to leave, she'd be gone by now. And what, I asked myself, could an old-timer like me possibly do to help her, anyway? How could I protect her from a husband decades my junior? And what if he found out she and I had spoken—wouldn't that make him even angrier? What if, because of my interference, he did something even more violent than he'd already done?

I worried about so many facets of the situation that once again I wound up taking no action.

And then one evening I woke up in the middle of the night. I lay still in my bed, my eyes closed, asking myself what it was that had awakened me. A few minutes passed, and then I heard her voice. It was very soft, a whisper from the depths, each word seeming to erase the one that came before it. I slid out from beneath my blanket and quietly got to my feet. I followed the sound to the living room, then into the hallway. I paused a moment inside my door, leaned against the wooden frame, and tensed in order to better capture the faint whispering from downstairs. It was so hushed that it would have been easy to ignore. I cautiously unlocked my door, careful to make no noise, and peered out into the stairwell. It was pitch-black except for a narrow strip of light that came through the window in the front door down on the ground floor. I pushed my own door open a bit wider and inched my head through the crack. My attention was drawn to a movement one floor below me. It took another second for my eyes to adjust to the darkness, and then I realized that it was the owner's wife. She was lying on her stomach, crawling on hands and knees up the stairs toward me. She seemed to be pulling herself upward with her arms, as if her legs were no longer working. Her hair stuck to her face in wet stripes. She breathed heavily but almost without sound, as if she didn't want to be overheard. Then she apparently became aware of something behind her and stiffened, just for an instant. Her features froze in an icy fear that crackled through her, and I suddenly saw that her hair wasn't wet but drenched with blood. It streamed from her hairline, trickled down her face, pooled at the bottoms of her eyes. She couldn't see me, I knew. She shivered and sighed, her fingers clawing the steps to pull her more quickly upward.

And that's when I saw him. He was leaning against the doorjamb, his arms folded across his chest, watching her in utter silence. Then he leaned forward and, without a word, grabbed her by the ankles. He dragged her down the stairs and, in continued silence, back into their apartment. Her eyes and mouth gaped wide open, but still she made no sound. Just before she disappeared from my sight, it seemed as if she stared straight up into my face. He shut the door noiselessly, and the quiet of the night was absolute, as if it had swallowed her whole.

The next few days, I was immersed in a somberness inappropriate to a person of my years. For some time, I had observed my surroundings with a sort of lighthearted resignation, and I was quite satisfied with that attitude. But now this darkness, this violence, had penetrated my walls. I sat in my armchair for

long hours and watched the crowns of the tallest trees swaying gently in the wind. I remembered how, only a few months
earlier, the older ones had been cut down, had vanished from
the park after living there for decades and had quickly been
forgotten, and how their disappearance had offered light and
air to those that remained. *This park*, I thought, *just like this
house, just like this city I know so well . . . everything changes, but
at heart it remains the same.*

Everything is irreplaceably what it is. Nothing yields.
Nothing bends to the world's violence.

The following day, I waited for the owner's wife. Each time
I heard the front door open, I hurried to the stairwell to see
who it was. The third time, it was her. She was coming up the
stairs, a blue-and-white shopping bag in her hand. I started
down, holding carefully to the railing. Although I moved as
quickly as my tired legs permitted, she reached her apartment
door before me. She glanced up at me for a moment, surprised,
and offered me a slight nod as she slid her key in the lock.

"Ma'am?" I said, inwardly cursing my old bones for not
being faster.

She hesitated, visibly reluctant, the knob in her hand.
"Yes?"

A few steep steps still separated us. It seemed to take
an eternity before I reached her, but fortunately she waited.
When I finally got there, I had to catch my breath. I leaned
a hand against the wall, held up the other in a gesture that
pleaded with her to grant me a moment to compose myself.

"Yes?" she said again, and she sounded irritated. Much of
her face was concealed by large sunglasses, which I expected
her to remove now that she was indoors, now that we stood
side by side. But she kept them on and wore no visible expres-

sion. Her skin was as pale as I remembered, her lips pressed tightly together, leaving no room for emotion.

"Is your husband home?" I asked when I was able to speak.

She shook her head and turned to go inside.

"No, wait, it doesn't matter. I mean—I actually wanted to talk to *you*."

She seemed distracted. I got the strange feeling that she anticipated I would strike her.

"I wanted to tell you that I know. I know what he does to you. Is there anything I can do to help?"

Her mouth opened very slightly, but she promptly closed it again. I still couldn't read her expression. She swallowed and said, "He can't help it. It's his heart."

"He has a heart condition?"

She nodded. "He takes medication, and it has side effects. Sometimes . . . sometimes he's not himself."

"Why don't you leave him?"

She lowered her head and whispered, "I don't dare."

"But you want to?"

She nodded without saying anything, then turned away from me abruptly, as if shocked by her own response.

After that conversation, I was determined to help her. I had done nothing in my life for which I needed to be embarrassed, but also nothing to be proud of. This, as I neared my finish line, would be my gift to the world. I devised a plan, and practiced the appropriate expressions of hysteria before the mirror. It wouldn't be easy, but I hadn't felt so keyed up in years.

The next day was a Saturday. It was ten minutes to six in the morning. I sat on the edge of my bed in pajamas and robe. I stood up and took off the robe, examined myself in the hall mirror, then went back to my bedroom and put it back on. Between the trees, the park outside was a dark gray. It wouldn't be long before the light would shift and daybreak would come. I checked the clock on the windowsill. Eight minutes to six. The owner would be fast asleep. It was time to act.

I picked up the telephone receiver and waited for the trembling of my hand to subside. Then I dialed his number. It was awhile before he answered, his voice hoarse with sleep. "Hello?"

I took a deep breath and screamed, as loudly and hysterically as I could, trusting that, newly awakened, he wouldn't recognize the sound as rehearsed: "Rats! Rats! There are rats in my apartment! You have to come up!"

"What? What are you . . . do you know what time it is?"

"They're in the attic! I can hear them scuttling around all night long, and now they're in the walls! I'm scared!"

"Can't it wait? It's—"

"No! No, it can't wait! Please come now, I can't stand it!"

"All right, calm down. I'm on my way. Jesus!"

He hung up. I set down the phone and waited, shaking with excitement, until I heard his apartment door open below. I took a breath and burst out into the stairwell with all the emotion I could muster. "There must be five or six of them!" I screamed at him, while he was still climbing the flight of stairs between us. He looked at me with irritation tinged with suspicion. I must have appeared crazy, with my white hair sticking out in all directions, my wrinkled pajamas, my unkempt robe hanging off my shoulders. "It's horrible! Disgusting! I've always been terrified of rats. And now they're in the ceiling. I can hear their nails scratching the wood, they probably have a nest of babies by now. The filthy beasts must be everywhere, and they eat everything. What do I do if they come into my apartment? What do I do?!"

"Calm *down!*" he ordered, and for one moment I thought he was about to hit me in the face. He didn't, but he studied me with unconcealed contempt. "I can't think if you keep on like that." He went on staring at me, and I realized that, in addition to contempt, there was also a certain interest glimmering in his gaze. He surely believed I had gone mad. Alzheimer's, if he was lucky. Then he'd have no trouble getting me out of the building.

I lowered my voice a bit. "Please, can you look in the attic? I'll never get any sleep."

He glanced up at the ceiling above the stairwell.

"There's a hatch," I said.

"I know," he sighed, and he reached for its metal handle. When he pulled on it, flakes of white paint and clouds of dust rained down on us. The hatch, I knew, hadn't been opened in years. The folding aluminum ladder above it was a cheap model. The previous owner hadn't wanted to spend a lot of money on a mechanism that would rarely, if ever, be used. It rattled coldly as it unfolded. When it was fully extended, it left little room for us on the landing. Its feet settled barely two inches from the topmost step of the stairwell. It was an unsteady contraption he would have to climb, thanks to the fears of a hysterical tenant, so early in the morning that he hadn't yet taken his medication.

I watched him furtively as he leaned one hand against the wall, the other pressed to his chest. He was panting, just a little. I was so close beside him that there was no need to shout, but I did so all the same. "Do you hear that? Do you? Rats!" I shoved him roughly, and he jerked away from my touch.

"Jesus, would you calm the fuck down?" Any vestige of politeness was gone now, and he stared at me in fury. "If you don't relax, there's nothing I can do."

"Sorry," I gasped, trying to look frightened.

He shook his head and examined the ladder. He raised a foot to the bottom tread and tested its strength. "Wobbly," he muttered. "Hold it steady, would you?"

I ducked beneath the ladder and grabbed onto it with both hands. The owner groaned a bit and slowly began to climb. He was so close to me now that I feared he would hear my heart pulsing against my ribs. I had to wait for the exact right moment—this was what it all came down to. He had to be as high as possible, to make his fall as long as possible.

When he reached the top tread and raised his right foot to feel for a next one, I took a deep breath and shrieked gibberish at him as loudly as I could while shaking the ladder violently. He struggled to hold on, but I shoved my hands between the treads and beat against his chest. He swallowed a cry and lost his balance. I went on screaming as he fell. He hit his head and tumbled backward down the steps before landing with a heavy thump on the bare wooden floor in front of his own apartment door, one flight below.

I stopped shouting and, panting heavily, peered down at him.

His door opened, and his wife appeared. She saw him and then, astonished, looked up at me. "What—?"

"He fell," I whispered. "Is he dead?"

She dropped to her knees and touched his throat. Then she rose, both hands covering her mouth.

"Dead?" I asked again.

She nodded, her face etched with horror.

"Go back inside," I said. "I'll call the police."

Not waiting to calm down, I dialed the emergency number and used the same overexcited, frightened tone with which I had talked to the owner. After hanging up, I went to stand at my window. I drew a deep breath and was not dissatisfied to note the profound serenity that came over me. The clock on the sill told me that it was three minutes after six. Eleven minutes had gone by since the last time I had stood there.

The park was still dark, though daylight was already peeking out between the treetops. In the distance, a siren sounded. I waited, and it seemed as though—if I paid close enough attention—I could see the night hide itself beneath the benches beside the trees. As if, right before my eyes, it disappeared behind the walls of the park.

# SOUL MATES

BY CHRISTINE OTTEN

*Tuindorp Oostzaan*

They were on our doorstep at ten after six this morning. I know the exact time because a fraction of a second before the bell rang—one short, two longs—I woke up and looked at my iPhone. 6:10. It was just getting light. I knew it was the cops. I mean, you just *know*. I heard Mom's bedroom door creak, her footsteps on the stairs, the murmur of voices. So I splashed some water on my face, sprayed my pits with Axe, and got dressed. I was calm. At times like this, my emotions just sort of freeze. I grabbed the Prada jacket Miriam gave me, slipped my bare feet into my Pumas, and went down. I'm a good boy, I am. I tried to ignore Mom's expression; if there's one thing I can't stand, it's that exhausted, disappointed look she gets in her eyes. *Can't I ever have a moment's peace?* Instead, I focused on the crew-cut heads of the two detectives standing in the doorway, their hands deep in the pockets of their ugly, cheap H&M jackets, and said, cheerfully as I could manage, "Good morning, gentlemen, and what can we do for you today?"

You could see them thinking, *This is one polite Algerian.* You always gotta stay a step ahead of them. Be the strongest, the smartest, don't let them figure you out, and most important: keep your anger under control. I learned that at kickboxing. Not too long ago, I got pulled over on my moped on the Meteorenweg because I was supposedly driving too fast.

I was heading to the Mandarijnenstraat to deliver six *frikandels*, three croquettes, a deep-fried *bami* slice, a couple of kebabs, and fifteen euros worth of french fries with mayo. I guess they were having a party. So, anyway, I was in a hurry, nobody wants soggy fries and lukewarm *frikandels*. I don't understand how anyone can stomach that disgusting haram shit in the first place, but whatever, not ours to reason why. The point is, I got pulled over. Must have been the cop's first week on the job. "Sir, you're driving much too fast." We both knew it was bullshit, I wasn't doing more than fifteen miles an hour, twenty tops, we both knew the only reason he flagged me down is I look like a Moroccan—a Marrow Khan in Tuindorp Oostzaan, I'm a poet and I don't know it!—but whatever. He whips out his little citation book to write me up, and I say, "I'm terribly sorry, officer, but my grandma is sick, she's in really bad shape, and I don't want her to be alone, that's why I'm in a rush."

When he hears me talking in complete sentences without a hint of an accent, his eyes practically pop out of his head. "Oh?" he says.

"She lives right around the corner here, on the Zonneplein." Which is 100 percent true: Mom's mother lives on the Zonneplein, upstairs from a Turkish grocery.

So the cop waves me on, and that's the end of it. Which is why I say: you have to stay a step ahead of them. Don't give 'em the chance to fuck with you.

Anyway, I had a good idea why the detectives were at our door. See, the Chink's been missing for five days now and the Mercury's been shuttered, although the old gook normally opens up at noon 'cause he don't miss a chance to cash in on the lunch trade. He didn't tell me he was gonna be gone: no e-mail, no text, nothing.

When I showed up for work five days ago and he wasn't there, I tried his doorbell—he lives upstairs from his snack bar/Chinese takeaway, see. I was only inside his apartment one time, and the stink of grease made me want to hurl. He really needs to do something about his ventilation.

So I got no response when I rang, and there wasn't any lights on I could see. Pissed me off, because it was payday, and man does not live by tips alone. For the last couple months, the old guy and me have had a little side deal. "Call it hush money," is the way he put it. I never asked for nothing extra. Didn't need to. The old guy read in my eyes that I knew the score. I mean, I'm not *stupid*. He never should have asked me to fetch that box of croquettes from the freezer, the fool.

All those bricks of brown and white powder hidden among the frozen snacks and fries! Street value? I have no idea. Jesus. I mean, you want to play gangster, at least you could be a little careful about it. Fine, well, anyway, the way I saw it, we had us what you call a win-win situation there. And I could use the extra cash. Him too, apparently. The Mercury Snackbar on the Mercuriusplein ain't exactly a gold mine, if you catch my drift. Until he gets the windows washed and loses those disgusting orange plastic stools and the greasy Formica countertop and does something about the ventilation, he pretty much *needs* a little sideline if he wants to stay afloat, you see what I'm saying?

I understand the Chink. He's gotta think about his future. He's not gonna wind up some old geezer wasting away in that pitiful apartment on the Mercuriusplein, not when he could live out his golden years in Malaysia or Hong Kong or Singapore or wherever the hell he comes from. Am I right? So I figured he emptied out his bank accounts and was having himself a roll in the hay with some Chinese hottie in a massage parlor off in Whereverland. I was actually kind of proud of him. I wasn't worried about our deal, or about the cops implicating me in his drug trade, because there was absolutely no paper trail or anything else pointing my way. I'm the delivery boy for the Mercury Snackbar, and that is *all* I am.

Except, with those two cops standing there awkwardly at the door, I began to feel just a wee bit sweaty.

The older of the two—you could already see the male-pattern baldness making inroads on his temples—cleared his throat. "We're sorry to bother you so early, but I'm afraid we have bad news. May we come in?"

*No way*, I thought. But Mom automatically took a step back. I could see her fear in the slump of her shoulders inside her pink robe. She grabbed my face and started whining like a wounded animal. "Where did I go wrong, Armin? You were always such a sweet little boy!" I was afraid she was about to keel over, so I slung an arm around her to keep her on her feet. I mean, I *am* the man of the house. But I guess I can't blame her for projecting her shit onto me.

"Calm down, Ma," I said. "Don't worry. Let's hear what the officers have to say."

To make a long story short, the Chink was dead. At least the detectives *thought* it was the Chink they'd found hacked to bits and the bits deep-fried, "considering how close the dumpster in the Maanstraat is to the Mercury Snackbar, and his contacts in the Chinese tongs." The only thing they could say for sure at this point was that what they had found was definitely human remains, though they were in such a state they weren't sure it would ever be possible to positively identify the victim. Somebody from the neighborhood had called it in. His little Staffordshire terrier had started barking and howling when they came in sight of the dumpster. The smell was pretty ripe, they said.

The older detective must have seen the dismay in Mom's eyes, 'cause all of a sudden he put a hand on her shoulder and said they were 99 percent sure it was the Chink, and they hoped the techs would come up with like a molecule of DNA that would lock in that last 1 percent. No such thing as a perfect crime, he said, puffing out his chest, "there's usually a loose end or two, we know that from experience," looking like he was starring in an episode of *CSI*, like he was some kind of a big shot. "We don't want you folks to worry now, ma'am, do we? Tuindorp Oostzaan's such a quiet little neighborhood, where nothing ever happens." I could hear the contempt in his voice. On the downtown side of the IJ, they think we're all hicks up here in Amsterdam-North.

So I told you I sort of freeze at times like this, right? My friends don't call me Ice for nothing—after the old rapper/actor with the pigtail from *Law & Order*, you know? Maybe the story was a little too crazy to believe. Even Mom just stood there crying silently instead of busting out screaming. But I realized pretty quick that the cops weren't out to tie me to whatever had gone down. When you're in their headlights, you *know* it. They were pretty chill about the whole thing. Just said they'd appreciate whatever I could tell them about the Chink, seeing how I was the Mercury's scooter boy and all—I wanted to correct them and say *moped* boy, but I didn't think I ought to interrupt—and I saw the old guy pretty much every day, so maybe I could help them with their inquiries. I told them I thought the Chink was out of town for a couple days, he said something about needing a break, checking out the tulips at the Keukenhof, yadda yadda yadda, and running a Chinese takeout/snack bar in Tuindorp Oostzaan ain't exactly what you call a sinecure, right? Meanwhile, the little gears in my head are spinning overtime, you know what I mean?

See, something told me maybe the deep-fried dead guy was *not* the Chink, after all.

Maybe I watch too many cop shows. On TV, nothing ever turns out the way you think it will, right?

But there was something else. Which is why I'm writing all this down, not as evidence but as a sort of testimony, in case something happens to me. For Mom's sake, you with me? Ain't nobody I love more than her, not even Miriam.

I don't know if I can call Miriam my girlfriend, exactly, since she's married and all that. She and her husband and their two little girls live in one of those villas on the Kometensingel, a fancy place next door to the house where our family doctor used to live. Once upon a time, Mom was the cleaning lady there. So one night they order a double portion of chow mein from the Mercury. I deliver it, Miriam answers the door, and the rest is history.

Trust me, Miriam is not just some ordinary chick. She is what I'd call a perfect ten. From our very first date, though, she told me she was never ever gonna divorce her husband, 'cause her own parents split when she was fifteen and she wasn't gonna put *her* girls through that kind of trauma. That's class, am I right?

Her husband's a lung doctor in some hospital up north. His name's Ed. He's forty-four. (Just so you know: I'm twenty-four.) I only know him from Miriam's stories and his Facebook page. Soon as the detectives left, I went online: his most recent photo was posted yesterday, from a bar, right after the Ajax–Sparta game. He was grinning into the lens with this smug doctor expression on his face and a glass of beer in his hand, an Ajax scarf draped around his neck, like, *See how normal I am?* You could almost hear André Hazes singing in the background. That's why he bought that house in Tuindorp Oostzaan—to prove what an ordinary guy he is. Miriam told me his whole bio. Ed's dad worked in the metal foundry on the Distelweg; the five of them lived in this dreary little bungalow on the Pomonastraat. Ed was a nerd, so after high school they told him he could go to college and he grabbed the chance. Props to him and his family, I gotta give them respect. If my loser of a father had half the guts Ed's dad had, I could've . . . nah, never mind, I don't want to go throwing stones.

Anyway, when Miriam met Ed he was a member of like a fraternity—you know what I mean, a group of students who were ashamed of their origins and put on high-class accents like they were part of the royal family. At first, she said, she thought it was kind of cute, that Ed was trying so hard to fit in. She told me she saw right through his act and decided she could help him "grow into himself." I mean, bullshit, right— and she knew it was bullshit even at the time. But a woman like Miriam's gotta have a project. Sometimes I think maybe I'm her newest project, but at the same time I think, *What the fuck?* I'll tell you what: she's *my* project. I love her.

Miriam and me come from two different worlds. Her mother was something high up at the university, and her father was a bigwig at Nestlé. When she was growing up, they moved to a new country every couple of years: Egypt, Canada, Nigeria, South Africa, Russia, Morocco. I mean, she's a woman of the world. Sometimes she tells me, "Ed's a real Tuindorper, totally white-bread. But you, you've got that Algerian blood." She has this tone when she says it, like, *This is heavy, man.* And the look in her eye, yowza. I don't know exactly what it all means, but so what? The bottom line is, it's pretty great with us between the sheets, if you follow me.

But I digress.

I love Miriam, you with me? And I know she's stuck between a rock and a hard place. Hey, put yourself in her position: your hubby's cheating on you with some pretty young intern while you sit home and look after a couple of kids. That'd make you nuts, am I right?

So, okay, this is where the story really begins.

From the first time we ever did it—Ed works irregular shifts and I'm pretty flexible, so she texts me when it's okay to come over—she's spilled her guts to me. I'm not so dumb I believe in love at first sight, but *something* just clicked between Miriam and me. "Soul mates," she calls us. That's such a Miriam thing to say. "We're both outsiders," she tells me. "We understand each other." It don't bother me she's fifteen years older. Just the opposite: I think older women are sexy, they know exactly what they want in bed.

Shit, I'm getting off track again. Focus, Armin!

So Ed's fucking this intern, right, and Miriam finds out about it. She confronts him. He goes all guilty, all pitiful, all *I'm sorry, you're the one I love, it don't mean nothing*, and he begs her to forgive him. And she *does*, the dope.

Okay, fine, I know what you're thinking: she's cheating on him too. To which I say, *Well, who started it?* Miriam was lonely. Can you blame her for taking comfort from a guy like me? A guy who at least *listens* to her?

As my mom's only son, trust me, I have learned how to listen.

So Miriam forgives Ed. But meanwhile, Ed goes right on nailing this intern every chance he gets. They're snorting coke—possibly coke they get from the Chink, what do I know?—and Ed don't realize right away the woman he's boinking is the devil in disguise. But then, see, the bitch commences to blackmail him. *If you don't leave your wife and kids, I'll tell the hospital administrator what you've been up to. I'll say you forced me into it. Abuse of power.* Shit like that. So you've got a doctor riding the coke train and banging an intern: Ed would definitely lose his job and probably his medical license or whatever you call it. I got all this from Miriam.

So once again, Ed fesses up, only this time Miriam plays it smart. She "forgives" him, she says, but now she has a plan.

"You're my sweet revenge," she tells me, this one time after we do it. We're smoking cigarettes in bed. Ed's working a double shift, and the girls are at his parents'. "You're my secret weapon."

Tell you the truth, that comment shook me up a little. It wasn't so much what she said but the way she said it, the bitterness in her voice, and the way she looked . . . like I wasn't even there, like I wasn't lying right beside her in the bed.

Anyway, Miriam doesn't trust Ed no more, but she doesn't want to leave him because of the kids. So she goes all detective on his ass: when he's in the shower, she checks his e-mail and his texts. And that's when the shit really hits the fan.

*I'll kill Miriam if you don't divorce her.*
*You'd better get rid of your daughters. My patience is running out.*
*You're mine!!!*
*I hate Miriam.*
*Miriam's a cunt and has to die.*

And then there are Ed's wimpy responses:

*Calm down, sweetheart.*
*I need more time.*
*I love you.*

This is all pretty recent, by the way. I was with Miriam just last night, and she brought me up to speed.

So now I gotta be careful what I write. I don't want to screw anybody over until I'm 100 percent sure. I know what it's like to be blamed for shit I didn't do. I mean, how many times have we had the cops at the door because so-and-so made a crack and everybody's all, *It must've been Armin who done it?*

How am I supposed to prove I *didn't*, right?

I mean, come on!

Look, I figure *you'd* probably freak if you found out your husband's lover wanted you dead, right? So I told Miriam maybe she ought to report it. Which, by the way, sounded really weird coming out of *my* mouth. Report it? Like the cop on the corner is your friend, right? But I just didn't trust the situation. I was worried about Miriam.

"This is private," she said. "I don't want the girls to hear anything about it. I'll deal with it." And then she climbed on top of me and drove me out of my gourd with her tongue. We fucked like we never fucked before, like . . . well, like wild animals. It was like Miriam squeezed herself *inside* of me. She bit me, licked me, raked my back with her long sharp nails, sucked my balls—Jesus, I thought I was about to black out—and meanwhile she whispered all this shit I figured was meant to stir me up and make our coming even more explosive, words and sentences I didn't really absorb—you know what

I mean, we all say weird stuff when we're excited. I mean, I get it that Miriam wished the bitch was dead and I'm not a baby, I've got a pretty rich imagination myself, if you get my drift, I've downloaded some illegal videos—you know, where Somebody A really *hurts* Somebody B, hits her, beats her with whips, cuts her with razors, tortures her—snuff films, I mean, that shit's fucked up.

Anyway, I didn't think much about the fairy tale she told me last night until those cops showed up this morning, but since then I can't get it out of my mind.

And I can totally see it happening.

Miriam waiting outside the hospital for her husband's chippie. Inviting her for a cup of coffee so they can "talk things out." Driving in Miriam's mint-green MINI Cooper convertible from North Holland down to Tuindorp Oostzaan, the wind in their hair, it's actually much too cold to be driving with the top down but Miriam wants to teach the bitch a lesson, *she's* wearing a leather jacket and a cap, she's prepared, she snuck the Mercury Snackbar's keys out of my pants pocket the day before, when I slipped out of bed to take a dump. Miriam parking the car somewhere on the Meteorenweg, and the two of them strolling to the snack bar, Ed's cunt grossed out when she sees the Mercury's grimy windows, *This is where you want to go for coffee?* The Chink's already long gone, Miriam knows that because I told her. Fine, so she holds the door open for the bitch, gives her a little wink, they're in this together, they understand each other, they both know Ed's a piece of shit and they'll figure a way to get through this, but the second Miriam locks the door behind them the nightmare begins. Miriam's thought of everything: the ropes, the bread knife, the chain saw, she switched on the fryer before she headed north so it would be nice and hot by the time they got back, she don't leave nothing to chance, and meanwhile the cunt's all shitting bricks and begging Miriam to let her go, but Miriam's got her chained to the meat hook that's attached to the kitchen ceiling by then, like a dead pig, like a dog— the Chinks eat dog, don't they?—her mouth duct-taped, and while the bitch shivers from the cold and the terror, Miriam goes to town, one finger at a time, one toe at a time, the blood dripping into an old-fashioned iron bucket, the cunt turning yellow then gray then finally white and blue and she's not dead yet, her left shoulder jerks when Miriam slices a chunk of meat from her leg and tosses it into the boiling oil in the fryer—can you imagine watching this happen to *you*, you know you're gonna die and there isn't a fucking thing you can do about it, just hope you'll pass out soon—but Miriam goes at it for hours, big pieces, torso, thighs, arms, she trims them to size with the chain saw and one by one the hunks of meat and bone and hair and guts and everything all disappear in the boiling oil.

You understand, I see the situation in a different light, now that the cops have come and gone.

*You're my sweet revenge. You're my secret weapon.*

See, Miriam's always sort of been a mystery to me. A woman like that, a woman of the world, so . . . *smart*, so well spoken, and beautiful too, even though she's just past forty, I never met nobody like her in my life. We might have come from different planets. You see where I'm going with this?

Is it possible the detectives showed up at *her* door before they came to mine? Like maybe yesterday, so she already knew about the mess in the dumpster before we got together last night? She lives practically right around the corner from the Mercury, she's a steady customer, I drop off an order of chow mein like two, three times a week. The detectives must know that if they're halfway decent at their jobs.

They go around the neighborhood door-to-door asking questions, don't they?

Meanwhile, I never once noticed my key to the Mercury was missing, so maybe Miriam made the whole thing up. I mean, maybe she's gotta fantasize shit like that to keep her frustration from driving her nuts, what do I know? Her husband's rich, but money don't make nobody happy. Status, neither. I know that much by now. And her whole story could have come straight out of a bad episode of *Midsomer Murders*. Mom watches that show every Wednesday night.

I get it, Miriam wanted the bitch out of her life, but even if she *did* decide to waste her, even then, she would have just run her down with her MINI, wouldn't she, or gotten a gun and blew her brains out? Wouldn't she? I mean, I just don't see Miriam going to town with a fucking chain saw. I don't think she'd even know how something like that *works*.

I know what you're thinking: *Why don't you just go ask her?* Ask her what's the real deal and, boom, case closed. But see, here's the thing: we don't have that kind of a relationship. I never ask her *nothing*. I just listen.

I mean—and I'm not talking about my relationship with the Chink here, that was pretty clear-cut, no surprises—I mean, it sucks the old guy got chopped into mincemeat and all, but that's the chance you take when you get in with the tongs, he knew the risk—but the idea that I dumped myself into this rich-people's soap opera, what does that say about me?

I love Miriam and all, but what about my self-respect? What about my pride?

Maybe this whole thing's some kind of a sign. Whatever really happened, my job at the Mercury Snackbar is gone. I am now footloose and fancy-free. I could just hang out for a while, see which way the wind blows. Nothing's stopping me from trying something completely new, stepping out on my own. Maybe computers? Or I could take over the Mercury and run it myself. Get rid of those shitty plastic stools, put in some decent ventilation, turn it into a hip new takeout place. Snackbar Armin, something like that, everything 100 percent halal. I bet there's a market for that in Tuindorp Oostzaan, especially if I hire a couple of kids with scooters to make deliveries all over Amsterdam-North. Why not?

I got all that hush money from the Chink saved up. Plus the tips Miriam always gave me—not just for the chow mein, but after we screwed too, now that I think of it.

Every cloud has a silver lining, right?

Am I right?

On the other hand, there's no way I'll ever hook up with a woman like Miriam again, that's for sure.

And what we have, that has to be love. I mean, the sex, the way she trusts me . . .

We're soul mates, aren't we?

I mean, *aren't* we?

*This story was inspired by an actual Amsterdam murder case.*

# PART III

*Touch of Evil*

# DEVIL'S ISLAND

BY MENSJE VAN KEULEN

*Duivelseiland*

Amsterdam has changed so much since smoking was banned from bars, restaurants, and public spaces. Walk, bike, drive, or take the tram or bus across the city and you'll see knots of people out on the sidewalks, clouds of smoke billowing above their heads. Cold weather, heavy wind, gloomy surroundings, the blare of traffic—nothing seems to bother them, especially not when a bunch of them are clustered together. I guess misery *does* love company, after all.

I am mildly asthmatic, so not a smoker, but after Jacob—who's one of my oldest pals—was deserted by his girlfriend for a stage director, I've sometimes found myself part of such a group. See, it turned out not to be such a great idea to have Jacob over to my place to unburden himself of his woes: the walls of my apartment are thin, and the later it got the louder he wailed . . . not to mention what his damn chain-smoking did to my air. Going out on the town with him wasn't an ideal solution either, because I have to get up early for my job, but I couldn't just tell the poor schmuck to deal with it, because, I mean, he was truly hurting.

The last time he turned up at my door was three days ago. I was exhausted, and I'd just fished a package of soup out of the freezer—comfort food, right?—when the bell rang and there he was, unshaven, face pale as a ghost. When I asked him if he'd eaten, he told me food was the last thing on his mind, and I stashed my soup back where it had come from.

"Let's go," I said, pulling on a jacket and leading him outside.

"Thirst never sleeps," he muttered.

"Hey, we're not gonna spend the whole night drinking. I've woken up with enough hangovers, thanks to you."

"Pain never sleeps either, but you're better off with an aching head than a rat gnawing at your heart."

"You'll get over it, Jake."

"You say that every time I see you, but the rat just keeps on gnawing."

I wanted to tell him that accusing me of repeating myself was a clear case of the pot calling the kettle black, but I was afraid that'd result in more screaming about how nobody understood him, and he couldn't live without Martha, and he was so lonely, and he wished he was dead—or, like we'd been through two weeks before, him collapsing to the ground and weeping like a little baby.

"Come on, let's go find something to eat," I said, steering him by the elbow. "And a beer," I added quickly, before he could begin to protest.

We turned into the Pieter Baststraat and passed a storefront that had the name of our little neighborhood lettered on its plateglass window.

"Devil's Island," Jacob growled. "If only. I wish the devil really existed, I'd pay him a little visit, right this second. Sure, fine, go ahead and laugh. But I mean it: I'd sell him my soul if he'd make Martha come back to me." He scoped out the storefront a second time. "What *is* this place, anyway? Another barbershop? Do we really need more barbers? How often do people have to get their hair cut?"

At that, he bent his head mournfully, but before he could

start in on how Martha always used to cut his hair for him, I told him he was overdue for a hearty dinner.

"Booze," he said, and then, as we passed the cigar store on the corner—a prime location, right across from Café Loetje—"booze and a smoke."

I pushed him through the door into Loetje, which has evolved over the years from a small café with billiards to a restaurant three times its original size—though sometimes you still have to wait an hour or more for a table. They were full that night, not even a couple of stools at the bar, but one of the servers recognized me and gestured it'd only be half an hour or so before we'd hit the top of the list.

A minute later, we were back on the sidewalk, each with a glass of beer, surrounded by half a dozen smokers—mostly thirtysomethings and fortysomethings—who I figured for realtors or some other well-paid professionals. Two of them were women, having a girls' night out. Jacob gulped his brewski, alternating swallows with deep drags on a cigarette. Across the street, the Old Catholic Church loomed, swathed in darkness.

"Got a match?" came a voice from beside me.

I turned to say I don't smoke but realized the guy was talking to Jacob, not me. He held a cigarillo between slender fingers.

"Sure," said Jacob, reaching for his lighter. It took him three or four tries to produce a flame.

"Much obliged, friend," said the man.

That *friend* seemed a little presumptuous, but Jacob smiled.

"These things taste better when lit with a wooden match," the man said, exhaling smoke in the direction of the church. "But who carries those old-fashioned lucifers around in their pocket these days? I love the smell of them, though, that momentary blast of sulfur. Would you like to try one of mine?"

"Thanks," said Jacob, and he lit the proffered cigarillo with the stub of his cigarette.

I hadn't heard a polite word out of Jacob in quite some time—and spoken to a stranger, no less. I took a closer look at the man. He was not unattractive, with black hair slicked back to just below the collar of his obviously expensive jacket. All things considered, I would call him a rather elegant fellow.

"May I pose a question?" The stranger's gaze flicked from Jacob to me to the other smokers. "Did any of you happen to know a gentleman who lived in this neighborhood, a certain Van der Meer?"

"Van der Meer," said a smoker who had overconfidently left his jacket inside. "You mean the professor?"

"Indeed I do."

"Don't waste your time looking for him: he's dead."

The man nodded. "A heart attack, I know. Does his widow ever patronize this establishment?"

"Yolande?" said one of the women. "No, I haven't seen her since he passed. When they used to eat here, I always looked the other way, and not just because he ordered his steak so rare the blood dripped all over his chin."

"Gross," said her girlfriend.

"I took a class from him once, and he was what you call a real skirt-chaser, totally annoying. I think *she* was one of his students—she was at least twenty years younger than him, maybe thirty."

The man nodded again, and this time blew a perfect smoke ring that drifted lazily skyward.

"When he was out here smoking," the woman went on, "I made sure to keep my distance. But I think he finally quit.

The last few times I saw them here, he stayed inside. I'll tell you, he seemed crankier about it every time."

"They lived in a big house up the street, right where the Museum District begins," said one of the men, grinding out a cigarette with his shoe. "It came on the market three days ago, and somebody bought it without even asking to see the inside. No surprise, really: this neighborhood's red-hot."

Two names were called, and most of the smokers took one last puff, stubbed out their cigarettes in the standing ashtray, and headed into Loetje.

The few who remained moved closer to the door and went on talking, which left Jacob and me alone with the stranger.

"I bought that house," he said calmly. "I've been looking for a suitable home in the city for some time. I don't care for hotels, I'd much rather have a place of my own."

"Jeez," said Jacob, and I thought I heard a note of admiration in his voice.

"You bought a house without checking out the inside?" I said. "That seems a little risky."

"Oh, I know the place well—I paid a call there not long ago. It's quite lovely, and there's a marvelous art collection on the walls."

"I assume the art doesn't go with the property. Or are you some kind of dealer or collector?"

"Both," he said with a smile. "Which is why I spend so much time traveling. When I finish my business here, I'll return to my country house outside Seville. I may stop off in Paris, I have a little pied-à-terre on the Place Vendôme."

He exhaled a plume of smoke that came straight at me and sent me into a fit of coughing.

"Please forgive my filthy habit," he said. "I forget that others might not appreciate the bouquet of fine tobacco as much as I do. Van der Meer ultimately had a problem with it too, which is why he had to give up smoking. Of course, that wasn't his only problem."

"You mean his wife?" Jacob guessed.

"In a way. She was, as you heard a few moments ago, quite a bit younger than he. At first, that was precisely what attracted Van der Meer to her, but their situation changed as he got older, and for the last few years it had all become—how shall I say it?—rather disastrous."

"What do you mean, *their situation changed?*" asked Jacob. "She didn't stop being younger than him."

"Yes, but that was the point, you see. He began to blame her for making him feel like an old man."

"Sounds like she's better off without him."

"Well, I wouldn't say better off." The man grinned, and—unlike Jacob, who had unbuttoned his jacket—I suddenly felt a chill.

"Explain that," I said.

The stranger flicked the stub of his cigarillo over the bike rack and into the darkness. "Well, I was sitting in a café, she happened to be sitting alone at the next table. She accidentally spilled her drink, I handed her a napkin, and—I don't know why, but I seem to attract people with a need to get things off their chests. Or perhaps *I'm* attracted to *them*. In any case, she told me her story. The bottom line was that her husband was a sadist who was making her life hell. There was no way he would agree to a divorce, and she couldn't possibly leave him, because she had nowhere else to go and she couldn't support herself on her own—she was a French tutor, and not many children seem to select that language these days. How, she asked me, could she ever get free of him? Well, a nasty old man with a weak heart, the world certainly wouldn't be any worse off without him."

"Are you saying you offered to *murder* him?" asked Jacob eagerly.

"That's a strong word, friend. I wouldn't call it *murder* to send a man on his way without ever laying a finger on him. I asked her about his weaknesses, and she mentioned something I thought I could use."

"And that was?"

"Religion." The man took a fresh cigarillo from his inside pocket and waved it at the church. "Van der Meer was a devout atheist who seethed at the sight or sound of anything remotely pious. I immediately devised what seemed to me an appropriate plan, and I presented it to her. Might I trouble you again for a light, friend? And here, have another yourself."

The man laid a hand on Jacob's wrist. Neither of them paid me the slightest attention.

"That very evening, I appeared at their door. She admitted me, as prearranged. That in itself infuriated Van der Meer, the idea that she would permit a stranger to invade his sanctum. I informed him, quite humbly, that I was there to return a book. 'A book?' he said. 'I never loan out my books.' 'I didn't borrow it,' I said, 'I found it lying beside your trash can.' I extended it to him, and he cried out in horror: 'A Bible? What makes you think that belongs to me? I've never owned a Bible in my life!' 'That's very strange,' said I, 'for your name is inscribed in it.' His face turned bright red, and he shrieked, 'Take it away! Remove that wretched volume from my sight!' I said, 'The seven plagues of Egypt will afflict you, brother, if you insult God's word in such a detestable manner.' He cursed at me and screamed, 'Get out, you vile liar! Get out!' I stood before him, opened the book, and showed him his name. And that was the coup de grâce. His eyes rolled up in their sockets, he shook uncontrollably, and he collapsed to the ground, stone dead. But let me tell you what happened next: his widow began to dance. She was now a wealthy woman, she exulted. She would sell the house, it would surely bring at least two million euros, she would travel to sunny climes, indulge herself in cruises, I can't remember the full shopping list. I began to feel pity for the corpse. After this tasteless exhibition, she telephoned for an ambulance, her voice trembling, and—without so much as a thank you—showed me to the door."

"Women," sighed Jacob. "Such heartless creatures."

"You are exactly right, friend. We must beware their treachery. Well, I offered 2.3 million for the house, and the paperwork awaits completion. The professor left behind no power of attorney, so the widow Van der Meer is required to make an appearance at the signing. And that will be difficult."

"Is she already gone?"

"Not quite. Her . . . departure still needs to be attended to. I would value some assistance, and if you're inclined to volunteer I will reward you more than generously. You seem to be a man with a gray future before him, yourself in some need of assistance. Am I correct, friend?"

"Gray?" said Jacob. "My future's black, ebony. What can I do to help you?"

"This neighborhood is crowded with tourists, no one will notice two gentlemen strolling leisurely toward the Hobbemakade with a trunk on wheels. The canal there is surely sufficiently deep, and there are brief gaps in the traffic when the lights at the crossings turn red. She weighs 130 pounds at most, and is perhaps five feet nine or ten in height—or should I say that she *was* five-nine or -ten? I believe she must have been a jogger, since her long legs—once so alluring to Van der Meer's goatish eyes—were too tightly muscled for an ordinary steak knife."

"Jacob," I said, filled with revulsion, "don't listen to any more of this bullshit. Let's go inside, I'm cold."

"With the exception of a few soft spots, the rest is rather lean, tough meat. That particular part of the process is as yet incomplete, and I could certainly use your help there as well, my friend. It would be best, I think, to wait until the blood has fully coagulated. Van der Meer may well have decorated his home with the finest available artwork, but he doesn't seem to have paid much attention to the outfitting of his bathrooms. There are a number of broken tiles in the floor, and those will have to be thoroughly scrubbed."

"Jacob, seriously, don't listen to this lunatic!"

"If we can't fit her into the trunk, there's also a carry-on bag with wheels that we can use."

My name was called and, almost gagging, I said, "Please, Jacob, let's go in."

He didn't react, his eyes and ears riveted on the stranger, who whispered, barely audibly, "It's a nice little piece, the fabric is a Scottish tartan, so even if there *is* some blood, it won't show."

"Jacob, for God's sake!"

"Yeah, I, ah, I'll be right in," he murmured distractedly.

They seated me at a little table by a window. I peered over the top of my menu and saw them standing there outside, their heads close together. When a server came to take my order, I told her I was waiting for someone. She asked if I wanted a drink, and I said I'd have a glass of the house white.

When I turned my attention back to the window, they were gone. I have to admit that it was cowardice that kept me in my chair. I couldn't eat a thing, just sat there pouring glass after glass of wine down my throat. The place emptied out, the chairs were turned upside down and put on the tables, and I just sat there with no idea what to do.

\* \* \*

I tried repeatedly to reach Jacob over the next couple of days, but his phone went straight to voice mail and at night his apartment windows were dark. I kept asking myself what could have happened to him and was plagued by the most gruesome images. I even walked along the Hobbemakade a couple of times, searching for something floating in the water.

So you can understand how relieved I was earlier this evening when I walked into Café Wildschut—one of my regular after-work hangouts—and spotted Jacob sitting in one of the shadowy corners in the back room. And you can understand how surprised I was to see him in the company of a woman—and not just *any* woman, no, but the one and only Martha. They looked so lovey-dovey I decided not to disturb them, and I hesitated for a second, debating whether it would be the better part of valor to take a seat at the bar or just leave the place altogether.

At that moment, Jacob glanced up and saw me and waved. Smiling broadly, the two of them stood and approached me. Martha handed Jacob her glass of wine so she could wrap me in an exuberant hug. I smelled expensive perfume, and saw over her shoulder that Jacob's hair was freshly cut and he was wearing a sharp new suit that must have set him back more than he could possibly afford on his salary.

"How nice to run into you both," I managed.

"Back atcha," said Jacob. "We're gonna go out and grab a smoke. Come with, and we'll tell you about our plans."

A few seconds later, we settled around one of the high-tops on the terrace.

Martha squeezed my arm and said, "We're leaving tomorrow."

"Leaving?" I glanced at Jacob, who avoided my eyes. "I was afraid you were already gone."

He grinned and shook two cigarettes out of a pack. "We got fantastic job offers."

"What do you mean?"

"I mean what I say, my friend. Our worries are over. A new life awaits us."

"You'll come and visit us," said Martha.

"Absolutely," said Jacob. "Who knows, maybe there's a golden opportunity for *you* in the south of Spain too, and you can quit your stupid job."

He put the cigarettes between his lips and struck an old-fashioned wooden lucifer. The stink of sulfur burned my eyes, and he blew a cloud of smoke right in my face. I made my excuses with a gesture and hurried home, half-choking.

And as I lie here in the dark, unable to sleep, I realize that my gesture was also a wave of goodbye, because I'm afraid—no, I'm quite certain—that I'll never see either of them again.

# THE MAN ON THE JETTY

BY Murat Isik

*Bijlmer*

Some call us Amsterdam's deplorables. Others claim there are only junkies and dealers left in the Bijlmer, our neighborhood. That's a bit of an exaggeration, though it's true that we live in a godforsaken part of town mainly inhabited by those who can't find anywhere else to settle. It's also true that the storage rooms in the Bijlmer's apartment buildings' basements have devolved into the exclusive domain of the city's addicts.

Saleem and I knew we had to watch out, not just for the junkies, but especially for those lost souls who might loom up from out of nowhere and surround us. So we were on our guard the moment we set foot in the stairwells, and we stayed alert as we slipped through the narrow streets after dark. And ever since a guy whipped out his dick in the elevator and scared the shit out of me, I knew I had to get out of the Bijlmer, the sooner the better.

One day, Saleem and I were on our way home. His uncle was visiting, and he'd brought with him a wrestling video featuring our hero, the Ultimate Warrior. As we chattered excitedly about the mythical man with the painted face who'd stolen our hearts, I spotted something in the distance I'd never seen before: an object shimmering like mercury streaked along the bike path, like Marvel's Silver Surfer cruising from planet to planet on his cosmic surfboard. When I looked more closely, I realized to my disappointment that it was just an ordinary mortal on a racing bike. He approached us at dizzying speed, and—with his mirrored sunglasses, Spandex shirt and shorts, and futuristic bicycle—he was the closest thing to a professional cyclist the Bijlmer had ever seen. When he was thirty yards off, he began to slow down. He braked to a stop beside us and looked us up and down inquisitively. "Hey, boys," he said, his tone friendly. "I saw you walking and thought, *I bet those kids can help me*."

He removed his shades, and I stiffened at the sight of his eyes. Those steel-blue eyes. It was him! This was the same guy who, a few months earlier, breathing heavily and staring at me full of sick desire, had pulled his prick from his pants in the elevator. Did he recognize me too? I looked around, trying to decide which way we should run.

"I think I'm lost," he said, smiling.

*You are* definitely *lost*, I thought. I elbowed Saleem, telling him without words to keep walking, but he just stood there, not taking the hint.

"Where you trying to get, mister?" asked Saleem politely.

The man eyed us, grinning. Anyone who saw him would have taken his expression as sympathetic, filled with warmth and humanity. But I knew the dark desires that hid behind it.

"I'm looking for the Hoogoord Apartments, but these buildings all look the same." He began rubbing his upper thigh. And then I saw it: he had a huge boner, though he was totally casual about it, like it was built into his bike clothes and he always pedaled around the city that way. We had to get out of there. We had to get out of there *right away*! I poked Saleem again, harder. Pretty soon the guy would recognize me, and then he'd grab for me or . . .

"Hoogoord?" asked Saleem.

The man nodded patiently, and his grin broadened as my friend spoke.

"It's in the Bullewijk," said Saleem.

"Is that far from here?" the man asked sweetly, but I could tell he was faking, just waiting for the right moment to pounce. His hand slid to the inside of his leg, as if he wanted to call our attention to his wiener.

But Saleem was oblivious. "Not so far, not with a bike like that."

I shoved him so hard he almost fell down.

"What's your problem?" he demanded. "Why are you pushing me?"

I fought to keep my voice from trembling. "We have to go," I said, loudly and clearly. "Your uncle . . . he's waiting for us."

The man looked right at me now, and it was as if an icy hand crept under my shirt and slid up my back.

"Metin, would you let me tell the man how to get to Hoogoord, please?" said Saleem, his voice overly articulate, as if to prove he wasn't just some street rat. "My uncle can wait an extra minute."

I pulled him close, put my mouth to his ear, and whispered, "He's the guy I told you about, from the elevator!"

"Are you sure?"

I nodded, and said through clenched teeth, "Look at his shorts, dammit!"

And Saleem's gaze finally dropped to the guy's woody, still big as ever, probably stimulated by our innocence. Saleem's breath quickened. "Shit," he muttered, "we gotta get out of here."

"I'll go first," I whispered. "You follow me."

The man looked like he was about to dismount from his bike. "Something wrong, boys?"

"No," I said flatly. "We have to go."

"Yeah, we have to go," repeated Saleem, his voice shaking. "And you"—for a second I worried my friend was about to panic—"you want to go that way." He pointed back in the direction from which we'd come.

"That way?" the man asked.

I was sick with tension.

"Yeah, yeah," Saleem stammered. He leaned into me and whispered, "Should we run?"

"Wait," I said, though I didn't know what we were waiting for. Maybe I didn't want to throw the situation off balance. Maybe I was afraid the guy would lunge for us if we freaked out. "Just take it slow," I said, barely audibly, and started off for Saleem's building. "Come on," I said, loudly now, "your uncle's waiting for us."

Saleem eyed the man nervously. "Sorry, mister, we gotta go." But he stayed where he was, as if he needed the man's permission to give up his role of helpful guide to the Bijlmer.

"Hey, fellas, what's your problem?" The man suddenly grinned again. "You never seen a cock before?" He picked it up with his free hand, like he wanted to show us it was in good working order. "It's a penis. Your daddy's got one just like it. There's nothing wrong with a penis, is there?"

Saleem took off, running like I'd never seen him run before. I set off after him, yet I could barely keep up.

"Hey, wait!" the man called after us. "You're not upset, are you?" Next thing I knew, he was biking alongside me, totally relaxed, like he was cheering on a marathoner. "Boys, why are you running away?"

"Leave us alone!" Saleem shouted. "Leave us alone, you pervert!"

"What did I do wrong?" the man said. "I was just asking for directions."

I sprinted as fast as I could go, but he stayed right beside me on his bike. "Hey, you look familiar, kid." He stared at me intently. "Didn't we share a pleasant moment in the elevator?" I tried to go faster. "Yeah, you're the kid from the elevator!" His breathing suddenly grew heavier. "And now you're running away." He raised a hand. "Come on, kid, can't we just talk for a minute? I've got a Nintendo at home with like a hundred games."

I rocketed after Saleem, caught up to him, and passed him. I ran like a horde of hungry, hungry hippos were at my heels. I ran for my life. After maybe ten seconds, never slackening my pace, I risked a glance behind me, just at the moment the man gave up the chase. He braked to a stop and set off in the opposite direction, as if he'd decided at last to follow Saleem's instructions.

I stopped running and bent over, gasping, my hands on my knees.

"What are you stopping for?" Saleem demanded.

"Gone . . . he's gone."

We walked on quickly, hearts pounding, looking back every couple of steps.

"We have to call the cops," I said.

"First let's tell my uncle," said Saleem decisively.

Soon we arrived at Saleem's building.

"I'll call up and ask him to meet us when we get off the elevator."

I wasn't used to Saleem taking the lead—I was always the one who made the decisions in our friendship—but the role suited him surprisingly well. Saleem thumbed the intercom button longer than usual, then shouted that Uncle Imran should wait for us upstairs at the elevator door.

As we stepped into the car, I worried that the man might rush in behind us and pick up where he'd left off.

"Were you afraid?" asked Saleem, as the elevator finally jerked upward.

"No," I lied.

The car came to a stop, and the door was ripped open. A giant with his head shaved bald stared in at us.

"Uncle Imran," Saleem cried, "I am *so* happy to see you!"

His bulk filled the entire doorway, and his broad shoulders and huge forearms were those of a man who had been blessed with extraordinary strength. If I hadn't known he was Saleem's uncle, I would have shrunk back against the elevator wall.

"What has happened, Saleem?" His voice was youthful and soft, in contrast with his intimidating appearance. "Did someone hit you?"

"No, not that."

"Then what?"

"There was a man . . . he showed us . . ."

"Showed you what? Just *say* it, Saleem!"

"He showed us his thing."

"His thing?"

Saleem nodded.

"What else did he do?"

"He . . ." Saleem fell silent for a moment, and I wondered if I should take over the telling of the tale. Maybe Saleem didn't dare bring up this sort of thing in front of his uncle. "He was touching it. And when we ran away, he followed us."

"Where? Where is the bastard now?" There was rage in

Imran's voice. Rage and a determination to take revenge.

"He rode off on his bike."

"Where to?"

"Toward Hoogoord," said Saleem. "He was lost."

The elevator car shuddered when Imran stepped inside. "We'll find him."

Imran must have been at least six foot three, and with his apelike hands he looked like a laborer who spent his working hours hauling blocks of granite. Saleem had told me he worked in a garage. He played cricket like every Pakistani man, but he also boxed, and he was a star in both sports. One day he'd knocked out his sparring partner even though the other man was wearing a helmet. Since then, no one would spar with him anymore.

"Take me to the place where you last saw him," he said. "I'll teach him a lesson."

Saleem looked at me gleefully, but for some reason I felt uncomfortable. What would happen to the man if Imran found him? He wouldn't just politely ask the guy to give up his dubious hobby. No, he'd probably feed him a knuckle sandwich.

"Which way?" asked Imran when we got out of the elevator. Saleem led the way, walking quickly. We passed a group of black boys who stared at us in awe. "What you looking at?" snarled Imran, and they immediately turned away.

We approached the path where Saleem and I had sprinted at least three hundred yards. "He followed us on his bike all this way," said Saleem.

Imran laid a hand on my friend's shoulder. "Listen, you point him out to me the second you see him. Don't be afraid, he can't hurt you now."

But strangely enough, I wasn't worried about the man on the bicycle anymore. I was worried about Imran, about what he would do to the man. I summoned all my courage and asked, "Uh, what are you going to do when you find him?"

Imran snorted. "Like I said, teach him a lesson."

The way he pronounced the word *lesson*, his dark eyes flashing with determination, I knew it had to mean something painful, something accompanied by screams and desperate pleas. I flashed back to the gangster movies I'd seen, where things never ended well for people who were *taught a lesson*.

"But," I said hesitantly, "shouldn't we just call the cops?"

"The cops?" Imran guffawed. "No, we definitely should *not* call the cops."

Encouraged by his laughter, I dared to ask: "Why not?"

He shook his head and spoke to Saleem in Urdu. From his tone, I gathered that his words meant something along the lines of: *What are you doing mixed up with a sissy like this?*

Imran gave me a penetrating look. "Listen, boy, the police don't do anything but write reports. That's all they're good for." He tugged at his beard as if he wasn't completely satisfied with his explanation. "In Pakistan, the cops would beat the shit out of a bastard like this guy. Then he'd never do such a thing again." He pounded his palm with his massive fist to emphasize the thoroughness of the Pakistani police. "But the Dutch cops will sit the guy down, give him a cup of coffee and a slice of cake, and talk the situation over with him, ask him why he did it, explain the rules, tell him little boys are fragile creatures, that sort of bullshit. And then the dirty pervert gives them an understanding nod, and they offer him a ride home. But I'm telling you: you don't solve a sickness like this with polite conversation." He snorted, probably with revulsion and not just because he had something stuck between his throat and his nose. "If I've learned anything these last years in Holland, it's that you don't trust family matters to the cops. Let them write their traffic tickets and sit behind their desks scratching their fat asses until it's time to clock out for the day."

"Uncle Imran," Saleem said suddenly, "the same man frightened Metin in the elevator."

"The same man? In your building? The goddamn shitbag!"

"He asked Metin if he'd ever seen a grown-up's penis," said Saleem, suddenly without shame. "And then he showed it to him."

"The bastard!" snarled Imran. "And next time it'll be *you* in the elevator with him, or your little brother." A new sort of rage welled up in him. "Fucking hell, man! This is too much, this bloody pedophile has gone too far!"

As we walked on, Imran appeared more determined than ever. He was terrifying me.

After a while, Saleem said, "Here! This is where he talked to us."

Imran examined the place as if there might still be traces of the man to be found. He scouted the area like a detective investigating a case. Then he crouched down and pulled a loose brick from the pavement. "Let's go on," he said, the brick clutched in his hand.

Two hundred yards farther, I almost choked with shock. The man we were looking for was sitting on a bench on a jetty overgrown with weeds, gazing out at the canal. His racing bike was leaning against the bench. I couldn't believe my eyes. What was he still doing here? Why wasn't he long gone? Why would he take such a risk?

One leg crossed casually over the other, he sipped from a clear plastic bottle. And as he sat there drinking peacefully, looking out at the water, apparently enjoying the afternoon sun, for a moment I couldn't imagine there was anything really evil lurking within him. He was probably nothing more than an ordinary pencil pusher.

Saleem was a few yards out in front, and he hadn't noticed the man through the high weeds. And though Imran was looking around alertly, he hadn't yet seen him either.

What should I do? What else *could* I do but announce that I had spotted the guy we were searching for? Imran would make sure he never bothered us again. There'd be no reason for us to be afraid in our own neighborhood anymore. But what exactly would he *do* to the man? He'd said he would teach him a lesson, but did that mean just put the fear of God in him, or would he go further and work the guy over with his fists, like the Pakistani cops he had praised?

I hesitated and glanced at Imran, at the brick in his hand and the muscled arms that stretched the fabric of his tight black polo shirt. He walked clumsily for a boxer. He stomped his feet and looked more like a wrestler about to go on the attack.

What should I do? Saleem and his uncle had already gone past him. The man unfolded a paper sack and took out a piece of bread. He broke off a bit and tossed it into the canal. As the bread hit the water, a raft of ducks surrounded it with a great flapping of wings, but just before they got to it, a covert of greedy coots chased them off, their eyes red, their beaks sharp. The man was clearly enjoying the show, since he went on tossing bits of bread into the canal. Soon, a colony of seagulls joined the battle. The squawking and splashing got louder, swelled to a cacophony of sound. Saleem turned around to look, and his eyes slowly widened.

"That's him!" he shouted. "Uncle Imran, there he is!"

Not asking if he was sure, Imran stepped from the pavement onto the strip of grass that bordered the canal. He marched heavily toward the jetty, began to run, like a warrior who's suddenly recognized his enemy in the distance. He must have stepped on a pool of bird shit, because his legs flew out from under him and he lost his grip on his brick, which arced into the weeds. Imran's huge body landed with such a loud thud that it attracted the attention of not only the man but also the coots and ducks and gulls. He hauled himself upright, roaring with anger. He brushed off his jeans, now spotted with greenish-brown stains, and, cursing, wiped the bird shit from his hands onto his pants. And then he set off again at top speed, aiming for the bicyclist. Like a gladiator confidently entering the arena for his final battle, he leaped onto the jetty, which creaked and wobbled beneath his weight, and flung himself at the man, who by now, shocked by Imran's approach, had gotten to his feet and instinctively raised his hands.

Imran quickly grabbed the man by the front of his shirt and yanked him close. No one who might have witnessed such a scene would have expected the giant bald man to speak before punching his insignificant opponent's lights out, yet that's exactly what he did. Imran gestured wildly toward the two of us and demanded, "Why were you bothering these boys?" The question didn't match his wrathful appearance. It was as if the gladiator had stopped himself at the last moment to make sure the figure who'd appeared out of the dust clouds of the Colosseum was in fact another gladiator and not some innocent deliveryman who'd accidentally stepped through an open doorway into the arena.

"Who, me?" the man mumbled.

"My nephew says you've been waving your dick in his and his friend's faces."

The man stared at us, astonished. "What? No! I—I only asked them for directions."

Imran pulled him closer, and the man's heels left the ground. He dangled on his tiptoes, like a doll. "Are you sure?" It wasn't a question. It was a warning that threatened impending disaster, as if that hadn't already been announced.

"I was lost! I swear, I was lost, I only asked the boys for help!"

Imran shook him violently. "Don't lie to me, you bastard!"

"Let me go," the man whined. "You're hurting me. Let me go, I didn't do anything!"

"You showed two little boys your fucking cock!" barked Imran. "And then you followed them, you pervert."

The man tried to worm out of Imran's grip, swatting ineffectually at the hand that held him tight. When that had no effect, he jerked away, screeching. His fluorescent bike shirt tore, and he fell backward, leaving Imran holding nothing but a scrap of fabric, glaring at it in confusion like he was doing an impression of King Kong. The man scrabbled away, trying to escape.

"You're not going anywhere," growled Imran. "I'm not finished with you." He crouched down and grabbed the ripped shirt, but the man kept crab-walking backward, and the shirt tore off completely, leaving him naked from the waist up, flopping around on the jetty like a fish out of water, about to be gutted and fileted. Imran took hold of his wrist and hauled him to his feet as if he was weightless. The man struggled to get loose, pulling and hitting the hand that held him captive.

"Stop it!" Imran ordered, and he hit the man on the ear. "Stay still!"

But the man failed to obey, went on shrieking that Imran had to let him go.

Imran dealt a second blow to the bicyclist's mouth with the back of his hand. The man cowered in Imran's grip, his hands clapped over his lips, and then he seemed to go insane. He unleashed a fearsome cry, then sank his teeth into the hand that still held him and shook his head wildly, like a hungry caiman ripping the flesh of its prey in the brown waters of the Amazon.

It was weird to hear our mighty protector yelling like a wounded beast. His voice tormented, he snarled, "You'll pay for that!" He balled his right hand into a fist and smashed it into the man's left eye. There was the sound of bone cracking, and a hellish scream.

"My eye!" the man wailed. "My eye!"

At that moment, I felt an intense sense of pity for the man. I turned to Saleem, filled with concern, but he was hopping up and down, swinging his arms like a charged-up Roman citizen who'd spent the whole week looking forward to this battle and was now enjoying it to the max.

The man staggered, and only remained on his feet because Imran was holding him up. Suddenly Imran noticed that his hand was bleeding. He stared at it, unbelieving, his massive chest heaving. Then he returned his disgusted attention to the bicyclist and spat, "If you gave me AIDS, you fuck, I'll kill you!"

Imran swiveled his torso and hip and let loose another right-handed wallop. This one caught the man full in the nose, and there came again the crunch of bone. The man sank to his knees.

We had to do something before Imran really *did* kill him. We had to stop the slaughter. I yelled at Saleem, but he didn't react, just stood there transfixed by his uncle's merciless attack. Maybe he was reminded of the many times we'd watched our hero, the Ultimate Warrior, on the mat. But this was no theatrical wrestling match: a human being was actually being torn apart, and all we could do was watch.

As Imran kicked the man in the ribs, I grabbed Saleem's arm. "We have to stop him! He's gonna kill the guy!"

Only then did Saleem face me, the color drained from his face. "Yeah," he muttered, "but . . . what can we do?"

"Pull him off," I said. I dragged Saleem onto the jetty. As we came up behind Imran, he kicked the guy again, then a third time. It sounded like all the air was leaking out of the man. I shoved Saleem forward and said, "Do something!" But he just stood there, watching his uncle go to town. So I pushed him aside and approached Imran myself.

"Stop," I shouted, "you're killing him!" But Imran seemed not to hear me.

And right then I heard a shout from the apartment building on the far side of the canal.

"Hey, stop it!" a voice called. "Leave the man be!"

That gave me the encouragement I needed. "Please," I said, "stop, before you kill him. Have mercy!"

Imran whirled around, his expression furious, and when his eyes met first mine and then Saleem's, it was as if the gladiator's mask slipped from his face and he morphed back into a concerned uncle. Imran was still holding the bicyclist by a limp wrist. He glanced down at his victim one last time, then let him go. The man collapsed onto the jetty. His thin body convulsed.

Imran took a step toward us. "I'm sorry," he said softly, "I—I lost control." He looked at his bloody hand and wiped it on his shirt. "He shouldn't have bitten me. I was only going to rough him up a little."

The man dragged himself to a sitting position, looked around in a daze, and dropped his head to his knees. He sat there defeated, folded almost in half to protect his battered rib cage from further damage, his spine so slender it seemed it might snap in two at any moment. Again I felt pity wash over me.

Imran fetched his water bottle from the bench and held it out to him. "Drink."

Without looking up, the man took the bottle. As he drank, blood dripped from his nose down his chin and onto his naked chest. I figured his nose must be broken. As if he'd only now noticed it, he waved at a fanny pack lying on the bench. I picked it up, unzipped it, and found a ring of keys, three foil-wrapped rubbers, lip balm, and a pack of tissues.

Groaning, the man got to his feet. He seemed only barely conscious, with nothing left to lose. One eye was puffed shut, his nose was unnaturally bent and continued to bleed. Not saying a word, he held out his hand to me, palm up. I hardly dared to look at him, but as I gave him the pack of tissues, I couldn't avoid the sight of his chest all covered with blood. With a trembling hand, he pulled a tissue from the pack and pressed it to his nose. The white paper immediately reddened.

"You'll never see me again," he said. He dropped the bloody tissue to the jetty. "As far as I'm concerned, this never happened."

Imran nodded. "None of it happened."

The man picked up his water bottle, staggered to the bench for his fanny pack, and strapped it to his waist with some difficulty. Then, breathing heavily, he righted his bicycle and pushed it through the weeds to the path. Moaning, holding onto the handlebars with one hand, pressing the other to his ribs, he pulled himself onto his saddle.

Without looking back, he pedaled away.

# LUCKY SEVENS

BY THEO CAPEL

*De Jordaan*

The A4 was crowded, as usual. Felix had been stuck behind a brand-new Seat Ateca for some time. He could almost see the guy in front of him frowning in his rearview mirror at Felix's old Cordoba. It was time for a new car. There was enough money to buy one in the inside pocket of his uniform jacket. The problem was, it wasn't *his* money.

When he hit the ring road, the traffic got worse. Up ahead, somebody slammed on his brakes, and Felix barely managed to avoid rear-ending him.

*Eyes on the road*, he told himself.

Imagine getting into an accident with all that cash on him. Some of his brothers in blue would surely suspect him of being crooked. He wouldn't even be given the chance to explain himself. He shook off the thought and proceeded carefully to the exit for the S105—he still insisted on thinking of it by its traditional name, the Jan van Galenstraat—which would take him to his home in the Jordaan. The bureaucrats didn't care that the Jordaan was the best-known part of the city. They felt it was good enough to put a simple *Downtown* on the exit signs.

It had been an unusual day for Felix. He was on his way back from South Holland, where he'd attended the funeral of a fellow Amsterdam police officer. Every cop there had been in uniform, including detectives like Felix. Dark-blue jacket, peaked cap. That had caused an uncomfortable moment, later in the day. Coincidentally, he'd also had an appointment in The Hague, at the headquarters of the agency that ran the national lottery. Tickets were cheap, and if you were lucky, instant happiness. Felix wasn't a gambler himself, but today he'd walked in the door with a scratcher that had revealed a fifty-thousand-euro prize beneath its layer of foil. He'd bought it at the corner cigar store, along with two packs of filtered cigarettes and a magazine. Felix didn't smoke, and it wasn't a magazine he liked to read. The winning ticket wasn't his either, and that's why he'd collected the money in cash.

They'd been upset at the sight of his uniform. They were expecting a Mr. Felix de Grave, and what they got was a cop. He'd cleared up the confusion, but there'd been another misunderstanding when he left. The woman who showed him out was surprised by his pale purple car. She'd anticipated a police cruiser, not this sad old jalopy. She'd just been telling him that lots of winners bragged the first thing they were going to buy was a new vehicle, but most of them wound up sticking their winnings in the bank. She seemed to think that banking the fifty thousand euros would, in Felix's case, be a mistake. She didn't say it in so many words, but he could read it in her expression when she got a look at his car.

They'd already thought it was odd that he'd wanted the money in cash. The unspoken suspicion was that he didn't want his wife to know about his win. Felix wasn't married, but the money was indeed intended for a woman. The winning ticket belonged to his neighbor, which was really nobody's business. It was Felix and the neighbor's little secret.

Many of the streets in the Jordaan—Carnation, Laurel,

Rose—are named after flowers. Misnamed, really, because the neighborhood was originally a wasteland, with long, narrow alleys and canals that dead-ended where the world-famous seventeenth-century Canal Ring begins. Nowadays, you need to be well-off to live in the shadow of the Western Church's bell tower, since the realtors do their best to make it seem as if the Jordaan is a part of the Canal Ring.

If Felix leaned out his living room window, he'd be looking right at the church's Westertoren, which for the older Jordaaners would be good reason to burst out in song. Ever since the neighborhood began to attract a demographic that was still disparagingly referred to as yuppies, the tower had been considered an annoyance, thanks to the fact that, every fifteen minutes, day and night, its carillon played a little tune. For the tourists, the tower was a beacon, guiding them to the Anne Frank House, which stood just around the corner from the church, on the Prinsengracht. Every day they lined up, waiting their turn to go inside, the line usually stretching along the canal to the tower. Felix's across-the-street neighbor, who was generally to be found hanging out the front window of her apartment, observing the passing scene below, never ceased to be surprised by the enormous interest in the Frank family's WWII hideout.

"There's nothing to *see* in there," she told anyone who would listen. "I should charge admission to come look at *my* house. I'd be rich!" She loved daydreaming of wealth, and the fact that Anne Frank had come to a tragic end—which gave the Frank House a dramatic attraction hers couldn't hope to compete with—didn't seem to interest her.

As he turned into his street, Felix wondered if he ought to honk his horn to notify his neighbor of his arrival. Probably not necessary, he decided. She peered out her window the whole damn day, so she'd be sure to see him. Especially today, since she knew where he had gone.

Except, to his surprise, she wasn't at her usual post. When he pulled up to his garage door and, just to be sure, looked up, he saw that her window was closed. The garage door, on the other hand, stood wide open.

Felix lived on the second floor of a building whose ground level had originally served as a sort of workshop for a company that manufactured lampshades. The company's name still appeared on the gable in white script letters. At the time he moved in, the garage was being used to house a street organ belonging to the previous tenant, an old friend of Felix's grandmother. When he left for a nursing home, Felix finagled permission to move into his apartment. Not long after that, the street organ disappeared, and he was permitted—for an extra monthly fee—to take over the ground floor. These days, a storage area like that was worth its weight in gold. Hardly a week went by that he wasn't asked to sublet part of the space. His upstairs neighbor had long been permitted to stash his bicycle there and Felix had graciously agreed to continue that arrangement, and he had more recently succumbed to a plea from a couple who lived across the street and pedaled their kids to school and other activities on a traditional Dutch cargo bike, which had to have *someplace* to sit when it wasn't doing taxi duty. In point of fact, he had succumbed to the wife after first refusing an identical request from the husband. Felix thought the husband, who claimed to be some kind of financial consultant, was a bit of a bullshitter, and—as a cop—he didn't care for bullshit.

With a little maneuvering, it was possible to squeeze both his Cordoba and the cargo bike into the space. The upstairs neighbor complained that this made it practically impossible for him to get his bicycle in and out, but he was one of those Amsterdammers who have raised complaining practically to an art form.

Felix saw that the woman from across the street was standing beside her cargo bike, her back to him, and he got out of his car to see if she needed help.

"You just getting back or heading out, Iris?" he asked.

His voice startled her, and she whirled to face him. "Felix! Have you heard the news?"

"Are congratulations in order?"

He knew she was being considered for a promotion to a senior position at the bank where she worked, but various factors were delaying a final decision. Maybe she'd finally gotten the approval she was hoping for.

But he let go of that idea when he saw the expression on her face.

"You *haven't* heard," she said, and began to cry.

"Hey, what's wrong?"

She was still wearing her work clothes, and she wiped away tears with the sleeve of her gray pin-striped suit. What could have happened? One of the kids fell down the stairs? Her husband got caught messing around with one of her girlfriends?

"Fetty's dead."

"Dead?" He felt a shock ripple through his body, and for a moment he found that he couldn't breathe. Fetty couldn't possibly be dead. He had a thick wad of cash for her inside his jacket pocket.

His hand went to his chest, and he felt the bulge of the money. Was it possible for a pile of bills to have stabbed him? The pain slowly ebbed.

"What are you saying? Fetty's *dead?*"

"It's so awful!"

She had no idea how awful it was. The lottery money belonged to Fetty, the neighbor he'd expected to see leaning out her window. It was no wonder she was called Fetty. She was shapeless and fat from head to toe, and she could barely make it down the stairs to the street. Felix was one of the neighbors who ran regular errands for her. Aunt Corrie, who lived right next door, helped with the everyday chores, and Felix took care of Fetty's weekly luxuries. Every Saturday, he stopped at the cigar store to buy her two packs of Stuyvesants. Filtered, she always reminded him, as if she was afraid the company might have suddenly started manufacturing *unfiltered* Stuyvesants. So, two packs of smokes, with filters, a copy of the weekly magazine *My Secret*, and two scratchers. The lottery tickets always had to be Lucky Sevens, because—according to her—that was her lucky game.

Her invariable habit was to open one of the packs of cigarettes in his presence and offer him the first Stuyvesant, which he always politely refused, at which point she lit it and smoked it herself, taking shallow puffs that she immediately exhaled. One of his aunts had smoked exactly the same way.

The next part of their Saturday-afternoon ritual was her asking him for a coin, which she would use to eagerly attack her scratchers. Meanwhile, Felix would page listlessly through the new issue of the magazine, which seemed more often than not to be filled with stories of pregnant women who weren't sure if the baby was their husband's or the neighbor's and other nonsense that would, in his opinion, have been better *kept* secret.

Their routine usually ended with Fetty's disappointed cry: "No luck!" This time, though, their visit had unfolded differently.

Felix thought at first that she'd had a heart attack. But

her explosive reaction turned out to be pure excitement, not a medical emergency.

"Felix, look! Two fifty-thousands! My God, all those zeroes! And look, the last number ends with zeroes too. It can't be another fifty thousand, can it? I can't look. You finish it for me."

He had scratched away the last bit of foil, and the two of them sat there and stared at the winning ticket looking back up at them from the table. The winning ticket Felix had taken to The Hague and cashed in for his housebound neighbor.

"It's a winner! A winner!" Fetty had screamed, and she'd grabbed Felix by the arms, hauled him up from his chair, and danced around him like a schoolgirl. "We won! We won!"

Later, he'd run into Aunt Corrie on the street. "You two were certainly kicking up a rumpus," she'd said. "I was afraid the glasses in my kitchen cabinets would get smashed. Did she have a little too much to drink, Felix?"

"Now, Corrie, the woman's entitled to a little fun once in a while," he'd said. And that was where he'd left it. He wasn't going to tell the neighborhood Fetty'd won fifty thousand euros.

"Vladimir's still at the police station. I thought you were him a minute ago. Why are you wearing your uniform? He called me and told me he had to go with the detectives, so I should pick Max up from his piano lesson. I wasn't expecting to go out again, I didn't even have time to change. I just put on some sneakers, and here I am. I must look ridiculous."

Felix had noticed the bright red sneakers. They were indeed a sight, but he was more interested in her husband.

"You're telling me Fetty didn't just die on her own? And Vladimir had something to do with it?"

"No, of course not. He just found her. And then the police

came." She hesitated. "Is it true Fetty came into a lot of money? Vladimir said he heard she won the lottery."

Felix had worried Fetty wouldn't be able to keep her good fortune to herself. "Was Fetty killed?" he asked. "Is that why the detectives were here?"

Iris began to cry. "I don't know," she said. "Aunt Corrie told Vladimir she thought Fetty was *in clover.* I'm not sure what that means—I still don't understand a lot of your Amsterdam slang. I just want to know when Vladimir's coming home. He called me at work, I was in the middle of a meeting. He said there was a funny little car outside the building, a handicapped car. What are those things called?"

"You mean a Canta?"

"That's it. He thinks we ought to buy one, because you can park on the sidewalk, then we wouldn't need to bother you with the cargo bike. What am I supposed to say to that? Anyway, I was in a meeting, I couldn't really talk. And then he called back and said he had to go with the policemen because they found Fetty dead."

"They?"

"Him, I mean. But I don't know for sure. All I know is Max is waiting. I have to call his piano teacher. But first I want to hear Vladimir's voice." She looked straight at him, wiping tears from her eyes with her sleeve. "Felix, can you call the station for me? You're a cop. Maybe they'll tell you something."

"You already tried? Did you call Vladimir's cell?"

"Yes, but he didn't pick up. And the woman at the station wouldn't tell me anything. She said they don't give information over the phone."

"You go fetch your son," Felix told her. "I'll see what I can do."

\* \* \*

"I still dream about him," Fetty had said when she was finished dancing and dropped, breathless, back into her chair.

She was so excited she tried to light the filtered end of a Stuyvesant, but Felix stopped her just in time. He wasn't sure who she was talking about.

"He's in trouble, and I can't help him. Can you believe it, Felix, sometimes I wake up sobbing? But now I really *can* help him." She fell silent, gazing straight ahead, beginning to sniffle. "If I only knew where he was," she said. She grabbed Felix's arm. "You're a detective. You know how to find a missing person. And I have money now. You can help me. You can find my little boy for me. You'll do it, won't you?" She'd let go of his arm and picked up the ticket, stroking it like a pet.

He sat there and listened to the story. Long ago, Fetty had been a live-in maid for a doctor and his family, and one of the doctor's sons had gotten her pregnant, then denied ever having touched her. The family was Roman Catholic, and the boy's father had refused to help her. It was too late to end the pregnancy, and she didn't know where to turn. The father's patient list included a home for unwed mothers, run by nuns, and he made arrangements for them to take her in, which at least was *something*.

"And that's where you gave birth?"

Yes, but she couldn't remember a thing about it. According to Fetty, they had sedated her. It was better that she never even see the child, they told her. She had to sign a paper giving up custody. God had arranged for the baby to be taken in by a good family, they said. That would erase the shame the devil had caused by putting the child inside her in the first place.

"I woke up, and they acted like nothing had happened. I

lay there weeping for days. They were witches, Felix, but there was one nun who took pity on me. She told me she had prayed for God to look after my son."

He understood that the events she was recounting had taken place forty years in the past.

"You can give *him* the money, Felix. And keep some for yourself, for your trouble. I trust you. You're the only one I can ask for help. People tell you things. You're a policeman."

She was being overly optimistic. In fact, most people had a tendency to say nothing when a cop showed up at their door.

"Here," she'd said, "you take the ticket. You know what to do. I'm counting on you. Help me find my little boy."

Felix swung his garage door shut and looked across the street. There was nothing left to be seen of the day's drama. The ruffled sheets still hung in Fetty's front window. Not long ago, someone farther up the street had passed on. Everyone knew about it, because the curtains had been taken down and white sheets hung in the windows. Many of the longtime residents said the Jordaan wasn't the Jordaan they remembered anymore, but the old customs linger.

The Westertoren's bells began to ring. It was the day of the weekly concert, Felix realized. Life went on. The carillonneur was known to be a Beatles fan. The bells played John Lennon's "Imagine." Yes, indeed, imagine . . .

Only then did he notice that someone in the house next door to Fetty's was waving at him. Aunt Corrie, naturally. She saw him notice her and opened her window.

"Felix," she called, "I'm coming down!"

Fetty had been fat and shapeless, where Aunt Corrie was fat but big-boned with more hair, which she dyed blond and wore piled atop her head. An Amsterdammer, Felix knew intuitively which women to call *Auntie* and which were *Ma'am*. Explaining the difference to an outsider would be a mission impossible.

Aunt Corrie's eyes were puffy from crying. "Oh, Felix, I can't believe it, gone just like that. And then the police at my door and that young man from up the street—what was he doing there? You must know all about it, don't you?"

He could tell she was angry at herself for not immediately rushing next door to gawk. She'd been in her bedroom vacuuming and had heard screams, but she'd thought they were coming from the television, which was tuned to one of those shows where a host brings on people who are embroiled in some kind of family feud and knows exactly how to stoke the fire. By the time she returned to her living room, another program had begun and the racket had stopped. She'd looked out her window and seen Iris's husband go in Fetty's door. And then, later, a police car had pulled up outside.

"Well, that's when I knew there was something wrong. But who could have guessed what it was? That poor woman. She'd finally hit the lottery, she told me so herself. You don't think that had anything to do with it, do you, Felix? I hope not. She sent me out to buy a ridiculously expensive bottle of liquor for her. Usually, she only drank lemon gin. But she'd written the name of it on a piece of paper for me, otherwise I never would have remembered. A bottle of Highland Park whiskey, she wanted. You don't buy something that pricey if you haven't had a real windfall."

She pronounced the name of the whiskey *Higg-land*, but he understood what she meant. It was his favorite brand. Fetty had asked him what she could give him as a thank you.

Aunt Corrie was not impressed with Iris's husband. Neither

was Felix. He'd always had the idea that Iris was the bread-winner in that family, and no idea whether or not the husband worked at all. He was certainly a world-class gabber. He'd told Felix once that he was named after a famous writer, and the implication was that he too was destined for great things.

"Vladimir," he'd said, "after Vladimir Nabokov. Maybe you heard of *Lolita*? He wrote that. My father was a big fan of him."

Felix had stood there and listened, though he had no idea why the man was telling him the story. It was not a good idea to arouse the suspicions of a detective. So Felix had done some sleuthing and discovered that the man's middle name was Ily-ich, which suggested that he had in fact been named after Lenin, not Nabokov. Of course, that didn't mean he would harm a hair on his neighbor's head. But Felix knew anything the man said had to be taken with a grain of salt.

"Iris is worried about her husband," he explained. "He called her and said there was a Canta parked on the sidewalk."

"A red one?" asked Aunt Corrie. "That must have been her brother Koos. He's got a bad leg, so they let him drive one of those little things. But I thought they weren't speaking, I haven't seen him around in forever. Was he here?"

Felix didn't know. Fetty had been a good woman, accord-ing to Aunt Corrie. But her brother was a scoundrel, only showed up when he needed money. Money for booze.

"Was he here today?" Corrie asked again.

Felix said the only thing he knew was that a handicapped car had been spotted in front of the house.

"I'm surprised he hasn't sold that little car for booze by now. It must have been Koos. Funny I didn't see him."

He'd stashed the lottery money in his gun safe and hung his

uniform in the closet. Back in civilian clothes, he was on his way with his colleague Dirk Blokdijk to the farthest corner of the Jordaan, just past the Palmgracht. Given that *gracht* is Dutch for *canal*, you would expect the Palmgracht to be a waterway, but the original canal had long since been filled in, and all that was left of it was the name.

"You went to the funeral?" said Dirk, a sturdy detective who preferred dogs to people. "And then came home to a dead neighbor? Some job we got, right? But whatever, we just keep on keepin' on. So where's this Koos Jollema you want to talk to?" He leaned out the Cordoba's passenger window and yelled, "Come out, come out, wherever you are!" Then he turned back to Felix. "Just Koos, huh, no middle name? His baby sister had one: Fetty Sjoukje Jollema."

Felix had always assumed that *Fetty* was a nickname. Amsterdammers loved nicknames, and one look at Fetty told you exactly where hers had come from. In fact, he'd always thought she was called *Fatty*, just spoken with an Amsterdam accent.

"An original Frisian name, Felix, a name to be proud of."

It sounded like Dirk might himself have Frisian blood in him.

"Supposedly died of a heart attack."

Which might well have been the end of the story, except the case had turned out to be not quite that simple. The coroner found bruises on her throat, and her apartment had been ransacked.

"And we caught a guy goin' through the place."

The guy was Vladimir. The officers who'd responded to the call had found him in the living room. Fetty lay stretched out on the carpet, and Vladimir was digging around in an open drawer.

"He handed us this bullshit story that some other guy had threatened him with a bottle right outside the dead lady's door, then took off in a handicapped car. He'd been walkin' past the house when he heard a scream, which is why he went up, to make sure the neighbor lady was okay. So what were we supposed to make of that, Felix? We stuck him in a holding cell so he could think over his story. Anyway, we were too busy with other cases to deal with him, if I can call *this* a case."

"His wife says he wanted to ask the man about his Canta. She's worried about him."

"I was locked up in a cell, my wife would worry too."

"You could have let him call home and tell her what was going on."

"Come on, Felix. We're cops, not the Salvation Army." Dirk gave him a sidelong glance. "You knew Fetty. She have anything worth stealin' tucked away in her drawers?"

How was Felix supposed to answer that question? Instead, he avoided it. "Let's see what the brother has to say for himself. What was he doing there? He hadn't been to see her in years."

"What I hear, he's not the kind of guy you invite over for tea. He's done time, Felix, two years for aggravated assault—way back when, but still. Not to mention several arrests for public drunkenness."

Koos Jollema lived at the end of the Lijnbaansgracht, the slender canal that formed the western border of the Jordaan. The city wall had once stretched along the far side of the canal, but in later years it had been replaced by a long row of cheap rental units squashed side by side.

There were plenty of similar one-room apartments in the Jordaan too. They were claustrophobic little dumps, which was why so many of their residents spent much of their time in the neighborhood cafés. Which, according to one of his neighbors, was where they were bound to find Koos.

"One hundred percent chance he's drinking himself stupid at the Van der Kruk," she told them.

And, sure enough, they spotted a red Canta right around the corner from the Café Van der Kruk, on a side street where little had happened over the last few hundred years, other than a steady decline. The café itself was shabby enough to fit right in, nothing more than a room in which to sit and drink. In addition to the bar, there was a scattering of tables, each topped with a length of Persian carpet that wasn't antique, just old. It was quiet inside.

The bartender was a heavy man with a few remaining strands of black hair combed over the top of his head and plastered to his scalp. He knew what Felix and Dirk did for a living before they even opened their mouths.

"Koos, you got company," he called. "Cops. You been fucking the apes in the zoo again?"

Koos sat alone at a table next to a door along the back wall.

Dirk headed toward him. Felix stayed put by the front door.

"Relax," said the bartender. "That's the bathroom. No windows, no way out. And he can't run, anyway."

Fetty's brother struggled to his feet. He was a little fellow with a deeply lined face and baggy pouches beneath his eyes. He staggered out from behind the table, and they saw that he dragged his right leg when he walked. He was clearly drunk.

"She send you after me?" he growled. "Jus' 'cause I took a bottle of her whiskey? She don't have enough to bitch about without that? I should've smacked her in the mouth with it and knocked that guy's block off, the dirty yuppie." He saw Felix looking at his leg. "Yeah, why don't you take a picture? That fucking bastard knocked me from the deck down into the hold. I could've died. My knee never did heal right. And they said it was *my* fault I stuck a knife in him. And then my sister just totally wrote me off."

"We'd like to talk with you about your sister," said Felix.

They brought Koos back to his apartment, but once Dirk saw the condition of the place he insisted they go elsewhere. "This joint's a pigsty! My dog would turn up her nose. And Brother Koos stinks to high heaven. Good thing your car's already a wreck, Felix. At least it can't get any worse. Come on, let's take him someplace nice and quiet."

Felix agreed. The only thing he could see in the apartment that wasn't filthy was the opened bottle of whiskey on the table. He tried a cabinet door in the kitchen, looking for a glass, and his hand came away sticky. Koos apparently put things away without bothering to wash them.

"There's no money here, so he can't have stolen any," Dirk said. Of course, Felix already knew where Fetty's money was.

They saw Koos staring at the whiskey.

"Take it along," said Felix.

Dirk wasn't so sure. "You don't think we'll get in trouble?"

"*He's* not going to tell anyone."

It was a brief ride to the Palmgracht, with Koos in the backseat, a small glass of whiskey in his hand. Dirk sat beside him. Koos looked ready to fall asleep, but Dirk poked him in the ribs to keep him upright.

"Come on, pal. This ain't a cab here."

They listened to his story. Koos denied having killed his sister, but he showed no empathy or sorrow at her death.

"She was my sister, sure, but she was a nobody. Yeah, I grabbed her by the throat, but I didn't hurt her. She shouldn't've blown me off like she did. Wouldn't even let me have a shot of her whiskey. But *she* called *me*, you know? I mean, I don't have a phone, but she called my neighbor and had her go get me, and then she told me this big story how she'd come into a shitload of money, so now she could make it up to her bastard son. Well, fuck him, he don't need money up in heaven, they taught me that in Sunday school. Now she can spend the rest of eternity up there with him. He can show her around, he's been there long enough to know the ropes. That's what I went to her place to tell her. 'It's not true,' she whined, 'it's not true!' I was lying, I wasn't gonna get a cent of her money. What was I supposed to do, just sit there and take it?"

Dirk glanced at Felix. "You have any idea what he's talkin' about?"

"Hear him out."

Back when Fetty had given birth, Koos was a merchant marine. Had Felix and Dirk ever heard of Bandar Abbas? A port city on the Persian Gulf. Hell itself couldn't be hotter or grungier. When his ship docked there, he'd found a letter from his sister waiting with the news. It was months before he was back in Holland and got the story straight from his sister's mouth.

"No kid and no money. They just kicked her to the curb, that fucking doctor and his fucking son. Stick your dick inside some dumb little girl, blame *her* for everything, and then take away her baby."

He'd shown up at the doctor's door and convinced the man to give Fetty two thousand guilders. Then they'd be done with each other forever. The only condition was Fetty had to come collect the payment herself.

"And she wouldn't do it. Said it was blood money. I tried to talk her into it, but she flat-out refused. We could have shared it: a thousand guilders for her, a thousand for me. But forget about it. I should have choked the little cunt then."

"But you waited almost forty years to do it," said Felix.

"I always been able to look out for myself. I didn't need her."

"You got two years' room and board from us," Dirk said. "And the way I see it, pretty soon the state'll be takin' care of you again. Only I don't think you'll be sluggin' down any more expensive whiskey for a while."

Koos ignored the remark. "She won the lottery, she told me. And now she was gonna find her little boy."

"The little boy you told her was dead?"

"Like I know if he's alive or dead? But what else could have happened to him? She never heard a peep out of him, all those years. Wouldn't *you* go look up your real mother, if it was you? Wouldn't you? All she had to do was set some of the dough aside for me. But no, not her. Just show me the money, I said. Show me the ticket. It wasn't none of my business, she said. You'd think she was scared I'd steal it. And then she started screaming I should get out. She wouldn't even give me a damn drink." He looked hungrily at Dirk, who was holding the bottle, and Dirk in turn looked at Felix. Who nodded.

"Okay," said Dirk, "one more. Call it your last meal."

While Koos drank, the two detectives left him alone.

"So now what?" said Dirk, once they had parked and gotten out of the car. "We're supposed to believe the sister was still alive when he left?"

"He choked her," said Felix. "He admits it, we both heard him say so. And his sister's dead, no doubt about that. I say we arrest him on suspicion of manslaughter, book him, and charge him. The rest's up to the court. Let's go."

"What about the neighbor?"

"He'll testify he saw the brother leaving the apartment."

Dirk glanced down at the bottle he was still holding. "And the whiskey?"

"Dirk, you've been a cop longer than me. The man confessed. He won't complain we let him wet his whistle. The whiskey doesn't come into it. Hand it over."

Felix took it and poured it down the gutter, then tossed the empty bottle in a trash can, along with Dirk's glass.

"What a crying shame," said Dirk.

Felix knew it wasn't just the liquor that was worth crying over, but he kept that thought to himself.

The lottery money had been paid out in five-hundred-euro notes. They were spread out on Felix's kitchen table, a hundred of them. He gathered them together in a nice neat stack. It wasn't his money, but whose was it? Did he now have a claim on it? He sighed and put the bills back in the safe with his gun.

He could have used a shot of whiskey, but all he had in the fridge was a bottle of Coke Zero.

"Here's to you, Fetty," he said aloud, standing at his front window and raising a glass to the darkened apartment across the street. He was still thinking about the money.

He remembered a song his grandmother used to sing: *Money isn't happiness—at least it isn't yet—but the more of it you gather, well, the closer you can get . . .*

He realized that he was humming the tune. He reopened his gun safe and spread the bills out again on the table.

The television was on, and he looked up from the money to see an ad for the new Seat Ateca. Was that a sign from above?

The money's rightful owner was dead. She didn't seem to

have left a will, so her estate—such as it was—would go to her legal heirs. No way that would be the son she'd given up for adoption, even if the boy—a man now, somewhere in his forties—was still alive. And the courts would disinherit the brother who had very probably been responsible for her death. Who did that leave? There was no written record of Fetty's agreement with Felix. He had bought the lottery ticket, and he had cashed it in.

He sighed, once again piled up the fifty thousand euros, and locked them away.

"Fetty, I'm going to drink a whiskey in your memory after all," he announced, taking his jacket from the coatrack. They carried Highland Park in the café up the street. He knew that from personal experience.

Maybe he'd just leave the money where it was for a while. Sometimes problems solve themselves, if you let them sit. Of course he knew better, but for now he was in no mood to go on thinking about it.

He pulled his apartment door shut behind him and headed down the stairs. The Westertoren's carillon began to play. The bells tolled for everyone, but in Felix's mind they rang for one old woman in particular.

# THE STRANGER INSIDE ME

BY LOES DEN HOLLANDER

*Central Station*

*Monday*

Ted Bundy came again last night.

Ted always comes around midnight on Sundays, every other week for a year now. He says I'm his friend, his *best* friend. I'm proud of that. It's great to finally have a friend.

Mother says I have to take a shower. She says she can smell me, and that other people will say I stink and blame her. Mother's been nagging me more and more lately. She says I eat too many eggs. Eggs are bad for my cholesterol, according to her. The blood vessels in my brain will get all sludgy. She also wants me to go back to getting my meds by injection, because the pill I'm supposed to take every week is bad for my stomach. I don't like needles, and the pills never actually *get* to my stomach. I don't need them anyway, but try explaining that to someone who believes God knows best and medication can make the negative thoughts in your head disappear.

Mothers. There ought to be a law.

Against mothers *and* caseworkers.

I can't stand anybody who has anything to do with the psychiatric profession. They think they know everything about your mental ability, they label you without any idea who you really are, they ask questions and arrange your answers in their spreadsheets, and—presto!—they slap you with a diagnosis you carry around for the rest of your life. And of course you're stuck with *them* for the rest of your life too.

Caseworkers should all be exterminated.

My mission is scheduled for this Thursday. The woman will be wearing a short brown leather jacket, a tight black skirt, black stockings, and high-heeled black boots. She'll have long blond hair, and here's the important thing: it'll be parted in the middle. Ted really made a point about that middle parting.

The place: Amsterdam's Central Station, track 13B. The time: Thursday, between 11:30 a.m. and 2:37 p.m. Not one minute sooner, not one minute later.

Ted knows he can count on me.

The first time he came was the night before my eighteenth birthday. I woke up and saw him standing in a corner of my bedroom.

I wasn't surprised, and I was aware that I wasn't. It would have been normal if I'd screamed and run out of the room, because I can really overreact when I'm startled. Instead, though, I just lay there in my bed and folded my hands behind my head and asked him who he was.

"They call me Ted Bundy," he said.

"Is that your name?" I asked.

"I was born Theodore Robert Cowell, but it was changed to Bundy when my mother married a loser and he adopted me. You can call me Ted." There was laughter in his voice.

"What's so funny?" I wanted to know.

"Me, being here. You, letting me in." He looked at me

with an intense expression in his eyes. "Letting me *inside* you, do you understand?"

I didn't.

It got very quiet in my room, and I didn't know what he expected of me.

He came closer. "They stopped me," he said. "I want you to pick up where I left off."

At that moment, I heard Mother in the bathroom. I turned my head toward the sound. Water ran out of the tap, then stopped. The toilet flushed.

When I turned back, Ted was gone.

Anja, the psychiatric caseworker I have to see every month, always asks me if I hear voices or have visitors. She wouldn't ask that if I'd just ignored Mother always grilling me about who I talk to late at night. But I had to go and tell her someone was coming to see me, someone *she* couldn't see. She should have known that was private information, not something she was allowed to pass on to anyone else, but Mother doesn't understand things like that. It doesn't surprise me when every man she goes out with winds up dropping her. What *does* surprise me is that, with all those guys, she's only had the one child: me.

Mother lives in a world of her own.

I don't give the caseworker a hard time. I'm polite, I answer her questions, I tell her I take my penfluridol every week. It's important I stay calm when she asks me trick questions. I know for a fact she's trying to trap me.

*Tuesday*

Ted told me about track 13B months ago, and today I went to take a look at it.

Mother had a migraine this morning and stayed in bed. She can't stand the least bit of light or sound when she gets a migraine, so I shut the living room drapes, made sure the windows were latched, and disconnected the doorbell. Then I snuck out of the house.

She didn't come right out and say so, but she made it clear that the migraine was my fault. In her indirect way, she let me know that I'd disturbed her sleep by making a racket until all hours, not even quieting down when she banged her cane against the wall that separates our rooms.

See, Ted showed up again last night, which was a surprise. When I realized he was there, I tried to make a joke: "Don't you have days of the week up there in Eternity?" I asked him, but I don't think he got it. I backed away from his angry reaction and apologized profusely. He raised his voice, and that made me start screaming. When Mother wouldn't quit banging on the wall, I begged him to calm down. I lowered my voice and began asking him questions. Open-ended questions, full of empathy. That helped.

He was clearly in the mood to talk, and to brag. Full of pride, he told me that, right before his execution, he confessed to more than twenty murders, but in fact his count was much higher. He explained what it had meant to him, the kidnapping, the raping, the killing, and he especially wanted me to understand how much he missed it, and how happy he was to be able to enter into me, and we were going to be a team. An amazing team that would always be there for each other.

I was so touched.

I feel this powerful connection to Ted, because we're both children of unwed mothers and we never knew who our fathers were. That's why I don't think it's weird that he picked me to be his special friend. And that's why I'll do whatever he tells me to. I won't be surprised if he shows up every night this week, though he didn't promise that he would.

He's always welcome.

I go into the Central Station by the main entrance. The gates from the main hall to the tracks never close, so I can walk right through.

There are two women in front of me, and they keep looking around. I go past them as quickly as I can and hug the right side of the expansive shopping area. First I check to make sure all the stores are in the right order. De Broodzaak: check. Swirls Ice Cream: check. Smullers: check. The Amstel Passage is closed. The Döner Company: check. No changes, so that's good.

There are two sets of fifteen steps up to track 13B. I have to be sure to remember to count them again when I come down.

My mission is so exciting! I can feel that it's all going to go just right for once. The woman I'm supposed to look for will be there. Everything will work out perfectly. I know it, and that sense of certainty makes me happy.

I've never been so happy in my life.

The man is only a few feet away from me, and I can smell his cigarette. "There are special smoking areas," I say, and I point to the standing ashtray not far off. He inhales deeply and blows a white cloud at my face.

I lower my head and count to ten. Every time Ted gives me a mission, he tells me not to raise my voice and not to argue with anyone. If I say something to this man . . .

I count to twenty.

I feel like Ted is watching me, but I can also feel Anja's eyes aimed in my direction. Let that frustrated caseworker find herself another victim! A piece of advice: make it somebody who'll give her a good roll in the hay. Somebody her big boobs will make all horny.

"Watch where you're going," a voice beside me snarls.

I'm standing next to a woman whose buttons are practically popping off her blouse. I mumble an apology and walk away.

As I approach the stairs, I see a woman in a short brown leather jacket coming toward me. Black skirt, black stockings, black high-heeled boots. Her long blond hair is parted in the middle. But it's only Tuesday.

I hurry down the thirty steps.

Mother has left me a note. She's gone to the beauty parlor and wants me to do the shopping. There's a list in the linen bag on the inside of the kitchen door. The money is in an envelope.

The thought hits me the second I touch the bag.

Mother is going to poison me. She's letting me do the shopping so I won't be suspicious, but she's already bought the poison, see? She tells me to get the ingredients she needs to make her endive stew with bacon, that way she figures I'll never stop to think how easy it'll be for her to stir the poison into the stew. She'll serve me a poisoned dinner, a meal I know *she* doesn't like and won't eat.

She wants to get rid of me.

I don't fit in here.

I wish Ted would come, wish just once he'd come during the day instead of at night. I could talk with him, explain my suspicions. He would give me good advice. Maybe if I sit very quietly on the sofa and stare straight down at the floor. I listen for his footsteps, not moving a muscle.

The clock in the hall strikes four. He's not coming. I'd better go do the shopping. But I won't eat the stew, not one bite. I won't let myself be poisoned. Not by *anyone*.

*Wednesday*

The new day is only ten minutes old. I slipped into the kitchen half an hour ago to make two cheese sandwiches. Mother loves cheese, so that's something she won't poison. And bread is safe. And butter. And milk. Anything Mother eats, I can eat.

She was insulted I wouldn't have any of the endive stew. She asked me what was going on with me, if I'm taking my penfluridol. She's always bitching about those pills. I have to stop myself from kicking a kitchen chair to bits.

I told her I had a stomachache and couldn't keep anything down. Then I went to my room and watched TV. With the door locked.

I'm positive Ted will come tonight. Maybe he'll tell me about the city where he was born. He's done that before, and that's why I googled *Burlington* tonight. I found out it's a city of interesting contradictions: it's the biggest city in Vermont, but the smallest biggest city in any of the fifty United States. When you think that Ted's not only a serial killer but also somebody's best friend, you can understand why he was born in Burlington.

I have to tell him I saw her in the station yesterday afternoon, a woman who fit the description for tomorrow's mission. Should I have talked to her? That question weighs on my mind.

He's told me many times how he approached his victims. If you go up to a woman and you're friendly but you don't bug her, most of the time she'll talk with you. But the best way to get her attention is if there's obviously something wrong with you: your arm's in a sling, you're using a cane and limping, you've got a big bandage on your head and you act like you're dizzy. Then they'll be all concerned, they'll ask if they can help you.

When Ted found out I don't have a car, not even a driver's license, so I can't drive women to some remote place and attack them there, he was mad at first. But later he said I was a new kind of challenge for him, and he gave me instructions I had to memorize but not write down. He decided the starting point would be Amsterdam's Central Station, and he told me which track and what the victim would look like. It wasn't until he'd come to see me a dozen times that he told me he wanted to concentrate on women who looked like the victims who'd escaped from him his first time around.

I have an old schoolbag that's just the right size to hold my bat. It has a long shoulder strap, so I can clutch it tight to my stomach when I carry it.

Up to now, my first seven tries were no good, because the women I was supposed to find didn't show up at the right track when they were supposed to. Ted says I have to pay closer attention, be sharper. Tomorrow is my eighth chance, and this time it's going to be just fine. I've already seen the woman, and I know she'll turn up right when she's supposed to. I'll bandage my left hand in the morning, and I'll walk with a cane. When the woman gets off her train, I'll catch her attention by the stairs, and I'll ask her to help me down. Halfway, I'll say I'm dizzy and I need some fresh air. Track 13B is close to the station's back entrance, and that's where I'll have the best chance to use my bat.

And to get away without anyone seeing me.

I know it's risky. But I'll take my chances. I'm not worried. Ted will protect me.

And if the woman I'm waiting for isn't arriving on the train but leaving on it, I'll just climb aboard with her. With my cane and my schoolbag. I'll sit near her and make sure she notices me.

Then I'll grab her right before the train pulls into a station. Or maybe it'll be better to wait until the train comes to a stop, so I can get off right away.

Thinking about the woman on the track, about finally carrying out my mission, is exciting. It's giving me a boner. I like the way that feels.

I hope Ted's coming tonight, and that he tells me more about what he did with the bodies. He is *so* cool!

*Thursday*

Ted didn't come last night. I'm really disappointed. It would have been helpful to discuss the plans for today one more time. Maybe he didn't show because he thought it would be too much of a distraction. Maybe he's afraid I'll back out at the last minute.

You never know.

My mission begins at eleven thirty, and I'll be sure to take a tram that'll get me to the station on time. Better to arrive half an hour early than one minute late. Because what if the woman turns up exactly at eleven thirty and I'm not there?

I have to get this right.

Mother thinks I look exhausted, and she wants to know why that is. I don't have a job, and I don't really *do* much, so why am I so tired? She thinks I don't get enough physical exercise but work myself up too much mentally. That needs to change, she says.

I'll have to find a way to fake her out.

She offers me homemade jam, and I say thanks but no thanks. She wants to know why I'm barely eating anything, do I still have a stomachache? And then of course she gets on my case again about changing my meds from the pill to an injection.

I try to tune her out and concentrate on my cheese sandwich and the glass of milk I made sure to pour for myself.

*Track 13B*, I think. *Woman with long blond hair parted in the middle. Brown leather jacket, tight black skirt, black stockings, black boots with high heels.*

The bandage and the bat are in my bag. I hid the cane in the bushes by the garden gate, I'll fish it out as I pass.

"She'll be here in half an hour," I hear Mother say.

I sit up straight. "Who'll be here in half an hour?"

"Your caseworker, Anja. I called her. You're not well, you need an extra visit. And a shot."

I get up. "Tell her I said hi. I have to go."

A second later, she's all up in my face: "You're not going anywhere until you've talked with Anja. I'm doing this for your own good, boy. You'll thank me later."

I look at her. She means it, she's not going to let me go.

But I *have* to go.

Why isn't Ted here when I need him?

The front door is locked. Where is the key?

Mother smiles.

I feel myself becoming calmer. Okay, fine, she has the key. It's obviously in her apron pocket. She always cleans the house after breakfast, and she's already wearing her apron.

It's almost ten o'clock, it's a five-minute walk to the tram stop, I might have to wait another five minutes for a tram, and then the ride takes twenty minutes. That gives me just enough time to get the key, and if she won't give it to me willingly . . .

I go into the living room and sit in my chair. Mother is puttering around in the hall. She's probably getting the vacuum cleaner from the closet at the top of the basement stairs.

The basement!

The bag with the bat is still in my bedroom, but the base of the lamp that stands on the armoire in the living room will do just as well.

I've put on a clean shirt and also a clean sweater. The key was indeed in the pocket of Mother's apron. The vacuum cleaner is back where it belongs, and so is the lamp. The basement door is locked. I can go.

The doorbell rings.

"I rode my bike," says Anja. "It's actually quicker than coming by car, so I'm a little early. Is it okay if I leave it outside?"

"You'd better bring it in," I recommend.

There's a detour, because they're working on the tramline. Signs show you which way to go.

I haven't ridden a bike in a long time, but I don't have any trouble. It's nice, the wind in my hair. I'm careful not to let the wheels drop into the tram rails.

I've got my bag on my right side. I bandaged my hand before I left the house. I have to hurry, because it's already five minutes to eleven. I pedal past de Bijenkorf, and I can see the station up ahead. I know for sure the woman will be there, and the thought gives me wings.

\* \* \*

The big clock in the station's main hall says 11:15. I'll leave the cane in my bag until I get to the stairs to track 13B. There's a strange noise behind me, and as I'm about to turn around to see what it is, a man in an electric wheelchair zooms by.

I'm panting a little.

Calm down, calm down, calm down.

Quickly check the stores.

There's the stairway. Count carefully, two sets of fifteen steps.

It's 11:25.

I'm positive I looked everywhere. I didn't miss her, she just isn't here. Didn't get off the train, didn't get on. This can't be happening!

The train that leaves Amsterdam at 2:38 p.m. is slowly pulling into the station. It comes to a stop. The doors open, and people come out. I have a good view from where I'm standing.

It's 2:37. The time is up. I feel all the energy drain out of my body.

And then I see her.

She walks past me, close enough to touch, and hurries to the train. I follow her without thinking, and the second I step aboard I hear the conductor's whistle and the doors whoosh closed behind me. She heads for the first-class compartment and holds the connecting door for me.

I lean on my cane.

"You should sit down," she says.

I obey, and see that she takes a seat in the middle of the car.

It was one minute later than the end time I was given, but I don't think Ted will have a problem with that. I found her, and inside my head I'm cheering. She's sitting there talking on her phone, laughing.

But not for long.

Pretty soon, I'll be the one who's laughing.

We're the only passengers in the compartment. Ted must have arranged it that way.

I'm not happy about that minute.

But I've got her!

### What Day Is It?

I've lost track of time, and there's a gap in my memory. The last thing I remember is the woman on the train, the way she looked. After that, there was a lot of commotion, somebody dragged me away, I was in a cell, people kept asking me questions, someone told me I had to be examined.

I've got a room and a bed, but all the doors and windows are locked. The food is good. Everybody here is crazy, but the man who comes to talk with me three times a week is far and away the craziest. He tells me I tried to molest an old lady on the train, though I keep explaining that she was young. When I describe her, he contradicts me. The lady he talks about isn't blond with a middle part, doesn't wear a short brown leather jacket, no tight black skirt, no black stockings and high-heeled boots. When I say we must be talking about two different people, he says no, we're absolutely talking about the same person. So he's a total nutbag.

Each time he comes, he's got new idiotic comments. He thinks Mother has been dead for a year, and I haven't seen my psychiatric caseworker, Anja, since Mother died. He says I've been skipping my appointments, and he keeps insisting that, given my condition, isolation is my worst enemy, because if

I'm alone I don't have anyone to correct my behavior and my thoughts.

According to him, when Mother was still alive I used to take medication that kept the weird thoughts at bay. It's apparently pretty much a miracle I didn't go off the rails until now. If I go back on my meds, I can learn to think straight again. I'll have to go to trial, but a good lawyer should be able to convince the judge I wasn't accountable for my actions when I attacked the lady on the train. The shrink will recommend confinement in a psych ward. The doctor emphasizes that everyone wants what's best for me.

I'm allergic to people who want what's best for me.

When I very carefully describe what I did to Mother and Anja, the doctor doesn't react.

He ought to go take a look in the basement.

They force me to take the pills. When I refuse, I get a shot. The meds make me dull, I sleep away half the day.

Ted doesn't come to see me. Now that I can't do anything for him, he's abandoned me. With friends like him, who needs enemies?

### What Month Is It?

They're fed up with my continued insistence that Mother and Anja are in the basement. The doctor thinks it would help me to see Anja. She's coming this afternoon.

I bet she won't look too good.

They've decided that the meds they've put me on are too strong, so now they're reducing the dosage. But they make darned sure I swallow the pills. I have to put each one on my tongue, and after I swallow it the supervisor looks down my throat, probably all the way down my esophagus. I don't feel as foggy now, and I don't drag my feet when I walk.

And Anja's coming to see me.

Party time!

I sit beside the shrink and across from the caseworker nobody seems to realize is lying in my cellar. I have to admit she looks pretty healthy, and she doesn't seem to have had any work done. I probably ought to keep my mouth shut, otherwise before you know it they'll up my meds again. But I can't stop myself from telling her that even though she thinks she's sitting here, she's actually dead.

She leans a little closer.

I pull back. She stinks like a corpse.

She tells me everything will be okay, and she'll always be here for me.

Those words rock me, and I have to hold onto the table to keep from falling over.

How could I ever have thought Ted would leave me in the lurch? How could I have doubted his intentions? When I see him again, I'll beg his forgiveness on bended knee, if that's what it takes. The more I think about it, though, the more I realize he won't be mad. If he was truly angry, he wouldn't have sent Anja to me. The only explanation for her presence is that she's joined up with Ted. And I'm the only one who knows.

See, this is what friendship is all *about*.

Now I know for sure Ted's coming back.

With Anja.

I wonder, what will my next mission be?

# PART IV

*THEY LIVE BY NIGHT*

# SEVEN BRIDGES

BY MAX VAN OLDEN

*Grachtengordel*

L isa was running ten minutes late. Normally that wouldn't be a problem, since there were usually two of them on Saturdays—but now, in early March, there were so few bookings she had to prepare the tables on her own.

In the crew cabin, she changed from her wool sweater to a tight white blouse and put on an apron. She checked the schedule. A Delight cruise, twenty-two passengers. She could handle that—sometimes, even in the winter, they had as many as forty on board. She piled eight crates onto her service cart—six beverages, two glasses—and above those balanced the plastic bin labeled *Tableware*. She glanced out the window and saw people already lined up at the Pier F ticket office, waiting for the passenger door to open. Sighing, she pushed her cart out into the main cabin.

Starting at the back of *Princess Beatrix*, she set each table, as always, with place mats that indicated their route with a dotted line on a map of the city's canals, bottles of water, bowls of beer nuts. She looked up and spotted their guide approaching. Arno was a dope, but he was always willing to lend a hand. That was more than you could say for some of the others.

"Need some help?" he said as he stepped on board, and, without waiting for an answer, pitched in and started setting tables. The sound system was already on, and they worked to the syrupy tones of Laura Pausini.

They finished at a minute to four. Foreheads glistening with perspiration, they took up their positions on the dock, Lisa on one side of the door and Arno on the other. They smiled brightly at the passengers as they boarded. The four o'clock and six o'clock cruises mostly appealed to retirees and families, quiet customers who never made any trouble.

"Goodbody, every afternoon," Arno began his usual spiel. After two years of it, Lisa didn't even notice the joke anymore. Wim, their captain, steered the boat—long enough to hold eighty passengers, low enough to sail beneath the city's innumerable bridges—past the train station. Back in the kitchen, Lisa pulled soft drinks from the fridge and arranged them on her cart.

"The Central Station is built on an artificial island," Arno said, first in English, then in Dutch and French and German. "It was designed by the same architect who designed the Rijksmuseum, which is where you can find our most important Rembrandt paintings."

Pulling the cork from a bottle of Chianti, Lisa glanced outside. The sky was gray, and there were wisps of mist along the embankment. When Arno paused for breath, she heard raindrops patter on the boat's glass roof.

She thought back to that morning, that lovely morning with Timo. They hadn't gotten out of bed until ten thirty. She'd cracked open a can of Jus-Rol croissants and slid them into the oven. They'd only been together for three months, but Lisa was already spending so much time at Timo's place she had practically moved in. Her toiletries were in his bathroom, half her clothing hung in his wardrobe, she felt so comfortable she knew their relationship was the real thing.

"On your right is NEMO, the science museum, and underneath it is the highway to Amsterdam-North."

The passengers gaped at the vast green building that rose up from the water like the prow of an enormous oil tanker.

When she was with Timo, she lost all sense of time. After breakfast, they'd put on Netflix and continued watching *Stranger Things*, the series they'd begun last night. When you were in love, all you wanted to do was snuggle up together, all day long. And so they did, until the middle of the afternoon, when Timo had pointed to his wristwatch and she realized it was past time for her to leave for work.

They continued along the river, "the majestic five-star Amstel Hotel on your left, the Rolling Stones' favorite place to stay when they're in town." The passengers were always on the lookout for celebrities. In fact, was that Robbie Williams working up a sweat on the treadmill in the glass-walled fitness center? No, too tall. Probably just some businessman.

After they passed the hotel, the captain turned them around and set a course for the Herengracht. When she could make out the distant bridge that marked the entrance to the world-famous Grachtengordel—the Canal District—Lisa felt a rush of pleasure well up from deep inside her. Not because of the bridge or the canal, but because she knew it wouldn't be long now before—

First, of course, would come the Willet-Holthuysen Museum with its imposing latticed windows to the right, and then "the relatively new Waldorf Astoria hotel" on the left, but after that it would be barely half a minute before Wim throttled back the *Princess Beatrix* almost to a standstill to give the passengers time to point their cameras off to the left for one of the cruise's highlights: beneath the graceful stone bow of the bridge over the Reguliersgracht, six more bridges could be seen, each of them illuminated, stretching all the way south to the Lijnbaansgracht, seemingly stacked up one atop the other. Yes, the Seven Bridges did indeed make for a lovely picture.

Her own personal highlight came almost at the same moment as the photo op: some thirty yards before it, there was something to be seen that seven *hundred* bridges couldn't compete with—as soon as the boat slowed down and the passengers turned their attention to the left, she could blow unseen kisses to the handsome young man on the old houseboat not six feet to their right. For those ten or fifteen seconds, it would be as if she was home, with Timo, done with work for the evening, and the love that would wash over her would be so intense, so delicious, it would carry her through the second half of the cruise.

They were almost there: the first passengers were getting to their feet, their phones at the ready, and Lisa turned to face the scene where, just a few hours earlier, she and Timo had relished their warm, sweet croissants. The skipper slowed the boat. Another fifteen yards, ten. She ran a hand through her hair. Five more yards, and she would be able to see into the living room. Three . . .

Lisa's shoulders slumped. Timo wasn't standing at the window, waiting for her. He was on the couch, asleep. The TV was still on. She sighed, but her disappointment quickly melted into tenderness. *He's even cute when he's sleeping,* she thought.

It was natural that her boyfriend would need to catch up on his sleep over the weekend. He rose at six every morning and put in at least fifty hours a week at work, sometimes sixty. His own ad agency—he'd wanted that since high school. There were times that he and his team slaved over a pitch until two in the morning.

Behind her, the cameras began to click. She turned around, and almost got a selfie stick in her face.

The *Princess Beatrix* returned to Pier F at five thirty. That gave Lisa half an hour to prepare the boat for the six o'clock cruise. She'd have to hurry. The moment the last of the four o'clock passengers were gone, she gathered up the empty bottles, dumped the trash in a large plastic bag, replaced the dirty place mats with fresh ones, checked the tables and the restroom. Arno helped her restock the drinks, and she wound up with a couple of minutes to sneak a cigarette on the back deck before the next load of passengers boarded.

With her imperturbable smile, Lisa took orders, refilled the nut dishes, snapped pictures for everyone who asked. Meanwhile, her thoughts were filled with Timo.

He was so different from Stefan. Timo was the complete opposite of that bastard she'd somehow stayed with for two and a half years. In him, she found everything her previous boyfriend had been unable or unwilling to give her: attention, tenderness, great sex. And the things she'd resented in Stefan were absent from Timo: egotism, self-righteousness, emotional distance. Opening a container of chocolate milk, she asked herself for the umpteenth time why she had let herself suffer through a relationship that, if she was honest, she had never for one moment truly believed in. The only answer she could come up with was simple cowardice.

Walking down the aisle with two bottles of Heineken in her hands, she heard someone say the words "Waldorf Astoria." She delivered the beers and returned quickly to the back of the boat. Once they passed the Waldorf, everyone would be looking ahead for the Seven Bridges. Lisa took up her usual position by the window, but then changed her mind. She opened the door to the back deck and was greeted by a chilly gust of wind in her face. There were puddles of water on the wooden benches. Rain dripped from the Dutch tricolor that hung out over the black surface of the Herengracht, as if the flag had just been fished out of the canal.

They approached Timo's houseboat. Inside the *Princess Beatrix*, passengers were getting to their feet, angling for a better view. Ten yards to go. She wished she had a cigarette but was afraid the captain might smell it.

Two more yards.

One.

"Can you give me a hand, please?"

Lisa whirled at the sound of the voice. A man stood in the doorway. He was having trouble staying erect, thanks to the thin elderly woman clutching his arm.

"My mother needs to use the lavatory," the man said apologetically. "She's ninety-four."

The old lady seemed about to collapse, and a moment later Lisa was on her other side, propping her up. The woman looked up at her gratefully and managed to right herself.

Lisa looked back. The houseboat was already far behind them, and the distance was steadily increasing.

For the remainder of the cruise, her cell phone burned in her pocket. She wanted to call Timo, just to hear his voice and tell him she loved him, but each time she thought she might be able to slip out to the back deck, someone ordered a drink or suddenly *needed* to know what tram to take from the Central Station to the Leidseplein.

She let Arno help the passengers disembark by himself. That was against the rules, but Wim was nowhere to be seen.

When she told Arno she had to make an important call, he merely shrugged.

Timo didn't pick up. "Sorry I missed you," she told his voice mail. "I was helping an old lady into the bathroom. With all the old folks on board, sometimes I feel more like a nurse than a server." She dropped her voice to a whisper: "You look really sweet when you're asleep. I'll see you next time around!"

The candlelight cruise was not her favorite. It was harder to work in the dark, especially back in the kitchen. And the passengers were more critical, more impatient. During the day, no one complained if they had to share a table with another couple, but in the evenings there were often people who refused to sit with strangers. Sometimes they even left the boat and demanded their money back. Then of course there were always a few who took the forty-euro "all you can drink" offer seriously, and there was nothing to be done about that: "all you can drink" did, in fact, mean *all* you can drink.

The electric candles were on the tables, and the dishes of beer nuts had been distributed. When Wim closed the cabin door and Arno picked up his microphone to welcome the passengers, she took one last look at her cell: nothing from Timo. She stuffed it back in her pocket and asked the first couple what they wanted to drink. By the time she got back to her service cart, she'd already forgotten their order.

The weather had worsened. Arno had to turn up the sound system to be heard over the rain, and it was so windy the waves on the Oosterdok shook the boat from side to side. With two bottles of wine in her hands, it was hard for Lisa to negotiate the aisle without bumping into the tables on either side. Arno recounted the legend of the Skinny Bridge: a couple that kissed on or under it would stay together forever. A minute later, as the bow of the *Princess Beatrix* swept beneath the bridge, dozens of phones and cameras clicked off selfies of smooching tourists. Lisa couldn't find it within herself to smile at the sight.

She was thinking of Timo. And, strangely, of Stefan.

It hadn't ended well for them. But there had been nothing left of their relationship, other than the fact that they still slept in the same bed. Stefan had withdrawn into himself, barely spoke to her. Apart from the occasional mechanical sex, there was no intimacy between them. No wonder she had fallen so hard for someone new.

It hadn't taken Stefan long to notice that she had metamorphosed into a new and reenergized version of herself, a Lisa who spent more and more time away from their apartment, who when she *was* home seemed to be constantly hunched over her phone texting. In retrospect, she realized why she had behaved so recklessly: without being consciously aware of it, she had *wanted* her affair to come to light as soon as possible. Which was precisely what had happened.

The cruise had another hour to go. Lisa walked up and down the aisle with plates of Dutch cheese cut into cubes and dotted with mustard. Passengers nudged each other and oohed and aahed over the toothpicks topped with red-white-and-blue paper flags.

"This is canal?" asked an older Japanese gentleman, pointing at the dark water outside the window.

"No sir, this is the Amstel River. We will turn into the canals very soon." She looked ahead to orient herself. In the distance, the red neon letters of the Koninklijk Theater Carré were visible. She explained their route: first they would sail past the Carré and the Amstel Hotel, then they would turn around and retrace their path, go back under the Skinny Bridge, and then turn left into the Herengracht, the most elegant of the city's three main canals. "Ten minutes, sir, maximum, until we're there." The man nodded politely and translated the explanation for his wife. Satisfied with her own professionalism, Lisa moved on.

There hadn't been an explosion, more of an *im*plosion. A change came over Stefan, subtle but inescapable, definitive. She knew she'd have to say goodbye to their little studio, the first place she had ever lived with a man. She felt guilty, miserable, but beneath all of that was excitement at the realization that she would now be able to bring her growing relationship with Timo out of hiding.

The *Princess Beatrix* passed beneath the Skinny Bridge. A young Italian couple sitting near her service cart struggled to take a kissing selfie. The volume of the conversations of those passengers who'd by this point downed three or four alcoholic beverages swelled.

Lisa snuck her phone from her pocket and checked the screen. No calls, no messages, nothing.

She looked at her watch. Quarter to nine. A little longer, and they would reach the houseboat.

As she served the next table, a memory welled up inside her. In her mind's eye, she saw Stefan's angry face. She was on her way to the elevator, a box of clothing and textbooks in her arms, and he stood in the apartment's doorway, watching her go. He took a step toward her, leaned closer, and she would never forget the single sentence he whispered in her ear: "You haven't seen the last of me."

White wine flowed over the rim of the glass, and the passengers sitting at the table jerked away from the spill.

"I'm sorry," she cried. "I'm so sorry!"

She whipped a dishtowel from her apron pocket and dropped to her knees. When she'd cleaned up the mess, she apologized yet again and shot a glance out the window.

Fifty yards.

It was raining hard. She hid herself away in the narrow passage leading to the restroom. The boat slowed, the passengers looked around excitedly, figuring out where to stand for the best possible shot of the Seven Bridges. They were nearing the houseboat. In the darkness, it looked like a black shoebox, with thick cables mooring it to the embankment.

In the flickering blue light of Timo's TV, she could make out the outline of his bookshelves, then the painting on the side wall.

Then the couch.

She couldn't believe what she saw: Timo's arm hanging off the edge, his head bent slightly to one side—it was all the same. Timo was lying in exactly the same position she'd seen him in four hours earlier.

Four *hours*.

The only thing that stopped her from screaming was the fact that, at that moment, a girl tapped her on the shoulder and said, "Would you mind taking a picture of us? With the bridges in the background?" Lisa stared at her for two full seconds, as if the girl had appeared out of some other dimension, before taking the proffered cell phone. She clicked off three shots, numb, and managed a weak smile as she handed the phone back, but the moment she turned away, fear overwhelmed her. She felt it accelerate her heartbeat and breath, and her hands trembled so badly she had to clasp them together to stop the shaking. She was afraid her legs would give out beneath her, and she held tightly to the handle of the door leading out to the back deck to keep herself upright. She peered out the window at the houseboat, already far behind them, and for just an instant considered diving into the water and swimming back. But for what purpose? To say a last goodbye?

The passengers had returned to their seats, the boat was picking up speed, it was time for her to get back to work. She ran her hands through her hair and grabbed a bottle of wine and began to refill glasses.

All she could see before her was Timo's face as she had just now glimpsed it. Was his expression merely relaxed in sleep . . . or was it frozen in death?

*He's not dead,* she thought. *There's nothing wrong. He shifted in his sleep a few times over the last four hours and wound up the way he was before.*

For half a minute these thoughts calmed her, but then the panic reasserted itself. She kept on working, but she was on autopilot.

She heard Arno say something about the blue of the imperial crown and glanced outside. They were passing the Western Church. She shook her head. She had completely missed their transit from the Herengracht to the Prinsengracht. She tried to remember something of the last ten minutes, *anything*—an order, a glimpse of the canal—but her mind was completely blank.

Arno started talking about the Anne Frank House. In half an hour, they would be back at the pier. She would clean up faster than she'd ever cleaned before.

When they docked, Arno apologized and took off. His son was sick, he explained. Lisa forced herself to empathize. Inside her head, she caught herself praying that Timo was merely sick too. Perhaps he was unconscious. Was that possible? Some sort of temporary condition that would resolve itself the moment she shook him out of it?

As the passengers got to their feet and shrugged into their jackets, she reached for her phone. No calls, no messages. She speed-dialed Timo's number. Then again, and again, and each time her call went to voice mail she had the same thought: *I'll never hear his voice for real again.*

The boat was empty. Arno and Wim were gone. The rain had slackened, but the wind was stronger, and the *Princess Beatrix* thumped against the rubber bumpers. The dock was deserted, the café shuttered. A single light burned in the office, at the Damrak end of the pier.

Lisa raced up and down the aisle like a madwoman, brushing tricolored flags, brochures, and crumpled napkins from the tables. She scrawled the date on the front of an envelope and dumped the contents of the tip jar into it and licked the flap. She packed empty bottles and glasses into their crates and stacked the crates on the back deck, ready to be transferred to the trash cart. In five minutes she was finished—but she decided to call once more before jumping onto her bike.

Breathing heavily from exertion and nervousness, she pressed the icon beside Timo's name and waited for the ring . . . and then her eyes narrowed. From somewhere in the distance came the sound of music. It was faint, barely audible beneath the wind, but it was unmistakably Eminem's "Lose Yourself"—Timo's ringtone.

A warm glow spread from the pit of her stomach up through her body, and she shivered with relief, her terror turned in an instant to joy.

Far ahead, past the row of darkened tour boats, she saw a figure step into the light from the office. It cast a long shadow that moved toward her. The guitar riff echoed off the wooden pier. She was still holding her phone to her ear, but it suddenly felt different against her skin. It was as if she were hugging Timo's dear face to her own.

The music stopped as her call was answered.

"Hey," she heard, and the phone almost dropped from her hand. It wasn't Timo. It was Stefan's soft, icy voice, and at the same moment she recognized his walk. "I see you," he said. "Thanks for calling."

She broke the connection.

"You should have seen this coming!" he shouted over the wind. "You're next, darlin', you hear me?"

Lisa pulled back behind the cabin door and peeked around the edge of its frame. Stefan had reached the *Prince Claus*, the next boat over from the *Beatrix*. He was gaining fast, his steps determined, staring straight ahead. It felt like he was staring right into her eyes.

She eased out of her heels.

"I'm going to reunite you with your boyfriend," Stefan said coldly. "You two belong together!"

She reached behind her back and untied her apron. It dropped to the deck.

Stefan was at the bow of her boat. Carefully, without making a sound, Lisa slipped to the other side of the deck. She climbed onto one of the wooden benches, ducked down to stay out of sight. The wind ruffled the surface of the black water, stirring up tiny foam caps. Stefan was still talking, so loudly it sounded like he was standing right beside her.

"You dumped me, you fucking bitch! Now I'll dump you! You're gonna be fish food!"

There was the screech of metal on metal.

She raised a foot to the gunwale, her arms stretched out to the sides to maintain her balance. She brought up her other foot and stared down. She could smell the water's chill.

"*Look* at me when I talk to you, bitch!"

She straightened, then pushed off with all the strength she could summon, as if she were diving into a pool at the start of a race.

She tucked in her chin, exactly as her swim coach had taught her, and the one second she hung in the air stretched out as if someone had adjusted the dials on the laws of nature.

Just out of reach, she could see Timo's face, could see the two of them together, entwined on the couch in the living room of his houseboat.

The vision enveloped her like a thick warm blanket, and it was so beautiful, so grand, that when she hit the water she never even heard the shot.

# THE GIRL AT THE END
# OF THE LINE

BY ABDELKADER BENALI

*Sloten*

A farmer found her with her head facing southeast, toward Mecca, as if in prayer. The stretch of reclaimed polder land is on the edge of the city, ringed by fields and narrow irrigation channels. Amsterdam's last remaining milk cows graze in the marshy meadows. I sometimes bike out that way, when I've got nothing better to do. When my yearnings are too strong to ignore.

Geese—a constant nuisance at nearby Schiphol Airport—also feast on the grass. If there's one good place in the city to dump a body, this is it. In my head, I divide Amsterdam into places where you can safely hide a body and places where you can't. They told me it was my job to think like that. But it wasn't just my job, it was my way of making sense of the world.

Somebody once left a tourist-office folder with information about the area at the station. Thanks to that, I knew more about the place than the rest of my colleagues put together. As I roamed around the scene, I felt myself dissolving into thin air, so that less and less of me remained.

This was where, in the olden days, criminals were exiled. They were forbidden to set foot back in the city. Out here, they were no longer Amsterdammers, they no longer existed. Someone had ruled that they were no longer permitted to exist.

Modern-day Amsterdam sees a murder victim a week, and that week it was her turn. I saw her in my mind's eye, standing at the tram stop at the end of Line 1, beautiful, mortal. I thought of her as the girl at the end of the line, but she wasn't really a girl; she was in her early twenties, a woman. In life, it would have been impossible to miss her. I thought she was lovely. Lovelier than I would ever dare to acknowledge.

A reminder of the city's old border still stood there, a tall pole that had once held a road sign, rising out of the mist like a sternly pointing finger. The farmer found her body not far from the pole.

Nadia. A lovely name.

The pole was mentioned in the tourist-office folder. I was never good at history. Unless someone explained it to me, I couldn't understand. But *this* interested me. Because it hit so close to home. Things that hit close to home give me a chilly feeling of excitement. Like a bucket of cold water flung in my face.

It had rained heavily. She lay on the wettest section of the farmer's field, a worthless bit of land no one bothered with. Not too far off, the farmer kept llamas and horses. It was a desolate place. The trucks that rumbled by on the nearest road seemed to come from nowhere, heading for some other nowhere. Far off, jets rose from the airport's runways. Something inside me said those planes were crowded with the guilty, but none of them knew what it was they were guilty of.

In her pockets we found a key to a bicycle lock, a plastic tram card, a wrapped peppermint from a restaurant, and a torn ticket stub for the Pathé De Munt's showing of *12 Years a Slave*. I'd seen that movie myself. It had disturbed me. Black people in America were treated like animals. Nadia's ticket brought back the powerful scenes of torture.

At the Meer en Vaart police station, my report got a luke-warm reception. They wanted to know if I'd visited the parents yet. That task fell to me, since I was "one of them," as the guys put it, and better suited to deliver the terrible news. My colleagues automatically assumed I must know every Moroccan in the city. You knew one, you knew 'em all, right? That was why I'd been hired in the first place, wasn't it, to put my Mocro background to good use, to offer the police an entrée into what was otherwise for them a closed-off world. Around the station they spoke of *affirmative action,* but never when I was within earshot. I got that from Ali, who was Turkish and told me everything. "They have loose lips when I'm around," he said. "It's not like they want me to hear it. It's just they don't even notice I'm there anymore."

How was I supposed to tell the family their daughter had been found facing Mecca? There was no question of rape. Her carefully manicured nails had jagged tips, as if she'd been trying to escape, like a rabbit clawing its way out of a burrow that had suddenly flooded. I couldn't get that image out of my head, but I wouldn't share it with her parents.

Talking to them was supposed to help us find a starting point for our investigation, some clue that would eventually lead us to the killer.

When Nadia's father let me in, I expressly asked that his wife—who was watching from the kitchen—join us, and then I took them aside to break the news. "She was lying with her head toward Mecca," I consoled them. "Under the eyes of her Creator, she became the victim of a terrible crime. He sees all."

We sat there for a time, in silence, staring at nothing. No one moved. There were no questions. There were tears, there was weeping.

Nadia's mother got up to make tea.

Then the father said, "The Creator has taken her to His bosom. May Allah receive her with mercy."

We drank tea.

I asked Nadia's parents for her bank statements. They had no such documents. They had nothing belonging to their daughter. The mother talked about her, the father sat silently by. He looked like my father. At that age, they all look like my father. Worn out by life. The subsidized housing in which they had lived for so long had aged them. Not enough space. What I had feared turned out to be the case: they had little or no knowledge of their daughter's life.

I knew girls Nadia's age—I'd dated some of them—and they all lived double lives. What they were up to outside the home was terra incognita to their parents. They never revealed who they hung out with, what they did.

This gave Nadia's killer a definite advantage.

Her parents kissed my cheeks when I left. They had appreciated my understanding of their situation. But it hadn't gotten me anywhere. Somehow, though, I had enjoyed my time with them. I was convinced I would be able to solve the case. They reminded me of my own parents, except mine would never have given me such a warm welcome. Who needs or wants a cop in the family?

One of my colleagues complimented me: "You fit right in. We couldn't do that. You made real *contact* with them." I was an outsider accepted into the police force's inner circle specifically because I was an outsider. If it all turned out right, I'd be a hero. If I failed, the fault would be entirely mine.

"We didn't get anywhere," I said. "They don't know their own daughter."

"It had to be someone in her circle who did it," Ali said drily. "What did you find in her phone?"

"Girl stuff. Nothing suspicious."

"Then she must have had another one. Her killer must have taken it." Ali proposed a hypothesis: "She was cheating on her boyfriend—or pretending to—and he caught on. She was a smart girl, plenty smarter than he. Maybe she texted him at the hookah bar. Maybe he was stoned. Anyway, he got pissed off. Arranged to meet her outside the city, said there was something he had to show her. She was naive, right, didn't have it in her just to break up with him. Figured she'd do him this one last favor. Girls like her are experts at confusing the issue. This'll make the investigation more complicated. Even her best girlfriends didn't know her secrets. There are girls like her all over this neighborhood, all coy and shy inside the family but vamps and divas out on the town. On their way home, they change back into whatever's acceptable. And nobody has a clue what they're up to."

I gazed at him. Ali thinks fast, talks fast, forgets fast.

"Bullshit," I said.

"You'll see. It's complicated, boss." He held up his hands and moved them apart. "Think big."

What was she doing out there in the dead of night, on the border between the city and the countryside? What was a beautiful young woman looking for in one of the loneliest parts of Amsterdam? What was she *thinking*?

Back at the station, I printed out my report, stapled the pages together, and dropped it in my out-box. Perhaps the results of the DNA testing would be helpful. If she'd fought her killer—and it looked that way to me—some traces should have been left behind.

For the rest of the day, I lost myself among the shoppers. It was spring, the sun wouldn't set until late, there were plenty of people out and about. It didn't feel like Amsterdam. No tourists. No canals. No women in summer dresses walking their dogs. It felt like a different city in a different country, where there was so much space and light that it was easy for the population to act as if no one else existed. Here and there I spotted pretty girls waiting for a tram. For the longest time, I used to suppress the urge to talk to girls like that. Until, one day, I decided that it really didn't matter what happened. Sometimes they'd ignore you, and then you'd feel like shit for a while. Sometimes they'd welcome your advances, and that could be the start of something very nice. I no longer suppressed the urge. But here in New-West, I had to be careful. I *was* somebody here.

Downtown, I used to go after pickpockets—I was good at it, it was an exciting period, I still think about it every day. The time before my transfer to Meer en Vaart was like a dream. I did great among the shoplifters, because I wasn't your typical undercover cop. With my three-day stubble, my worn leather jacket, my beat-up sneakers, I could have been an illegal alien on the make. There in Amsterdam's crowded streets, I could use my appearance to capture guys with criminal intentions.

I was the child of Moroccan immigrants who'd been visibly shocked when I told them I'd been accepted into the police academy. They warned me about flying bullets and murders, told me I'd never be home for dinner, which would make it hard to develop a good relationship with a peaceful girl. Emotional blackmail. I figure a *little* blackmail can be a sign of love, but too much blackmail can scar you. There's a thin line between a little and too much. I have to admit that I carried the scars, though I tried not to make a big deal of it.

Where did I get the idea of becoming a cop, they wanted to know. They'd always heard me cuss out the police—*They've got it in for Moroccans, but they let the white offenders slide*—so why this change of heart? Should I tell them about my instinct, my almost infallible ability to see who was cool and who was up to no good, who was a crook and who wasn't? Sure, try to explain that to your parents, who are Berbers from the Rif Mountains. My father had bad memories of the police back home. "They speak Arabic to us, they insult us, they take our money. The authorities sic them on us to fill their own pockets. Vultures."

Sometimes I'd follow some guy down the street, because he seemed to fit the description of a murderer. Even with my friends, I asked myself who was running a racket and who was on the up-and-up. It bothered me that I couldn't share this with anyone. I felt like a traitor.

"Mother," I said, "this choice brings me peace."

That would have to be enough for them.

And it *did* bring me peace. The training went by quickly, although I never told my parents how irrationally the other recruits grumbled about "my people," the Moroccans, the Mocros, the Muslims.

One part of our training happened at the academy, the other part came from the popular reality show *Detection Requested*. All the trainees watched it, and the next day it was all they could talk about.

What it boiled down to was that all Moroccans were the same, except me. I was different. One of my fellow trainees put it this way: "You fit in everywhere. You could be a suspect or a cop."

After I graduated and got my first assignment, I was shy, I kept things superficial, and the result was that my new colleagues didn't trust me.

They couldn't get rid of me, though: I was good. Maybe *too* good. So they transferred me. Something about excessive force, something about complaints from bystanders. I was just a little too assertive.

Sometimes it's pointless to resist the inevitable, because you know nothing's going to change.

There wasn't much for me at the Meer en Vaart station. Those first weeks, I missed not only the bustle of the city center, the anonymity, but most of all the old connections. The way we knew each other, the in-jokes, the speed with which things happened. We were a team. At my new assignment, I was left to my own devices.

Before too long, my desk was piled high with case files. My predecessor—who had retired—was old-school, which meant that few of his records had been digitized. The whole station was still stuck in the 1980s. The only real crime was bureaucracy.

By the end of my first month, Ali—one of the old-timers— had taken me under his wing. He was my big brother, and he took pity on the new kid. "Go here after your shift," he said, handing me a slip of paper with an address that turned out to be a blue-collar sailing club on the Sloterplas. The building was hidden behind trees, bushes, and a fence. When I turned up, Ali was already there, on his second beer. He'd exchanged his work face for a carefree joviality. He hugged me. "I'm a Turk," he explained. "We hug."

If he was looking for an after-hours drinking buddy, he'd picked the wrong guy. I don't drink. I ordered a mineral water. I really *shouldn't* drink, it's just asking for trouble, especially since I do things I'd be better off avoiding. Which is why I was in New-West now and not still in the heart of the city.

Ali cautioned me not to take the suspicion that dominated our workplace personally. The station had been going through an identity crisis for some years, caused by the treatment it received from headquarters. The station felt it wasn't being taken seriously, and that was the reason for the pain I could feel whenever I walked through the door. The city center had forgotten us, despite the recent increase in criminal activity. Organized crime ran illegal casinos, refugees streamed into our forgotten neighborhoods, once-proud buildings were degenerating into tenements, some areas were under the control of street gangs. "Let's say the problems of us brown people are a lower priority than the problems of the white people in the Grachtengordel."

Only when there'd been a gang murder did they come out our way to have a look.

"Then all at once we're New York, Los Angeles. The media show up, the social services stand around and nod thoughtfully. Put on their cool act. Shove us off to the side."

Of course, HQ *had* to put in an appearance when something high-profile happened. The rest of the time, they stayed nice and cozy in the Canal District.

"The canal ring's like an albatross around our neck," said Ali. "There's the world inside the ring—with all its glamour and wealth and success—and then there's the world outside the ring, with our six hundred creeps on the most-wanted list, our jihadis in training, our gambling dens, our money launderers, our meth labs, our tough guys and welfare cheats. They don't give a shit. Worse than that, *arkada*, they *like* it like this. They figure they can never get rid of evil altogether, but what they can do is give it a place to live. So here we are in Evil's Preserve. *Marhaba!*"

* * *

Now, in the distance, children were taking sailing lessons on the calm surface of the lake. The Sloterplas dominated the neighborhood. Wild horses couldn't drag me out onto the water.

"My kids are almost old enough for that," said Ali. "Pretty soon now, they'll start whining, 'Papa, I want to sail!'" He dreamed aloud of a boat of his own and brought his glass of beer to his lips. He could drink here without anyone watching him. "Social control, man," he said conspiratorially, and took another slug, and then another.

I knew this sort of drinking, the behavior of a man who didn't have the luxury of spreading his consumption out across the day, so he had to suck down as much as he could when he had the chance. If he was going to drink, it had to be here and now.

"Everything's got to be normal here. If you can't fit in, don't try to live here—go downtown. Every crime that happens here is explainable. But what happened to Nadia? That wasn't normal. They're all talking about it, even in the mosque. But it won't last long. People forget. They want things to go back to normal."

Ali was the only one of us who lived near the station. He grew up here. He lived in Old-Sloten, close to the lake. He could be home in a jiffy; you could get from anywhere to anywhere else in this neighborhood in a jiffy.

"Still, Old-Sloten's different," he said, "not like this. Here, nobody knows anyone else. That's the way things are now. They don't call us *Old*-Sloten for nothing. We're old. Even the newcomers. We make them old. I love that. I'm a traditional man. A man who appreciates the old ways."

He ordered another beer. I'd already seen him put away

three of them tonight, and he might have had more before I got there. Alcohol made Ali a better man. I envied him that. My parents caught me drunk once. They basically freaked out. I had "adopted the habits of the infidels." As far as they were concerned, I was already on my way to hell. I kind of enjoyed their reaction. Better drunk and in hell than sober among the hypocrites.

Ali confided in me that the Meer en Vaart cops would try to get rid of me as soon as possible. "Then they'll be happy. So don't be bitter if you have to move on. It's got nothing to do with you personally."

The kid was standing beside the school principal, waiting for me. They'd arrested his father on suspicion of money laundering, racketeering, and extortion. The trifecta. My colleagues had knocked in the front door of their house and found a lot of cash on the premises. They took the mother away too. One visit from the cops, and your whole family's gone. I was supposed to bring the kid to child protective services, since he was a minor. I made a wrong turn at first. There was traffic, and it was raining. Springtime was working against us.

The kid didn't speak, just looked out the window. I figured he had no idea what his parents had been up to, though you never really know. Someone had warned him to keep his mouth shut, but he suddenly seemed to realize I wasn't just some random guy.

"You doing okay at school?" I tried.

His face twisted. I wasn't his older brother or any other relative, I was a cop, even though I wasn't in uniform. He turned away, but I could see he was having a hard time of it.

"I used to want to be a doctor," I said. "Then you can help people get better. But I became a police officer instead."

"Nobody trusts a cop. You're all traitors." The look in his eyes was harder than granite.

"Who killed Nadia?" he demanded when he got out of the car. As if he were interrogating me. As if I knew something about it. Why do these kids all think the police are part of the problem?

I visited the other members of the family. Everywhere I went, I was received graciously. Maybe a friendly reception makes it harder to find the solution.

Her sisters told me she loved movies, but she never went out. I kept my own opinion to myself. She never hung around with bad boys. They'd never known a purer girl. Then they cried. The conclusion I drew from these conversations was that Nadia had kept her sisters in the dark too. They knew nothing about her. No details that could send us in a useful direction. Nothing.

Maybe she was murdered because she was so *present*, because she was dominant, because she was different. At least that's how her girlfriends described her: radiant, well behaved, defiant. There had to be plenty of guys in the neighborhood who were attracted to her. Everyone was absolutely convinced of the goodness of her character. She was an unusual girl, unique. That breeds jealousy. Killed because she was too good for this world. Something like that.

Her death had made Nadia a martyr. She had been promoted to sainthood. She would be held up forever as an example.

He was six years older than Nadia. They'd met at a Turkish restaurant she frequented with her girlfriends. He was there with his buddies. There was chitchat and flirting. The two of them began texting each other. They both loved Turkish comedies. He had a Turkish background. "I'm an Alevite," he told me. She was a Moroccan Sunni.

So she couldn't tell her parents about their relationship? He nodded.

Was it serious between them?

"She meant everything to me." A romantic soul, but I believed him. I could see in him the same sense of loss I'd seen in her girlfriends. "She was one of a kind. She didn't know how to lie. She lived from the heart. You don't meet many people like her."

I didn't pay much attention to whatever he said after that. What it came down to was that Nadia had been his guarantee against bad behavior.

But their relationship had been troubled. He wanted more time with her than she was willing to give. At last, a few weeks back, she had pulled the plug.

Had he been devastated?

No. In fact, he'd been relieved. He'd been wondering how long it would take before she finally acknowledged her doubts. He didn't have a steady job, no wealthy parents, no brothers to support him. He had little chance of making something of himself. "She woke me up. I never hated her, not for one second."

We *had* to believe him, he said.

Why do we always *have* to believe these people?

When I left him, we shook hands. His were dry, and rough as sandpaper.

The forensics report came in. No traces, which now suggested she hadn't fought against her attacker. The conclusion was that she'd been lured to her death by someone she knew. "The killing must have been premeditated. It was carefully planned by someone who knew what he was doing."

"I told you," said Ali. "Whoever did this wasn't normal. Wasn't from around here. But he had an eye for pretty girls."

Back on the street, I encountered two young Muslim men.

"*As-salaam alaikum*," they said.

"*Alaikum salaam*," I replied.

They introduced themselves. They were on their way to the mosque. Would I come by sometime, talk about my work as a policeman and what I contributed to society? "We are proud of you. You are one of us." They'd be happy to welcome me to the mosque. The House of Good. I didn't want to insult them, so I accepted their invitation. I would come. When I was ready, they said, when I was spiritually clean. When that day came, I would also call my parents.

That evening, I went to Ali's home. I was uncomfortable about those two Muslims. It was as if they knew of my torment. And there, in Ali's living room, I felt the earth shift beneath my feet. For the first time in months, I drank. By the end of the evening, I had no idea what I was saying. I talked and talked and talked. I rattled on about the young girls, my feelings of guilt, of rejection. I talked of death, said I hoped that when *my* time came I would be laid to rest with my head facing Mecca.

Ali comforted me. When I left, he looked at me differently than he had when the evening began. My only hope was that he would always be my friend.

I wanted to find out where that peppermint had come from, so I decided to go downtown. There were a number of places to get a quick bite near the Pathé De Munt. I went into many of them, ostensibly to use the men's room, and on my way out I took a peppermint from the bowl by the door. It was, of course, a fool's errand. She could have gone anywhere in the city that evening.

But I knew she'd been here. In the area around the theater. She'd had something to eat. To drink. She lived her life to the fullest.

In New-West, you didn't have the luxury to be naive. She'd told him everything about her life, her yearning to be free, her bossy brothers. Her sweet sisters. Her wonderful parents. And he had listened. Understood that she was suffering. She told him everything. Deep inside her was a human being in pain. Someone who couldn't see any hope for the future. The moment she stepped back inside her house, it was as if she'd confined herself within a glass cage. Running away wasn't an option; it would break her heart. She was a good girl. Honest. But where had her honesty gotten her? She was living a lie, deceiving her family. And some boy had taken advantage of her.

A few months later, I was pulled off the case. Despite my background and knowledge, I hadn't produced the result they'd expected. I rubbed them the wrong way. I wasn't the Mocro-cop they'd dreamed of, who would fit in among the Moroccan community. In my evaluation, they wrote that my familiarity with the killer's milieu and my ability to win the trust of its inhabitants had gotten in the way of my professional judgment, had perhaps even *prevented* the murder from being solved. They were ready to trade their approachable Moroccan man in for a more standoffish model. That's how I read it, those are the conclusions I drew. Not long after that, I requested a transfer and left Sloten.

\* \* \*

This all happened ten years ago. The case was never solved. The reports were filed and forgotten.

I've resigned from the police. I do something different now, though I still divide the world into places where you can safely hide a body and places where you can't.

Sometimes I dream of Nadia. I see her quite clearly, before she disappears into the polder. She says, *I don't know how I wound up here.*

A girl with too many secrets.

I believed that, with my background, I'd be able to solve her murder. I thought I was convincing enough to get the answers I needed, that the solution would simply present itself to me.

I was wrong.

Had she lived, Nadia would still be a mystery.

The only indisputable fact is that she is dead.

The rest is silence.

# GET RICH QUICK

BY WALTER VAN DEN BERG

*Osdorp*

So I tell Sayid pretty soon we'll be rich. In two hours. Maybe three.

He says he don't know what he'll do with his share. He says he can't imagine what a person *would* do with a fuckin' million euros.

We're at the Mickey D's on the Osdorpplein, and we got cheeseburgers in front of us, but I can't eat. I'm too hyped. "We can't do *nothin'* with it," I say. "We bust ourselves if we spend it. We gotta wait a month. Maybe two."

"Okay," Sayid says, but I can see he don't think it's okay.

"We don't spend it," I say. "That's lesson number one."

"Lesson number one at what school, man? The Uni-fuckin-versity of Stealing?" He looks over at the counter, where his kid sister stands behind the register, ringing up an order.

I remind him he's seen plenty of gangster movies.

"What are you tellin' me, gangster—we're gangsters now?"

I say I think we are gangsters now, and I open my jacket just enough so he can see the piece stuck in my waistband.

"Chill," he says. "That's way chill." Then he shakes his head. He reaches across the table and opens my jacket a little wider, so he can get a good look. "When do we gotta give it back?"

I tell him that depends on if we use it or not. "We use it,

we dump it in the lake. We don't use it, I'm s'posed to bring it back tomorrow."

"You got it from the Abduls?"

"Half," I say. "I got it from Abdulhamed. Abdulhafid didn't wanna give it to me. He said he promised my old man. Abdulhamed said he never promised my old man nothing."

"Chill, man. The Abduls are chill."

"They want a cut."

"What?"

"They said nothing goes down in Osdorp unless they get a cut."

"Shit, gangster, what'd you tell 'em?"

I shrug. "I told 'em they can have a cut."

Sayid shakes his head.

I say I've given this some thought. "They got no idea how much money's involved here, so we can tell 'em it was a hundred thou and slip 'em ten Gs."

"Why'd you tell 'em *anything*, gangster?"

I say, 'cause we needed the piece. "It wouldn't work without a gun, gangster."

"True dat."

I say I didn't tell 'em what we were up to. "They asked, but I didn't tell 'em. They said we should be careful, and I said we would. Then they asked again, but I ducked the question. If I'd told 'em, they'd know we're not after no hundred grand."

"Okay then," says Sayid.

I remind him we'll be rich in two hours.

"Rich or dead," says Sayid.

"Forget dead. Rich."

"Inshallah."

"Yeah, inshallah, gangster."

Then Linda waltzes into the Mickey D's and every guy in the place checks her out. Linda wears these skintight jeans, man. I give her a wave, and she heads over. "Hey," she says.

"Hey," I say.

Sayid stays quiet. He looks to see if his sister is watching— his people don't like him hanging out with girls like Linda.

I ask her if she's ready.

She shrugs. "What am I supposed to do?"

"Wave. When you see Patrick coming, you step out in the street and wave. He'll pull over. You get him talking, and we get in the car."

She says she doesn't know what he drives.

I say I'll point it out. "I'll give you a sign when I see him. All you gotta do is wave, and then give him a little chitchat."

"Okay," she says. "And what do I get?"

"A hundred euros," I say.

"Two hundred."

"All you gotta do is wave."

"And chitchat," she says.

"One hundred."

"He wants to marry you," Sayid chimes in.

"I know. Two hundred."

"Okay, fine, two." I stand up. "Let's go."

Linda climbs on behind me, and Sayid and me aim our scooters for the Osdorper Ban.

Here and there on the Ban are these clusters of shops. They got clusters like this all over Osdorp and the other New-West neighborhoods: used to be that the little groceries and cigar stores and bakeries were for the white people, but now the whites who still live in these parts go to the big supermarkets. So you got Turks roasting chickens on the sidewalks and stores selling hearing aids and Pakistani dry cleaners with their *hawala* banks in the back.

Patrick told Sayid and me he was making a run tonight. Patrick brags about shit like that, because he wants to impress us. He's been bragging about shit like that for a couple months now, but we never took him serious until somebody said we oughta take him serious. Told us he's been moving bags of cash back and forth between this one *hawala* here and another one in Rotterdam for months now, and he got the gig 'cause he's about the whitest white guy ever lived, he even drives a fucking Ford Focus. He brags about it in this weird robot way he's got, like he's not really human, you know, and when we kid him about it, he's the one laughs the loudest, but not exactly *real*, like he don't know what's funny and what ain't, like he's just guessing. He says he's saving up so he can ask Linda to marry him. I say maybe he oughta try going steady before he starts talking about getting hitched, but he says he already thought it through, and in the movies girls go for romance and bust out crying if you ask 'em to marry you. So it's better you ask 'em to marry you than go steady.

We park our scooters outside Snackbar Van Vliet. Sayid won't go into Van Vliet, he says they cook the pork in the same fryers as the french fries, but it's a good place to leave the scooters—there's always scooters parked there, and I figure we better leave our scooters someplace they won't stand out. I want to be professional about this, and I think that includes we put our scooters someplace they won't stand out.

I tell Sayid and Linda we'll wait across the street. Patrick will make his pickup at the dry cleaners, and then he has to take the ring road, so he's gotta come right past here. There's a parked van we can hang out behind. I tell Linda I'll let her know when I see Patrick's car, and I keep my eyes fixed on the dry cleaners. I check my phone and it's almost five. It's starting to get dark—it's winter, but not cold. Feels like it's gonna rain.

Without turning my head, I ask Sayid what're the odds we'd get pulled over if *we* tried driving for the *hawalas*.

"One in four, gangster."

"Maybe one in three," I say. "That's what you call racial profiling. What a world, right?"

"Are you two gangsters?" asks Linda.

I say society has made us gangsters. And then a blue Ford Focus pulls into the parking space in front of the dry cleaners.

"There he is," I say.

Behind me, I hear Sayid puking. Linda gives out like a little scream. I shoot a quick glance over my shoulder and tell him he's an asshole. I ask him does he want to be rich or not.

"I want to be rich," he says.

I signal Linda to come closer. "You see that blue car? That's him. So you step out in the street and wave him over, and when he rolls down his window you have a little chitchat. That's all you got to do. You understand me?"

She says she understands me. She's not *retarded*, she says.

"You'll get your money tomorrow," I say. I stay behind the van with Sayid, Linda goes to the curb, and she does just fine, plays a little with her phone, then looks up when she figures Patrick's on his way. She makes like she spots him and waves, steps out in the street, and Patrick pulls up in front of the van.

"Shit, it's working," says Sayid. "Shit, man!"

Linda walks around the Focus to the driver's side, where Patrick's rolled his window down, and she leans in, her elbows on the window frame, her ass in those tight jeans sticking out behind her.

"We grab the bag now?" asks Sayid.

I look at him. I say we get in the car and make him drive to a good place.

Sayid asks what's a good place. He says we can just as easy grab the bag of money now and head for our scooters.

I look across the street at our scooters parked in front of Van Vliet. I say Sayid's idea would call too much attention to us. "We were gonna do that, we should've parked the scooters on this side of the street."

"Come on, gangster, you didn't think about that?"

I tell him to shut up, okay? "Come on," I say, "let's climb in." I go up to the passenger side of the Focus and yank on the back door handle, but the back door is locked. Sayid bumps into me. I look at him. Linda's still standing there with her ass in the air.

"What the fuck, gangster?" says Sayid.

I grab the piece from my waistband, circle around to the driver's side, and pull Linda out of the way. She gives another little scream. I touch the front end of the gun to her head and tell Patrick to unlock the doors.

"Three hundred," Linda says.

Patrick looks from me to Linda, scared-like. "Don't hurt her," he says, and I hear the locks pop up. I pull the driver's-side back door open and nod to Sayid he should get in on the other side, next to Patrick, and I shove Linda into the car and she yells not so hard or she'll go straight to five hundred. I get in after her and put the gun to the back of Patrick's head and tell him to drive.

He doesn't react.

He's got his hands on the wheel, but he don't do nothing.

I glance to my right. Linda looks kind of cramped, pressed up against this big laundry bag. Nylon, colored vertical stripes. My old man uses the same kind of bags to store the stuff he sells at the open-air market.

So that's the cash.

Patrick just sits there.

I tap the back of his head with the end of the gun barrel. "Pat," I say, "drive."

He says he's not afraid of me.

Sayid, sitting next to him, looks from him to me and back again.

"Pat," I say, "you gotta drive."

"I'm not afraid of you," he says again, like the weird robot he is. I figure that's another reason he got this gig with the Pakis. He's so white he'll never get pulled over, and he's a weird robot you can't scare.

I point the piece at Linda.

Patrick watches in the rearview mirror. "Don't hurt her," he says.

I tell him Linda wants to marry him, but I'll blow her brains out if he doesn't drive.

Patrick starts the Focus and drives, and Linda says now she wants a thousand euros.

Patrick drives, and Sayid looks at me and says, "Where we going, man? Where the fuck we *going?*"

I say we need to find a good place.

Sayid says I ain't given this enough thought. "Shit, G, you shoulda thought about this."

"You didn't think about it either, did you?"

He says he ain't the brains of the outfit.

I say I never said I was neither.

Linda sighs.

"Turn right," I tell Patrick, but he doesn't listen. He keeps going straight.

I push the gun into the back of his neck. I tell him he better listen or I'll blow his brains out.

He don't react, just drives straight ahead. We come to the intersection with Meer en Vaart, and he finally pulls into the right lane. Off to the left are the new apartments where the rich white people live. To the right are the old buildings on the Ruimzicht where they used to live.

"Okay, good," I say.

"I'm not doing it because you say so," he says. "I'm doing it because it's my job." He turns onto Meer en Vaart, the cop shop on the right, and I jerk the piece down behind his seat. I tell him in a second I'll aim it back at his head.

Sayid turns around and rests his arm on the back of his seat and glares at me. "In a second you'll aim back at his head?"

"Come on, gangster, we *know* Patrick, right?"

He says what difference does that make. "For fuck's sake, man, we're ripping him off!"

Patrick says he knows us too.

"That's logical," I say. "We all know each other."

He says that means we'll have to kill him. Otherwise, he'll turn us over to the cops. He downshifts for the red light at the Osdorpplein.

Sayid looks at me and nods. "He's right," he says.

Patrick drums his fingers on the steering wheel. "I have to do my job," he says.

I push the gun deeper into his neck. "Pay attention," I say. "Make a right."

"I'm going straight," he says. "I'm going to the Lelylaan, and then I'm getting on the ring road, and then I'm driving to Rotterdam."

A car pulls up beside us, so I lower the piece again. The light turns green, and Patrick drives straight ahead.

I tell him, "It's time for you to get scared, Patrick."

"I'm scared already," he says. "But not of you." He looks in his rearview mirror.

"What?" says Sayid.

I turn around and see a big black Dodge Ram behind us. It's so close all I can see is the front grill.

"The fuck," I say. "Who's that? Who the fuck is *that*, Patrick?"

"That's the people I work for." He drives on, doing exactly the speed limit. Ahead of us is the back edge of the Osdorpplein, where a little while ago we were sitting at Mickey D's, which we never should have left. We definitely shouldn't've done *this*. To our left is the narrow side of the Sloter Lake. The water is black as death.

"Speed up," I say. "*Now!*"

He says he's going to do his job just the way they told him.

"Patrick, I got a fucking *gun* here."

He says he's not afraid of my gun.

Behind us, the Dodge Ram's engine races.

Linda screams again—I forgot all about her. I point the piece at her. "Patrick," I say, "I'm gonna shoot Linda in the face. Now *go*."

Patrick hits the gas. Linda and I are thrown back in our seats, and she swats the piece aside. "Just stop it," she says. Then she turns to the laundry bag behind her and unzips it. Bundles of pale purple paper: five-hundred-euro notes. "What's all this?"

"It's money," says Patrick.

I look behind us. We're about sixty feet ahead of the Dodge, but he's coming up fast. Patrick's Ford Focus is about as speedy as a horse and buggy.

Patrick runs a red light and somebody honks. He turns left into the Lelylaan. He looks over his shoulder at Linda and says he took this job for her. "I'm doing this for you, Linda."

Linda, meanwhile, is holding one of the bundles of money in her hands. "There has to be at least ten thousand euros here," she says. "At *least*."

The Dodge is right behind us again, its motor growling.

I take the packet of bills away from Linda and stuff it in my jacket pocket. "You get two hundred," I say.

The Dodge comes up and nudges our rear bumper.

I see Patrick looking at her in the mirror, and he says, "Are you getting paid for this?"

"Of course," she says.

Patrick jerks the wheel to the left and we shoot off the asphalt onto the tram tracks that run down the middle of the Lelylaan. Both the 1 and the 17 trams use these tracks but we're in luck, they're unoccupied at the moment. Off in the distance, though, I see a blue tram coming our way, and the Focus skids across the rails and bottoms out, steel scraping steel, but we keep on going and bounce onto the asphalt on the other side of the tramline where the traffic's coming toward us from the city center, and the cars jam on their brakes, their headlights lighting up the inside of the Focus. We go off the road onto the grassy hill that slants down to the lake, then roll down the slope doing at least fifty. I look back, and the Dodge is coming after us, but the tram that was approaching is there now and it smashes into the side of the Dodge and I think about a story I heard once about how some tram conductors, who get a week off to recover after an accident, don't bother to stop when there's a car in their way. I practically shit my pants, but I'm still thinking about that story.

We roll down the grass and Patrick steers the Focus to the left and onto the footpath that runs along the shoreline, past the tall letters they put there—*I amsterdam,* with the *I* and the *am* in red and the *sterdam* in white, so it sort of says, *I am Amsterdam*, ha ha, so the tourists who accidentally wind up out here know they're really still in the city—and across the water I can see the apartments on Ruimzicht where we used to think the rich people lived and now there's a bag on the rear seat beside me with two million euros in it.

"Where we gonna *go*, man?" asks Sayid, turning to me from the front seat. Then he looks past me to see if the Dodge is still there, but the Dodge has been rammed by tram 17. A kid on a bike in front of us swerves out of our way and onto the grass. From the light we're shining on him, I can tell our right headlight is out.

I got the piece in my right hand, and with my left I pat my pants pockets 'cause that's what I always do when I'm thinking. I can feel my keys, and in my head I go through it: my place, my aunt's place, the storage unit. The storage unit. We have a storage unit for the shit my old man sells at the market, and that's the perfect place to hide a bag full of money, in the middle of all those other bags that look exactly the same. I say we're going to the storage unit. I rest the barrel of the gun on Patrick's shoulder and tell him we gotta go to Slotervaart.

He says he'll decide where we gotta go. "My life is meaningless now," he says.

"You're full of shit, man," says Sayid.

Patrick comes to a stop on the sidewalk when we're back on Meer en Vaart. In front of us there's a row of duplexes that must have been pretty nice once upon a time, but now their balconies are all overflowing with crap. There are lights on in a couple of the apartments, though most people ain't home yet. Most people are still in their cars on either side of us. Everyone who passes stares at us: a car parked on the sidewalk, only one headlight working.

"My life is meaningless," Patrick says again. "I was saving up so I could ask Linda to marry me. But now I don't trust her."

Sayid and me both look at Linda. She stares right back at us. "What?" she says. "I did what you told me. I can totally be trusted."

I ask her if she's sure she don't want to marry this guy. She shakes her head. He sees her do it in the rearview mirror.

Sayid asks, "Pat, how much you saved?"

"Twelve thousand," he says.

"He's got twelve thousand euros saved," I tell Linda.

"How much did you want to have before you asked me?"

"Twenty thousand."

"That's a lot of money," says Linda.

"I'll never get it now," says Patrick. "I'm out of a job."

"That's a shame," says Linda.

I say he needs to head for Slotervaart.

Patrick looks back at Linda. "You don't think twelve thousand's enough?"

She's sitting next to a bag with two million in it. Patrick told us he carries two million every trip. She shrugs. "Maybe."

Sayid and I look at each other. I can see from his face he's trying not to laugh. I can also see from his face he's trying not to cry. He's scared.

In the mirror, I can glimpse what's happening on Patrick's face too. He's gotta figure this shit out, but he don't know how. "Come on, Pat," I say, "be smart. We're gonna stash this bag someplace safe. You're gonna lose your job anyway, we might as well be smart, right?"

He turns around in his seat and looks at me. He says I'm right. We might as well be smart, he says.

He sits up straight.

"Let's go to Slotervaart," I say.

"Let's not go to Slotervaart," says Patrick, and I can hear from his robot voice I might as well stop telling him where to go, even with the gun I got from Abdulhamed stuck in his ear. He inches his Ford Focus into the traffic on Meer en Vaart and heads back in the direction of Osdorpplein.

I look off to the right, at the Sloterplas, that weird man-made lake in the middle of Amsterdam New-West you have to drive all the way around to get anywhere. When we were kids, we used to swim there, because our parents wouldn't give us money for the public pool where all the white kids went, so us brown kids were the poor schmucks who had to settle for the dirty green water of the lake. Us poor schmucks with our brown skin who loved the white kids, because the white kids got to go to their activities in their old man's car, activities maybe their old man took them to because us brown kids were hanging out on all their streets and squares.

*Poor schmucks*, I think, looking at the Sloterplas while Patrick drives, this weird autistic guy, my pal beside him, me on the backseat with some dumb bitch and a bag filled with two million euros. Two million. Two hours ago we were at Mickey D's and we were poor, because we weren't smart enough like our cousins who went to good schools and applied for a hundred jobs at banks and insurance companies and finally got a job at the hundred-and-first place they tried because they had brown skin and funny names, but now that they finally got those jobs they had a future. The fuckers.

My future sits in a laundry bag on the backseat of a Ford Focus, and I'm sitting right beside it. Maybe I'll buy an apartment in one of those new buildings off the Ruimzicht, tucked in among the white families, and I'll laugh when the white realtor's eyes go all wide when I dump payment in full on his desk. Cash money.

"Patrick," says Sayid. "*Patrick.*" He looks at me and I shake my head—Patrick ain't listening no more. Sayid grabs the piece out of my hand and curses and sticks it in Patrick's face, and Patrick's hands tighten on the wheel and he stares right through the gun. "Here," says Sayid, "here, *look*, there's bullets in here and I'm gonna blow your fuckin' head off."

Patrick lifts his right hand from the wheel and rips the piece out of Sayid's hand. He glances at it, clicks off the safety, aims at Sayid, and then there's a big bang that makes Linda and me cup our hands over our ears and there's smoke and the stink of cordite and Sayid is screaming and there's a hole in the side window with a ring of blood all around it. Sayid goes on screaming. "You cocksucker!" he shouts. "Cocksucker!" He covers his face with his hands, covers his mouth and nose, and he looks at me and pulls his hands away and *his nose ain't there no more* and he asks how bad it is while the blood runs into his mouth.

I don't know what to say.

"*How bad is it?*"

"Your nose," I say. "It's your nose."

"*How* bad *is it?*"

"Your nose is—Jesus, it's sort of gone, G."

Linda pukes into the bag of money.

Patrick drives. "I'm sorry," he says to Sayid. "I was trying to blow your head off." He holds the wheel with his left hand, the piece in his right. He checks his mirror and says the Dodge is back. I turn around but don't see it. "There," he says, and he nods at the bike path between the road and the lake, and there's the Dodge, zigzagging a little, probably the tram threw off its alignment.

"Who's in there?" I ask.

Patrick says he already told us. "The people I work for. *Worked.*"

Sayid whines, his hands cupped over his face. "I gotta go to the hospital," he cries. "I really gotta go to the hospital, man."

Patrick looks at Linda in his mirror and says her name.

She looks back at him.

"You think twelve thousand's enough?"

She stares past Sayid at the hole in the passenger window and the blood all around it. "No," she says, "not anymore."

"You think two million's enough?"

"Two *million*? Where you gonna get that kind of money?"

I tell her there's two million in the bag. "You stupid bitch," I say.

"Don't insult her," says Patrick, and he glances over to the Dodge, which is keeping up with us on the bike path.

Sayid screams, his hands cupped in front of his face. "You stupid bitch!"

Patrick touches the barrel of the gun to Sayid's head and pulls the trigger.

Explosion.

Cordite.

Sayid's body slumps against the passenger door.

"Patrick," I say. "Patrick."

Linda sits pressed up against the backseat, her hands covering her eyes.

Patrick steers the Focus to the side of the road, bumps over the curb, and now he's right next to the Dodge.

"I'll shoot you later," he tells me, "but I can't do it now because you're behind me."

We're driving parallel to the new boulevard that runs along the short side of the Sloterplas—before last year it was just trees here, with a walking trail between them, but they cut down the trees and now they got expensive tiles and benches—and Patrick runs the Focus into the side of the Dodge. The Dodge is much heavier than we are, except the tram must have shook it up because it smashes into one of the steel benches and comes to a stop. The streetlamps cast a soft glow on the boulevard's tiles and on Sayid's blood.

Patrick puts the Focus in park and gets out and comes after me, but I jerk away and pull Linda in front of me and she screams, and I smell her puke and I think she's pissed herself. Patrick doesn't shoot.

At first I don't dare to look, but Linda pulls free and I see Patrick's on the other side of the car now, the gun—my gun— aiming at the Dodge, and he fires three times.

Linda and me sit up straight, and we see somebody fall out of the Dodge. Then we look at each other, and then we both look at the laundry bag with the two million euros, the laundry bag I could have stashed with the bags of my old man's shit in the storage unit. I try to wipe off Linda's puke and Sayid's blood. I grab the bag and she grabs it too, and I want to pull it away from her but two million euros is *heavy*, man. And for a second that's the whole world, the backseat of the Focus and our four hands on that bag, all that money so close, and for that second it feels like I ought to kiss her like it's a fucking movie. Then the door on her side swings open and Patrick yanks her out, and I'm so surprised I let go of the bag and it flies out with her.

I see Patrick drag Linda and the bag onto the boulevard and it's like I'm in a long dark tunnel and the tunnel feels safe—just leave me right here—but then Patrick sees me. He hunkers down and holds the piece in both hands and aims at the tunnel, my tunnel, and he shoots—there's a bang, but not so loud this time because I'm in my tunnel and he's outside, and I think about that bang while my shoulder is blown to fragments. I drop onto a bench and I die. I think I'm dying. My buddy's lying here in front of me and he's already gone, and I'm on my way. I open my eyes and lie on my back and look upside down out of my used-to-be-safe tunnel—it seems so long ago now, that feeling of safety inside my tunnel.

Patrick says something to Linda. I can't really hear it. She just squeals. She's lying on the boulevard in the glow of the streetlamps and she's squealing, and behind her I see the Sloterplas, its black water beautiful beneath the black winter sky, and I see the Dodge and the man who fell out of it, and he tries to sit up and he stares at me and I see the disappointment on Abdulhafid's face.

"I didn't know it was you," I say softly, and he didn't know it was me, either—all I told him was we were gonna score a hundred thou, he never thought I meant his two million.

Patrick stands up and grabs the bag of money and unzips it. "Two million," he tells Linda, loud, "*two million.*"

She shakes her head, sobbing.

I hear him say he's gonna ask her one more time. And then he asks her: "Linda, will you marry me?"

I hear her say no, soft, sobbing.

Patrick picks up the bag by its handles, and in the glow of the streetlamps I see him carry it to the water's edge. He drops the bag on the ground, then grabs it by the bottom and flips it over, and I can't see the bundles of five-hundred-euro notes drop into the lake but I think I can hear them, *plop plop plop,* quick splashes as the packets hit the water.

I laugh 'cause I still got one of the bundles in my pocket. How many bills are in a bundle like that? A hundred? I suck at math, but I figure it's gotta be a shitload of money, right?

Patrick walks back to Linda, who's lying on the ground weeping like a drama queen even though he ain't even shot her, and he asks her if she sees what he gave up for her. "Did you see that? I did it for you. Will you marry me?"

"No."

He grumbles and turns to Abdulhafid, who's lying next to the Dodge and who I figure is already dead, but Patrick shoots him in the head with the piece the other Abdul loaned me.

The gun's been used, so it's gotta go in the lake. I laugh again. I remember our scooters parked in front of Van Vliet. It'll be days before anyone finds them. I figured it would be professional to put them there. I laugh, and I keep on laughing.

Patrick hears me, and he comes back to the Focus, and I press my hand against my jacket pocket, against the bundle of five-hundred-euro notes, a hundred of them, that's four zeroes, so fifty thousand euros, and I laugh because I'm dying richer than I ever lived.

# STARRY, STARRY NIGHT

BY RENÉ APPEL & JOSH PACHTER

*Museum District*

Vincent slips his arm around Mila's bare shoulder and pulls her close. "So many stars," he whispers. "And so many more, so far away we can't even see them. Thousands of planets, millions of light-years away. It's unbelievable, isn't it?"

Mila doesn't reply. Not with words, anyway. She leans into him, kisses his neck, brushes his cheek with her lips, moves on to his ear, her hot tongue exploring its contours.

He groans with pleasure.

The two of them have been a couple for almost half a year. They met at the Escape, a nightclub on the Rembrandtplein, and their click was instant and overpowering. One of Vincent's old buddies has a tattoo on his left bicep of a heart with an arrow through it, and that's how Vincent feels, like there's an arrow piercing his heart. Sometimes he has to stop himself from checking his chest to make sure he isn't actually bleeding.

Everything changed for Vincent when he and Mila got together. For years, he'd been a hard-core party animal, and *animal* was the operative word: drunk with his pals every weekend, a steady diet of fights and vandalism and anonymous sex, anything for a laugh. His life was a carnival, illuminated by flashing neon, its soundtrack a pulsing heavy-metal beat. Hard to believe it was only last year that he, Roy, Marco, and Tommy had practically torn Greece apart during an alcohol- and drug-fueled summer trip to the islands. Jesus, you choked down the right cocktail of stimulants, you could party hearty for a week without sleep.

Now, tonight, Vincent gazes lovingly at his beautiful Mila. She looks awesome in a short leather skirt and low-cut tank top.

"Mmmm, don't," he murmurs. "You know that makes me crazy."

There isn't a hint of a breeze, nor a cloud in the sky, and he's aware that the sultry summer evening only adds to the hunger he feels for her. He slides his left hand beneath Mila's skirt and caresses the soft inside of her thigh, sneaking his fingers higher to brush the warm, moist cotton of her underwear. It's absolutely silent in this dark corner of the Vondelpark. Now and then a bicycle whispers past in the distance, but this narrow side trail is completely deserted except for the two of them.

The very instant he has that thought, a runner in a fluorescent green shirt huffs by, but Mila doesn't seem to notice the intrusion. Perhaps her eyes are closed. Here on this wooden bench . . . could they? No, you never knew who might appear out of nowhere, even at one a.m., like that jogger. The park used to be known as a meat market for gay guys on the make. Maybe it still is.

Mila licks his ear again. She sucks the lobe into her mouth and nibbles it gently. "You taste so good," she breathes. He feels the faintest pressure of her teeth. "I could eat you up."

His fingertips slip inside the elastic of her panties, and just as she bites down on his earlobe his cell phone rings.

"Ow!" he cries.

"Oh no," says Mila, "did I hurt you?"

Vincent fumbles for his phone. On its screen he sees the word *Senior*.

"Crap, it's my dad, I better take it."

Mila wriggles a few inches away on the bench and straightens her skirt, as if she's concerned her boyfriend's father might see her.

"What's up?" Vincent says.

There is a moment of silence at the other end of the line. Then he hears his dad's cigarette-hoarsened voice bark, "You make your deliveries?"

Always checking up on him, like he's a little baby, has to be watched every minute. Doesn't the old man trust him? And anyway, what's he doing up at this hour? Once you turn fifty, you're supposed to be in bed by midnight, for Christ's sake.

"Muntplein and Koningsplein are done," Vincent says. "I'll do Museumplein in the morning."

"You were supposed to hit all three of them tonight."

"What difference does it make? I'll be there before they open tomorrow."

"That's not our agreement," his father says. "First you promise me you'll do it tonight, now you say tomorrow morning. I don't nag you, next thing I know it's afternoon and it's still not done. We've been through this before, son."

"Not for six months, we haven't!"

It's true that Vincent has messed up in the past. Before Mila, he broke pretty much every promise he ever made to the old man. But that was then. He's a different guy now. Responsible. No more crazy parties, no drunken orgies, no pills, he hardly even drinks booze anymore, just a few beers when they go out to dinner. Mila has shown him he can live a better life. He *has* to behave himself, if he doesn't want to go back to being a total loser.

And his dad's business is a gold mine: kiosks on three squares in the heart of Amsterdam, perfectly placed to serve drinks and snacks to the city's hordes of tourists. Someday, when Daddy Dearest lies down for the big sleep—and given the two packs of Camels a day the old man inhales, it will probably come sooner than later—the whole enterprise will belong to him, and he'll live off the proceeds for the rest of his life . . . if he doesn't screw it all up.

"I want that last delivery made tonight," Vincent Senior grumbles. "You hear me, boy?"

"I . . ." He sees that Mila is eying him with concern. He presses the phone to his chest and explains what's going on.

"Do what he tells you," she says. "I understand."

She understands. For the first time in his life, Vincent has found someone who actually understands.

When he puts the phone back to his ear, his father is still talking. "Sure, Dad, whatever you say," he interrupts. "I'm on my way to Museumplein right now."


The Museum Square is a ghost town at this hour—all that's missing is a lonely tumbleweed blowing across the broad grassy area bordered by the Rijksmuseum to the northeast, the van Gogh and Stedelijk museums to the north, and the Concertgebouw to the southwest. The tourists are tucked away in their hotels, or hunched over glasses of beer in the brown cafés on and around the Leidseplein, or roaming the Red-Light District in search of excitement, adventure, action. But there is nothing for them here. The museums and the city's concert hall are all long shuttered for the night. The occasional car engine rumbles from the Paulus Potterstraat, a knot of locals chatters as they glide along the Hobbemastraat behind the Rijks on their black bicycles, homeward bound, and then silence again descends . . . before being irrevocably broken by the arrival of three boisterous young men, twentysomethings, dressed almost identically in T-shirts, jeans, and sneakers. Two of the three sport shaggy haircuts, the third has shaved his head.

"Whaddaya wanna do, Tommy?" says the bald one, whose name is Roy. There is a tattoo of a heart and an arrow on his left arm.

"Marco," says Tommy, "that cunt told you where the party is, right?"

"Yeah, lemme think. It's around here somewhere."

"Not in *there*." Tommy waves at the looming bulk of the national museum, the Rijks. "You guys ever been inside that dump?"

"On a field trip once," bald Roy shrugs. "I tried to ditch it, but they dragged me along. About a million stupid old paintings and whatever. Almost as boring as dinner with my folks."

"That shit's worth millions, though."

"I wonder anybody ever broke in there? You got any idea, Marco?"

Marco shakes his head. He gazes thoughtfully at the gigantic building, scratches his armpit, and shrugs.

"Man," says Roy, "I'm wasted. Let's get a cab."

"You see a cab around here?"

"Anyway, where we going? Why don't you call her, Marco? You got her number back at the Jimmy Hoo, right?"

"Jimmy Woo."

"Whatever. You call her, get the goddamn address. I'ma stretch out for a sec."

Roy reaches halfway along the tall plastic letters that spell out *I amsterdam*—the *I* and the *am* in bright red, everything else a glossy white that almost glows beneath the starry sky— grabs the crossbar of the letter *t*, and hoists himself up to sit with his back against the *t* and his feet propped on the top of the *s*. The modern font of the letters clashes with the museum's classical architecture, but who gives a shit, the tourist board put several of these fuckers up around the city for the American backpackers and middle-aged Germans and hordes of Japanese with their clicking camera shutters, and they lap it up like dogs attacking a bowl of kibble.

Marco reaches for his phone. "Shit, what was her name again?" He stares at the screen as if waiting for Siri to answer the question.

"I Amsterdam," says Tommy, using the bottom curve of the *s* to boost himself up onto the big red *m*. "That doesn't fucking *mean* anything."

Roy laughs. "Look at the colors, asshole. Read the red letters twice—it says *I am Amsterdam*."

"Bullshit," Tommy responds. "Read the red letters twice, it says, *I am I Amsterdam*. Now who's an asshole, asshole?" Then he shakes off the argument and says, "You got any left?"

"Any what? X?"

Tommy rolls his eyes. "No, any licorice. *Asshole*."

Roy fishes a small metal box from the pocket of his jeans and shakes it, letting the others hear the rattle from within. He slides it open and sings, in off-key English, "*The Candyman can, 'cause he mixes it with love and makes the world taste good.*" He takes out a little yellow pill with a smiley face stamped on one side, swallows it dry, and tosses the box to Tommy.

Marco is scrolling through his contacts. "That guy she was with," he says, more to himself than his friends, "Raffie? Robbie? Ronnie?"

A white delivery van with *Van Galen* lettered on its side turns from the Honthorststraat onto the square and pulls up beside the shuttered snack kiosk. Its headlights go out, the purr of its engine dies, the driver's door swings open, and a thin figure emerges.

"Hey, look who's here," says Roy, his face lighting up in a grin. "It's Vinnie Van and his minivan! Good ol' Vinnie—shit, what's he doing here in the middle of the night? C'mon, boys, let's check it out."

Marco puts away his phone. Roy drops down from his perch atop the *t*, Tommy rolls off the *m* and lands on his feet like a cat. The three of them advance toward the delivery van.

Vincent swings the van's rear door open. He'll lug everything over to the kiosk before unlocking it and stacking the goods inside. It's a ten-minute job, tops. But that doesn't much matter anymore, since Mila's already home, probably fast asleep by now. He pushes two crates of soda cans together and slides them out, and that's when he sees them coming toward him. Roy, Marco, and Tommy, now that's a fine how-do-you-don't. What are those jerks doing out here in the middle of the night? It's like they've been waiting for him, but of course their appearance has to be pure coincidence.

"Vinnie Van," says Roy cheerfully, "you're workin' late."

"Yeah, restocking."

Roy swings around in front of him, blocking his way.

"Move, will ya? I gotta take this stuff to the—"

"You forgot the magic word, Vinnie, my brother."

Vincent is tired, not in the mood to fool around. "Please," he says, swallowing his irritation. "If you don't mind."

"You see, boys?" says Roy. "Look how polite he can be. Our Vinnie's grown up into a good little soldier."

Vincent, burdened by the two heavy crates, heads for the kiosk's back door. Roy takes a step closer, bumping into him, almost throwing him off balance.

"Watch where you're going, Vinnie," says Roy. "You clumsy piece of shit."

Tommy and Marco stand there snickering stupidly, watching the comedy play out.

"We're goin' to a party," says Marco. "You comin' with, Vinnie? The more the merrier, right?"

Vincent holds his tongue. No matter what he says, they'll take it the wrong way. He sets down his crates and returns to the van for two more.

"What's the matter?" demands Tommy. "We ain't good enough for you no more?"

"Maybe his fuckin' girlfriend don't like us," Marco mutters. "Mila with the milky mammaries. You like to suck on those mammaries, Vinnie? She let you have a taste if you're a good little boy?"

Vincent shakes off the insult and goes back to the van for two cardboard cartons of chips. He can feel his old gang fall into single file behind him, swinging their arms like apes in the zoo, their sneakers slapping on the pavement amid staccato bursts of laughter.

"You need some help handling those big boys, Vinnie?" says Roy, and Vincent isn't sure if he means the boxes or Mila's breasts.

"I bet he does," says Tommy, going straight for the nastier of the two entendres. "I mean, anything more than a mouthful's too much for one guy on his own, right, Vinnie?"

Vincent sets down the cartons by the kiosk's back door, and when he straightens up and turns around, Roy is right there in his face, an evil gleam in his eyes. "I could use a snack and a Coke, Vinnie. What about you guys?"

"Sounds good," Marco smirks, and Tommy nods eagerly.

"Whaddaya say, Vinnie? We're still your buds, right?"

Vincent heads back to the van.

"Cat's got his tongue," says Roy.

"I want a snack and a Coke," Tommy whines, imitating a child.

"You can spare a couple bags of chips and a couple Cokes for your best pals," says Roy. "Remember that time in Crete when you puked all over your bed? Who cleaned that shit up for you, Vinnie? *We* did, remember? You were totally out of it."

"Yeah," says Marco, "and this is how you thank us?"

"Come on, man," Tommy urges, "I'm thirrrrrsty."

"We'll help you unload the rest of this crap and then we'll all head over to the party, have a couple *real* drinks, for old time's sake," Roy suggests.

Vincent shakes his head.

"We'll catch a ride with you, Vinnie Van. Hey, check it out, I got some X for ya." Roy holds out his metal pillbox, the yellow smiley faces glowing happily under the light of a billion stars, but Vincent turns away as if he hasn't even noticed.

"Jesus, you got *boring*, Van Galen. This is all that fuckin' Mila's idea, right? You get high and the bitch won't suck you off no more?"

Ignoring them, Vincent carries the last two boxes of snacks to the kiosk. Now there's just a few crates of bottled beer left before he can move it all inside and then take off.

If these three clowns will let him. *What did I ever see in these assholes?* he wonders.

"How much you make doin' deliveries, Vinnie?" says Marco. "Your daddy pay you decent, or you work for free 'cause you love him so much?"

Vincent doesn't react.

"Remember when you used to bitch and moan about the old fucker?" says Tommy. "I never heard you say one nice word about him." He reaches out and pushes Vincent's shoulder, not hard, just enough to be annoying. "Now all of a sudden he's your best friend?"

Roy moves to block Vincent's access to the van's back door. He's gritting his teeth, his eyes are wide open and darting from side to side, the pupils huge and black and glittering.

*Christ,* Vincent thinks warily, *he's already tripping.* He gestures at Roy to move, but the guy just stands there, bouncing up and down on the balls of his feet.

"Please," sighs Vincent. "Would you *please* let me through?"

Roy grins and steps aside, motioning Vincent forward. "Glad to oblige, Mr. Van Galen," he says with exaggerated politeness. "I wouldn't want to hinder you in the swift completion of your appointed rounds."

Vincent doesn't trust this, but he leans into the van and slides out two stacked crates of Heineken, the tourists' idea of Holland's finest. As he turns to the kiosk, the three boys close in around him. With the van at his back, there's nowhere for him to go. He doesn't know what they're planning—he doubts they're clearheaded enough to even *have* a plan—but they're obviously not going to let him through.

Roy suddenly takes a step back, opening a path. Vincent starts forward, and Roy sticks out a leg and trips him.

Vincent falls, and the two crates of beer go flying, crashing down on the asphalt. His palms sting, and there is shattered glass everywhere, though he doesn't seem to be bleeding. He looks up into the grinning faces of Roy, Marco, and Tommy from his hands and knees.

"Vinnie fall down, go boom?" says Roy, the picture of innocence, while his droogs giggle idiotically.

"Fucking assholes," Vincent mutters under his breath as he examines the smashed beer crates.

"You oughta be more careful, pal," grins Marco. "I think your shoelace came untied. That's dangerous."

"Dangerous," Tommy echoes. "You better tie your shoelace."

Picking carefully though the beer-splattered mess, Vincent sees that most of the bottles have broken. *Shit, shit, shit.* He gets slowly to his feet. "You stupid bastards," he says. "You're gonna have to pay for all this—"

Roy's hand whips around behind his back and snakes something out of his rear jeans pocket. There is a metallic *snick*, and Vincent sees a long blade glitter coldly in the starlight. "Your fuckin' shoelaces trip you up," he says slowly, "and you think *we're* gonna pay for it?"

Vincent puts out a hand to keep his old friend at bay, seemingly unaware of the broken bottle he is holding.

But Roy sees the threat and lunges toward him. Vincent jerks to the side, his hand flashing forward defensively.

There is a sudden scream, and for just a moment it is unclear which of them has made the sound, but it is both of them who have cried out, both who have been wounded.

They stand there in the Museumplein beneath the blanket of stars, swaying from side to side, Marco and Tommy looking on in dumbfounded horror.

A spray of arterial blood gushes from Roy's throat, and there is hot pain on the side of Vincent's head.

Roy drops his switchblade and crumples to his knees, clutching his neck in both hands, before toppling over.

"Holy shit," Marco breathes. "Come on, Tommy, let's get out of here."

As if by magic, the two of them disappear, leaving Roy and Vincent behind.

Vincent gingerly touches the left side of his head, where blood streams from a deep gash left behind by Roy's knife.

"You cut me!" he whimpers. "You fucking *cut* me!"

He collapses to the pavement and lies there weeping as Roy's body trembles violently for a long moment and then grows still.

The two of them remain there, side by side like a pair of lovers, until Vincent hears the wail of approaching sirens through the starry, starry night.

# ABOUT THE CONTRIBUTORS

*Willem van den Heuvel*

**KARIN AMATMOEKRIM** (Paramaribo, 1976) is the author of six novels, including the best seller *Het Gym* (2011) and *De Man van Veel* (2013), a historical novel about the life of Resistance hero Anton de Kom. A documentary about her sixth book, *Tenzij de Vader* (2016), was broadcast on Dutch television in May 2017. She also writes short stories and essays, and is currently working toward a PhD in modern literature.

*Danny Schwarz*

**RENÉ APPEL** (Hoogkarspel, 1945) published his first thriller, *Handicap*, in 1987, and has written twenty more, two of which have received the Golden Noose, the annual award for the best Dutch-language crime novel. In 2017, *Joyride en Andere Spannende Verhalen*, a collection of his short stories, was published, and English translations of his stories have appeared in *Ellery Queen's Mystery Magazine*, *Alfred Hitchcock's Mystery Magazine*, and several anthologies.

*Wouter Dasselaar*

**ABDELKADER BENALI** (Ighzazene, Morocco, 1975) is a writer, documentary filmmaker, and photographer. He emigrated to The Netherlands from Morocco at the age of four. In 2003, his novel *De Langverwachte* won the Libris Literature Prize, the most important literary award for Dutch fiction. His work includes novels, plays, poetry, and travel essays, and he has written extensively about Tangier, Henri Matisse, radicalism, and Marcel Proust. Today he lives in Amsterdam and Tangier.

*Dieter Rays*

**MICHAEL BERG** (Heerlen, 1956) worked for almost twenty-five years for Dutch public radio as a host, director, documentarian, and manager before moving to France and becoming a full-time writer. In 2013, he won the Golden Noose for *Nacht in Parijs*, and his *Het Meisje op de Weg* was the highest-ranked Dutch-language entry on Hebban's list of the best international thrillers of 2016. In 2017, he moved back to The Netherlands.

*Sanne Klein*

**HANNA BERVOETS** (Amsterdam, 1984) is a fiction writer and essayist. She has published six novels and is the recipient of numerous literary prizes, including the Opzij Literature Prize for *Lieve Céline* and the BNG Literature Prize for *Ivanov*. In 2017, she was awarded the Frans Kellendonk Prize for her full body of work. Translation rights for several of her books have been sold in the US and Germany. Her most recent novel, *Fuzzie*, has received glowing reviews.

**THEO CAPEL** (Amsterdam, 1944) has reviewed crime fiction in addition to writing it himself. After ten novels about Hank Stammer, who runs a collection agency in Amsterdam, Capel (writing as Erik Bolt) began a new series featuring Amsterdam policeman Felix de Grave; to date, there are two books in that series. "The Red Mercedes," a short story about Stammer, appeared in *Ellery Queen's Mystery Magazine* in 2004 and was reprinted in *Passport to Crime* in 2007.

**MARIA DE BRUYN** (Utrecht, 1949) has had a varied professional life, beginning as operations manager of a translation bureau, working as a desk and copy editor, and progressing to a career as a policy advisor, trainer, and writer after becoming a medical anthropologist. Her nontechnical translations have included a children's book and a comic book. She fills much of her time now with wildlife photography and blogging about nature.

**SIMON DE WAAL** (Amsterdam, 1961) writes novels and scripts. *Cop vs. Killer*, *Pentito*, and *Nemesis* were nominated for best crime novel in The Netherlands and Belgium, and *Pentito* won Belgium's Diamond Bullet. De Waal's script for *Lek* won the Golden Calf, and he wrote and directed a film version of *Cop vs. Killer*. He has worked for the Amsterdam police since 1979, including as a detective-sergeant in the homicide division since 1986.

**LOES DEN HOLLANDER** (Nijmegen, 1948) began writing prose and poetry at the age of eight, and in 2001 she won a short-story contest, which motivated her to write twenty-four thrillers, three collections of stories, a commercial novel, and three novellas.

**SAM GARRETT** (Harrisburg, 1956) has translated almost forty novels and works of nonfiction from Dutch to English, has been short-listed for some of the world's most prestigious literary awards, and is the only translator to have twice won the British Society of Authors' Vondel Prize (in 2003 and 2009). His translation of Herman Koch's *The Dinner* was a best seller in the US, UK, and Canada.

**MURAT ISIK** (Izmir, 1977) debuted in 2012 with *Verloren Grond*, for which he received the Bronze Owl for best Dutch-language first novel and was nominated for the Academica Literature Award. The book has been reprinted multiple times, and has been translated into German, Swedish, and Turkish. *Wees Onzichtbaar*, his second book, was published in 2017, and was selected as the NRC Book of the Year and nominated for the BNG Literature Award and the Halewijn Award.

*Lisette Chevalier*

**HERMAN KOCH** (Arnhem, 1953) is the author of, among others, *Het Diner (The Dinner)*, *Zomerhuis met Zwembad (Summer House with Swimming Pool)*, *Geachte Heer M. (Dear Mr. M)*, and *De Greppel (The Ditch)*. *Het Diner*, an international best seller, was translated into more than forty languages and was filmed in the US, The Netherlands, and Italy.

*Anneleen Louwes*

**CHRISTINE OTTEN** (Deventer, 1961) writes both fiction and nonfiction. Her novel *De Laatste Dichters* (2004), based on the lives of the legendary African American group the Last Poets, was nominated for the Libris Literature Prize and was published in English as *The Last Poets* (2016). Her latest novel, *We Hadden Liefde, We Hadden Wapens* (2016), was enthusiastically reviewed and has been adapted for the stage. Otten leads creative-writing workshops in Dutch prisons. She lives in Amsterdam.

*Fjodor Buis*

**JOSH PACHTER** (New York, 1951) is an American writer, editor, and translator. His own short crime stories have been featured in *Ellery Queen's Mystery Magazine, Alfred Hitchcock's Mystery Magazine*, and many other periodicals and anthologies since the late 1960s, and his translations of crime fiction by Dutch and Belgian authors appear regularly in *EQMM*. He lived in Amsterdam from 1979 to 1982 and returns often, although he now makes his home in Northern Virginia.

*Rebecca Jones*

**ANNELOES TIMMERIJE** (Amsterdam, 1955) has written several nonfiction books, beginning in 1992. Her first novel, *Zwartzuur* (2005), won the Women & Culture Debut Prize in 2006, and was followed by *De Grote Joseph* (2010), the short-story collection *Slaapwandelen bij Daglicht* (2013), and, in collaboration with Charles den Tex, the historical novel *Het Vergeten Verhaal van een Onwankelbare Liefde in Oorlogstijd* (2014), which was published in English as *Finding Her*.

*Esther Hessing*

Chiel Wevering

**WALTER VAN DEN BERG** (Amstelveen, 1970) spent almost forty years in Osdorp, the Amsterdam neighborhood in which he set his contribution to *Amsterdam Noir*, but he now lives in a village by a river with his wife and dog. He has published four novels: *De Hondenkoning* (2004), *West* (2007), *Van Dode Mannen Win Je Niet* (2013), and *Schuld* (2016), which was nominated for the Libris Literature Prize.

Anneleen Louwes

**MENSJE VAN KEULEN** (Den Haag, 1946) lives in Amsterdam. She writes novels and short stories and has published several award-winning children's books. Her first novel was *Bleekers Zomer* (1972), and her most recent was *Schoppenvrouw* (2016). Her books frequently appear on the long and short lists for literary awards, and her body of work has been honored with the Annie Romein, Charlotte Köhler, and Constantijn Huygens prizes.

Lawrence Mooij

**MAX VAN OLDEN** (Zevenaar, 1973) debuted in 2015 with *Lieve Edelachtbare*, a legal thriller about a young lawyer in training that won the Shadow Prize for the best Dutch-language debut crime novel of the year. His second book, *De Juiste Man* (2017), a psychological thriller that explores the subject of revenge, made the long list for the Golden Noose. Van Olden is himself an attorney with a civil practice.